call heaven to witness

BERNARD BERLIN

THE MUSSON BOOK COMPANY
TORONTO

The Musson Book Company
30 Lesmill Road, Don Mills,
Ontario

ISBN 0-7737-0010-2

Printed in Canada

For Isobel —

who waited so long.

ACKNOWLEDGMENTS

My most sincere gratitude to David J. Lewis, M.D., psychiatrist at the Royal Victoria Hospital, clinical director of the Allan Memorial Institute of Psychiatry, and an associate professor at McGill University, for his co-operation and advice.
To Doctor Luis Vacaflor, psychiatrist, Chief of Service at the Douglas Hospital, my deepest thanks for his patience and graciousness.

B.B.

CONTENTS

PROLOGUE

Jonathon Temple's life ended the day he got married. You think that's a peculiar thing to say? Maybe so, but when you know all the facts, you'll agree with me. And I saw it happen. I watched the events unfold, and I watched over the death throes. I doubt that there was any way I could have influenced or averted the outcome. I was simply an onlooker, and impotent.

Jonny and I grew up together. From the time we were both five years old, and our parents moved side by side in the west Montreal suburb, we were inseparable. All through school and college, and even afterwards, we were together constantly. We were more like brothers than friends. Sure, we lived in separate homes with our folks and slept in our own beds, in our own rooms. But we were together almost every waking hour of every day. Our interests were the same, we had the same outlook, our desires and ambitions were parallel. We had wonderful dreams and great plans for the future. Actually, from the day our parents had moved, we planned our future and it always included our being together and working together. They were good plans, workable plans, plans that would have fulfilled our lives. Of course, we were kids at the time. And, like kids, we could not foresee the day when, having grown to manhood, others would influence our lives and put an end to our dreams. In our young minds we would grow bigger and older, but we would remain the same, thinking alike. And our youthful dreams would never change.

But I'm getting ahead of myself. I can't start in the middle, because if I do, you won't understand what happened to Jonny and why. I'll start at the beginning and then you'll know why I said that Jon Temple's life was over the day of his marriage. It's really quite simple. . . .

CHAPTER 1

JONNY

As a child, Jonathon Temple was often referred to by adults as a man-child. Not in the sense that he was born a male, but in the sense that, even as a youngster, he showed the physical characteristics and the promise that were to mark him as a man. He was slender and wiry, his young body perfectly proportioned. He was tall and dark, his great shock of coal-black hair overhung a sensitive face that was both handsome and rugged at the same time. And his eyes were black, so black that the pupil and the iris were as one, piercing and direct. It was easy to visualize Jon Temple grown, and looking much the same. Jonny was an intelligent boy, personable and with a fun-loving sense of humour. He was a good student and an equally good athlete. You might say he was an all-round boy during his school days.

Jonny and I complemented each other. I was considerably shorter than he and inclined toward plumpness. I was also much lighter complexioned. No one in his right mind could ever consider me handsome. Open and frank, yes. Studious, yes, but never good looking. I wasn't much on athletics either and it was tough trying to keep up with Jonny in that department. But he was never condescending or egotistical. I was his friend and that was all that mattered to him. He accepted me as I was and was slightly protective in a loving, brotherly way. And I . . . I worshipped Jonathon Temple all his life.

We had decided that when the time came, we would both study law. And, of course, when we graduated, we would be law partners and make our fortune as the outstanding criminal lawyers in Montreal. It was a good arrangement. Jonny had many interests, but I was a bit of a bookworm in those days. It was decided that I would prepare the cases and Jonny would plead them. A perfect team.

There was only one thing about Jonny that bothered me, worried me really. Jon had a tendency to place women on a pedestal, all women. Good or bad, ugly or beautiful, warm or frigid, they were women. And, according to him, they had to be respected and protected and dealt with tenderly. It worried me because Jonny couldn't seem to distinguish between them. He treated them all the same and, sooner or later, he was bound to run into trouble. To put it in a nutshell, handsome Jon Temple, student and athlete, was the biggest sucker in the world where women were concerned. Perhaps this was an inheritance from his parents. Jonny's father, David, a nondescript merchant, always deferred to his handsome wife. Rose Temple, pretty and vivacious, ruled the Temple household with the determined air of a martyr, jealous of her role of leadership, resolved to carry the burden of saintliness sadly but resolutely. Jonny was taught, from a very early age, to respect his mother, to worry about her, to do all in his power to relieve her of some of her crushing burden. All this simply because she was his mother and a woman. It was not necessary for her to earn his love and devotion, she was entitled to it by virtue of having given birth to him. After all, as she reminded him very often, she had shed blood for him, and he was beholden to her for the rest of his natural life. It bothered me that Jonny accepted all this so meekly and uncomprehendingly.

I'll give you a for instance. As healthy, young males during our college days, we both naturally liked girls. We dated occasionally and were not averse to a little necking. But Jonny decided that was as far as we could go with our classmates. There were girls downtown, he said, who were used to all sorts of things. We could go the limit with them because they were professionals and knew the score. Better them than some innocent young college girls who could get into trouble. Well, one night, things having progressed to bursting, Jonny and I headed for downtown Montreal, chippy-hunting, as we called it in those days. It was kind of funny, because we knew what we were after. But the dance hall proprietors and the bartenders were scared off by our youthful appearance, and we got kicked out of one place after another. You see, they thought we wanted to drink and that was the furthest thing from our minds.

Anyway, we finally clicked at a little joint called the Porte D'or on Stanley Street. The boss man didn't bother us and Jonny got picked up almost immediately by a dark girl, good-looking in a cheap sort of way. At his insistence she got a friend for me. Now, the girls were quite ready to take us back to their place right away, but Jonny decided the right thing to do would be to wine them and dine them first. I didn't think it was necessary, and hated the idea of blowing all my weekly allowance in one night. But we ate and drank and treated the girls like queens. It amused the hell out of me that Jonny kept up a running conversation, touching on topics that the girls neither understood nor cared about. Francine, Jonny's girl, who was after all a businesswoman, decided that we should skip dessert and hustled all of us out of the Porte D'or. We walked a few blocks till we came to a crummy old apartment building that was Francine's place of business; her flat was three flights up.

The flat consisted of one room, sparsely and poorly furnished. The only pieces of furniture consisted of a single bed and a beat-up sofa, a small chest of drawers, and a lamp table with an old unshaded lamp on it. The room had a peculiar, musty odour to it and it took me several minutes to realize why. No food had ever been cooked or served there. It was a business place, period.

Francine lost no time in preliminaries. She had no sooner shut the door behind us when she began to undress. I was horrified to think that there was only the one room and that Jonny and I were to conduct our business with an appalling amount of togetherness. I looked helplessly at him, but he only shrugged and grinned. "Part of our course," he said. "Prescribed study for the senior year." The girls giggled and got ready for business. I got the sofa.

When we were ready to leave, Jonny thanked the girls courteously and elaborately. They thought he was nuts. We paid our money, Jonny insisting that we leave it on the lamp table, which was more delicate than handing it to them, and made our way outside to fresh air.

On the way home, Jonny was strangely sad and thoughtful. I bugged him and he finally said, "It's a damn shame. Those poor girls forced to make a living like that. I'm sorry for them Arnold, I really am."

"Oh come on Jon," I replied, "theirs is the oldest profession in the world. And did you hear them complaining? You must be kidding. They like what they do. Besides, you'd better start saving your sympathy for those who really need it." But Jonny was distressed all the way home. He seemed to want to assume all the guilt of society for those girls. That's the kind of guy my friend Jonny Temple was.

Anway, I didn't tell you this story to show what terrific casanovas we were in those days. It's what comes after this incident that's important, that'll give you an insight into the character of my friend.

It was quite late when we got home. But Jonny insisted I come into his house for milk and cake before we went to bed. Jonny's mother met us, suspiciously, at the door. Then came the inquisition: "Where were you boys tonight?" "Downtown, Mom." "Where, at the movies?" "No, not exactly." It would have been so much easier if Jonny had been able to lie a little. "Well, if not the movies, where?" "Sort of a dance hall, I guess." "You guess? Either it was a dance hall or it wasn't." "It was a dance hall." "What did you do there?" "Danced." "What else?" "Picked up a couple of girls." "That's what I thought." And then Jonny's mother launched into a half-hour harangue on the evils of picking up dance-hall girls and all the possible consequences.

During all that time, Jonny's father didn't open his mouth. I certainly didn't and neither did Jonny. And don't forget that all that flow of language was directed at a young man, almost twenty-four years of age, in his senior year at college, not a twelve-year-old kid. And then came the most fantastic, stupefying thing of all. Jonny's mother was able to extract a promise from him never to do that sort of thing again. I couldn't believe it. In a way, it was almost obscene, forcing such a promise from a grown man. But Jonny gave his promise, and God forgive me for my ridicule, he kept it.

For the next few months at any rate, we had very little time to think about girls, or much about anything for that matter. Jonny and I were cramming for our final exams. Anxious to do well, we studied day and night, hunched over our books until the small hours of the morning. Sometimes there was a few minutes break to munch sandwiches and drink milk by the gallon. But mostly it was study, absorbing, memorizing until our eyes almost bugged out of our heads. It was a good thing the exams finally came when they did — we couldn't have kept up that pace much longer. Well, the exams were written and the results were good. To everyone's relief, especially our parents', the day of graduation from law school finally came. The team of Temple and Berman was now ready to take on the world, and to show the legal fraternity how things were done. The future seemed very bright.

The night following the last exam, I wanted to go down-town and blow off steam, live it up. I wanted to make a real bash of it, eat and drink and maybe find some willing girls and all that sort of thing. But Jonny was reluctant, he had made a promise. We finally settled for a get-together at Jonny's house. My parents were invited and they brought over a bottle of wine. It was hardly what you'd call a gay evening. Two boys, slightly frothing at the bit, and two sets of fond parents, taking credit for what had nearly caused us to go blind and permanently hunched. But one good thing came out of the whole mess. My father, may his soul rest in peace, came up with the brilliant idea of treating me to a trip to New York for a graduation present and talked Jonny's folks into doing the same for him. It was decided that we'd take the train the next day and spend a week in New York before coming back to start our year as juniors in an established law firm.

It's strange when you come to think of it. That innocent trip, that token gift made a big difference in our lives, particularly Jonny's. And we couldn't see it at the time. Of course, we were young. We couldn't see into the future, nor did we care to. The young live for today. Perhaps that's the way it should be, I don't know. Anyway, that's the way it was.

We checked into the Park Sheraton and settled ourselves. Then we went downstairs for coffee and a hamburger, and looked through the New York newspapers to decide on what shows we wanted to see. We both wanted to see *Oklahoma*, the smash musical hit. So we made up our minds to go over to the theatre immediately and see if we could get tickets for the evening show. Now you talk about coincidences. About a block from the theatre, we bumped into Ronnie Bleeker, a boy we'd gone to school with — I'd forgotten he lived in New York. Ronnie not only said he could get us tickets for the show, but he knew someone in the cast and could get us invited to the cast party afterwards. All in all, the evening was shaping up pretty good.

The show was great and the party after even greater. It was a real thrill for us to meet and hobnob with the actors and actresses. We felt like we were really something, being guests at that party. And then she came in, the most beautiful girl I had ever seen in my life. The girl I would love vainly and hopelessly for the rest of my life, walked through the door of the hotel suite and every eye turned on her. Beautiful . . . she was breathtaking. She was of medium height, but with a stunning and lush figure. A madonna's face, a creamy complexion. But what knocked your eyes out was her hair, a glorious, piled mound of red hair that lit up her face and the whole room. I knew who she was. She was in the cast of the musical and her name was Blaze Scotland.

I recovered enough to glance over to Jonny, seeking his confirmation in what I saw and felt. And he was standing transfixed, his mouth open and gaping like a Friday night fish. He shook his head several times, as though to make sure he wasn't dreaming and then repeated, "Oh my God, oh my God, did you ever see anything like her in your life? She must be the most beautiful girl in the whole world."

We both turned at the chuckle behind us. It was Ronnie. "Don't get yourselves into an uproar fellows," he grinned. "She's the friend who got us the invites here. I've known her most of my life. Come on, I'll introduce you." He led the way and we followed, almost stumbling over ourselves in our eagerness.

Blaze Scotland was her stage name. Born Andrea Kellerman in Brooklyn, she had wanted only one thing out of life — to be an actress. Her talent and her stunning beauty had opened up the path for her. And now, a lead role in *Oklahoma* was her crowning achievement to date. She was destined to be a star of the first magnitude. "Andy," Ronnie called, "I want you to meet some college chums of mine from Montreal, Jonathom Temple and Arnold Berman." The smile turned on us was radiant as, with a tinkly laugh, she linked her arms through ours and led us over to the bar. "The hostess must buy her guests a drink," she said. At the sound of her throaty voice, we were floating up there among the clouds. At that moment we didn't want to come down, not ever.

I didn't have to be a doctor or a soothsayer to see that a chemical reaction was taking place between Jonny and Blaze Scotland. Their affinity for each other was growing by the moment and that was pretty obvious. I knew I was being relegated to a status of friend of the family, but such was her magnetism that I was even willing to content myself with that, just so I could be near her from time to time. As the evening wore on, she and Jonny got closer and closer together. If there is such a thing as love at first sight, that night was a damn good example. I ended up leaning on the bar watching it develop moment by moment.

"Arnold would you mind if we meet back at the hotel? I'm taking Blaze home." Jonny was talking to me, but he had a faraway look in his eyes as if he had just beheld one of the wonders of the world. I've never seen a guy fall in love so fast or so completely. But I sure couldn't blame him. I could only envy him. Half of New York was probably in love with Blaze Scotland in those days and would have counted Jon Temple as the luckiest man on earth.

"When she was a little girl, a teacher nicknamed her Blaze because of her hair," Jonny was saying, "and when she got her first part, she took her drama coach's last name, which was Scotland. So she became Blaze Scotland. What a fabulous name, what a fabulous girl, eh Arnold?" Jonny had come back to the hotel in a trance after taking Blaze home. Now he was slightly recovered and pacing the floor like a prowling bobcat.

"What can I say Jonny?" I replied. "She's just the greatest thing I've ever met."

Jonny put his fingers to his lips with wonderment. "She kissed me goodnight," he whispered. After a long pause, he turned to me. "You don't know the half of it Arnie," he said. "She's straight and truthful and sincere. And would you believe it? She doesn't even think she's beautiful. Can you imagine that, not thinking she's beautiful?"

"It's hard," I admitted, "she must be quite a girl. To look like her and to act like her and to be unspoiled too, she's got to be something special."

"I love her," Jonny said very softly.

"I know," I answered.

I didn't see much of Jonny the rest of that week. He was always running off to meet Blaze. He spent the days with her and every night he watched her in *Oklahoma*. And then he would take her to supper and eventually back to her place. That boy was really on a merry-go-round. In love! The guy was lost. Ronnie took pity on me and we spent the time together, making the rounds of New York like a couple of sightseeing bachelors on the prowl. But each night I waited in our room for Jonny, to hear him extol the virtues of his love. As I think back, I was really glad for Jonny; I'd never seen him so deliriously happy. But I was scared too. After all, a lot of plans, our whole future could go down the drain, depending on the decisions he and Blaze would make that week. I didn't have to worry on that score.

I wish I could tell you that the affair between Jonny and Blaze Scotland had a storybook ending. It would give me pleasure to be able to tell you that Blaze gave up her career for love of Jonny. And that Jonny was able to make financial arrangements with his folks so he could marry her and continue with his career back home in Montreal. That would have been simple and beautiful. But it didn't work out that way. You'd have to have really known Jonny to understand why, and then the reason would have been obvious. Jonny knew what lay ahead of him. He couldn't support a wife, certainly not a girl like Blaze. And he just couldn't ask his folks to support him, with a wife, while he was trying to make it. Blaze understood. So they vowed undying love for each other. Blaze promised to wait for him. And Jonny swore there would never be anyone else for him. At the end of the week they parted. On the train, going home, Jonny was strangely sad for a guy so much in love. It had nothing to do with the parting. I think he feared for the plans that had begun that week in New York.

Back home in Montreal, we became juniors in a law firm. We had to serve for a year while preparing for our bar exams. Assuming we passed the exams, we planned to open our own offices as soon afterwards as possible. For the first few months, Jonny wrote to Blaze several times a week. Her letters always saddened him and I ached for my friend. Then Blaze went on tour and the letters became less frequent, although they never stopped entirely.

We threw ourselves into our work. We were determined to be good apprentices and serve our time with as much distinction as possible. Actually, it wasn't difficult. We carried out our assignments with enthusiasm and, we were told, better than average competence. Several months went by without incident. And then I began to notice a change in Jonny. He had become more subdued; his sense of humour was lacking in spirit. At first I didn't know why. And then I did — because his dispiritedness increased in direct proportion to the decrease in the number of letters from Blaze. He loved her desperately and he saw his love disintegrating through time and space. He never mentioned it to me but he didn't have to. I knew Jonny. I knew what he thought and what he felt. I had known these things since we were five years old.

As I mentioned, Jonny had always been a good athlete. Now that the winter snows had come to Montreal, Jonny rediscovered his passion for skiing. He spent every spare moment on the ski slopes in the city and then began going up to the Laurentians at weekends. Somehow, I believe, the white snow, the high slopes, and the biting wind uplifted him, made his growing sense of loss more bearable. I hate to admit it, but I missed Jonny a lot on these outings. I was so used to our being together that I didn't know what to do with myself when he wasn't around. And to tell the truth, I relied on him for our good times. He was the idea man; he always came up with interesting, even exciting things to do. I just moped around when he was away skiing. And I wished to hell the winter would pass quickly so I could have my friend back. No dice. When spring came and the snows were gone, Jonny took up golf. He would come back from the course so dog tired that he'd go right home to sleep. I began to despair that our relationship would ever get back to normal again. And I grieved for both of us.

Nothing lasts forever. Slowly, imperceptibly, Jonny began to snap out of it. I guess the main reason was that we wrote and passed our bar exams. And the search for suitable office space and furnishings interested him tremendously. He made a deal with his father to borrow his share of the expense money with a pre-arranged schedule of repayments. That was the way Jonny did things. Everything had to be on the up and up. Most boys, including myself, felt our parents owed it to us to set up our first law offices, or medical or dental or what have you. But not Jonny. To him it was a loan and an obligation which he accepted cheerfully. Well, we got ourselves a pretty good deal in downtown Montreal and rented a three-room suite. There was a private office for Jonny and one for me. The third room was to be a combined reception office, library, and filing cabinet space. We had our names put on the outer door in gold leaf. To start with, we arranged for a telephone answering service. We finally got moved in. And now we were open for business.

If it hadn't been for the fact that we were both living at home, we would have starved to death. People don't exactly break the doors down bringing cases to fledgling criminal lawyers. It was months before we got ourselves a decent case to work on. We lost. It was months more before another case presented itself to us, one that we could sink our teeth into. We worked like dogs but we lost it too. I was just about ready to try some other form of law, one that might prove just a little more lucrative than the nothing we had earned to date. But Jonny wouldn't hear of it. He insisted that we were criminal lawyers, and as such, we were to hold out for cases that were our specialty, that we had trained for. I was never much of an optimist and was damn sure that Jonny had made one hell of a mistake, a mistake that could write finis to our careers before they started.

But Jonny was seldom wrong in those days. And he wasn't wrong that time either. He ran all over town, he cultivated people, he talked, promised, petitioned. And he got us cases. We pretty near blew our tops when we broke the ice and won one. And from that moment on, things got better. We began to win cases with increasing frequency. I made damn sure to prepare them carefully and thoroughly. And Jonny . . . Jonny began to emerge as a promising trial lawyer. His work in the courtrooms was a joy. More cases came to us and within a comparatively short time, we were becoming a couple of busy young lawyers, earning a decent living. I was happy, happy because I was with Jonny all the time again, happy because our youthful dreams were being fulfilled.

Jonny was completely crushed the day he read about Blaze Scotland's marriage. Now don't start blaming Blaze all over the lot. And don't curse her either. It wasn't her fault. It wasn't anyone's fault really. It came about because of a misunderstanding which is easily explainable. After all, a lot of time had elapsed since that week in New York. And the letters between them had become even fewer because of Blaze's constant travelling and Jonny's preoccupation with his own career. What's more, Blaze was now a big star. She was making motion pictures, both in the States and Europe. And don't forget she was an exceptionally beautiful woman. She was getting the rush act from all sides; there were plenty of men more than anxious to be Blaze Scotland's husband. Her love for Jonny began to seem like a half-remembered dream. And she believed that Jonny had forgotten too. She married some European nobleman and, according to reports, she was happy with him.

Jonny understood and forgave, but he was inconsolable for weeks after the wedding announcement. He went through the motions at the office, he did his job competently in court. Only the dullness in his eyes betrayed his inner emotions. I hovered around him like a trained nurse. And like a nurse, I had to understand the problem, recognize it for what it was, follow the prescribed treatment and never upset the patient. I didn't mention Blaze. What was the point? He knew that I knew his sorrow. I think he was glad I was around and glad too, that like old friends, we didn't have to talk about it all the time.

As a matter of fact, it was just about that time that I learned something new about my friend Jonny, discovered a trait in him that was to become more and more evident as he got older. Jonny had never been the greatest in the world at small talk. I was often surprised at how shy he could be in the company of strangers. If he didn't have anything special to say, he would keep quiet. Bored, uncomfortable, even distressed at inane conversations, he simply kept his mouth shut. He listened but he wasn't listening. Or maybe he was listening to his own thoughts, which he found a hell of a lot more interesting. Anyway, after he got over the initial shock of Blaze's marriage, he lapsed into silence. He must have figured there was no use in belabouring the issue. He was hurting so much inside that he had become inarticulate. He carried his hurt and his pain in silence; he talked about them to no man, including me. Afterwards, I always knew when Jonny was crushed by the perplexities of life, or hurting. He just withdrew into himself and didn't talk at all. Maybe, in his mind, he was groping for answers and, finding none, decided there were none to begin with. One other thing didn't help a damn bit at the time. The hit songs from *Oklahoma* were being constantly played on the radio, day and night. He couldn't forget if he wanted to. The song that never failed to shake him up was "People Will Say We're in Love."

It took a long time for Jonny to come back to this world. But, as with an operation, pain gradually subsided, the wound healed, the discomfort lessened. You always remember an operation but eventually, human nature being what it is, you forget the details, you decide it wasn't so bad after all, you dismiss the pain. Gradually, tentatively I began to suggest to Jonny things we might do, places we might visit, people we might see. At first he just wasn't interested. But I persisted and finally, perhaps to humour me, he began to go along with my suggestions. But he would never join me in a chippy-hunting expedition. Whether he was being true to his promise to his mother or to Blaze, I never knew.

As often happens, our most important case to date walked into our offices unannounced one late afternoon. The caller was a sharply dressed hoodlum who frequented a district known as the Lower Main, the southernmost section of St. Lawrence Boulevard, the main artery that divides Montreal into east and west. Jammed with cheap theatres, cheaper restaurants, and still cheaper nightclubs, it was the hangout for the unemployed, the dispossessed, the outcasts of the city. And a group of hoods, known as the Chain and Mail Gang, because of their penchant for wearing bulletproof vests, formed the hierarchy of the wretched community. There had been a murder on the Lower Main — it was in all the newspapers — and the alleged killer of a nightclub waiter, one Jacques Perrier, a leader of the Chain and Mail Gang, had been apprehended. He was sitting in Bordeaux Jail awaiting trial.

Our caller introduced himself as Franc Perrier, Jacques' brother. He reached into his pocket and produced a wad of bills. There must have been several thousand dollars there. He peeled off ten one hundred dollar bills and placed them on the desk. "Down payment," he said shortly, "for the defence. Get him off and there's plenty more where that came from." It was typical that he made no protest of innocence, offered no excuses. It was also typical that he took it for granted that we would take the case. Actually, I started to refuse but Jonny shut me up. And when I saw the reborn sparkle in his eyes and the expression of eager anticipation on his face, I stayed shut. Having Jonny whole again was more important than anything else.

When Franc Perrier left I turned to Jonny. "You know of course that the s.o.b. is as guilty as hell. It's an open and shut case as far as the prosecution is concerned. And I wouldn't like to lose this one. The Chain and Mail Gang might not appreciate it."

For the first time in many weeks, Jonny laughed joyously. "He's guilty all right, there were plenty of witnesses. But don't you see? That's the challenge of the whole thing. It doesn't matter to us whether he's guilty or not. Our job is to defend him. That's what we were trained for. That's what we get paid to do. And if we pull it off, with all the publicity, we're made. We'll have more cases than we know what to do with."

"And if we don't?" I asked.

Jonny laughed again. "If we don't," he replied, "we'd better get the hell out of this town." That was the beginning. That was how the firm of Temple and Berman became attorneys to the best-known people in town. As far as we were concerned, the best-known people were all hoods.

"It's impossible," I complained bitterly. "It just can't be done. We'll never be able to prove that sonofabitch innocent. At least three people will testify they saw him do it. The prosecution will make monkeys out of us. It could be the shortest murder trial in history."

Jonny had been pacing up and down the office, literally talking to himself. At my words he stopped and looked at me. Actually he looked right through me. "We can't prove him innocent," he mused, "but they can prove him guilty. Okay, so what course do we take?" It was quiet in the office for several minutes. "Got it!" Jonny yelped. "Look here Arnold, we don't have to prove him innocent at all. We can't anyway. But we can work like buggers to create enough of a shadow of a doubt in the minds of the jury to screw up the prosecution's case. That's all we have to do. If there's enough doubt, there can't be a guilty verdict. And if they can't find him guilty, they've got to reduce the charges or set him free. Either way, it's okay for us."

"Jonny, Jonny," I sighed, "it's so simple. All we have to do is find a way to create the doubt. But how do we do that?"

"There must be a way," Jonny replied grimly, "otherwise we'd better start packing."

Jonny's work in that courtroom was nothing short of brilliant. He went to work on the prosecution witnesses and before he was through with them, he had them gibbering like idiots. On cross examination they became completely confused, they retracted, they contradicted each other. Before the trial was over the court was a three-ring circus. I was sure the judge was going to have apoplexy. At some time during the trial he turned a livid shade of purple and stayed that way. Finally his language became purple too as he told the prosecutor off and informed him that the crown had failed to prove its case. The charges were dropped and Jacques Perrier walked out of that courtroom a free man.

I shuddered as I watched him leave, smirking and waving at the spectators, many of whom formed part of his gang. I hated to think of what he was liable to pull now that he had been exonerated by the processes of law. The Chain and Mail Gang was jubilant. Franc Perrier pressed an envelope into my hand as he left. It contained four thousand dollars. Jonny sat at the counsel table long after the others had left. He was exhausted and the fire had gone out of him. Like an actor after the curtain rings down, he was spent and listless. He would only catch fire again in time for the next performance.

The newspapers were full of the trial. And Jonny's picture

was quite prominent on the front pages. Suddenly Arnold Berman and Jonathon Temple were in demand socially. People we hardly knew invited us to dinner parties, cocktail parties, and other assorted social events. Peculiarly, Jonny insisted we accept the invitations, although I knew by now that he loathed affairs of that sort. "It's good for business," he would say, "that's why we have to go." So we went, but for Jonny it wasn't easy.

I think I mentioned before that Jonny had a good sense of humour. It was more than that really. What it was, it was a sense of the ridiculous, of satire perhaps. It was pretty evident when we started attending those parties. Jonny understood even better than I that we were being invited for two reasons. One was to satisfy the curiosity people have about so-called celebrities. The other was to enable them to bask in reflected glory. He knew damn well that they would tell others that they had met Jonny Temple and Arnold Berman, had dinner or a drink with them — "You know, those two young lawyers who handled the Perrier case so brilliantly."

In self-defence, Jonny wore a perpetual smile of amusement, which eased his conscience. But the guests, unknowingly, put it down to sophistication and a charming modesty. For example, at one party, someone remarked at how forceful and animated Jonny had been during the trial. Jonny replied, "Yes, but don't forget, Franc was sitting right behind me. If you had a gun in your back, you'd have been animated too." Another time somebody commented on how grateful Jacques must be to Jonny for his life. "True," Jonny answered, "and much more grateful than his next victim is likely to be." While the guests basked mainly in Jonny's aura, I was happier than I'd ever been. Jonny and I, partners. Things were good and they would get even better. But it doesn't always work that way. The clouds of the storm were gathering and they weren't very far off.

It was at a dinner party, given by people I don't even remember, that I first noticed Rita Stern. I noticed her because she was making a big play for Jonny. She was attentive, she was flattering. And for some reason I'll never know, Jonny was falling for it. It's true that Rita was attractive. She was quite tall, almost as tall as Jonny, and slender. She was darkly pretty, even though her lips were a trifle thin for her round face. And boy, did she know how to carry herself. Aristocratic, haughty are the best words to describe her. I found out later that her friends called her "The Queen of Sheba," not exactly lovingly. Even that first night, she took command of the party. She even rearranged the seating plan at dinner, so that she might sit beside Jonny. I was placed at the other end of the table where I could only observe, not interfere. She kept up a running conversation; Jonny didn't even have to try to get a word in edgewise. But I could see that he was completely captivated by her. Nausea swept over me. It wasn't only that I had taken an instant dislike to her. I was scared, plenty scared for Jonny. Instinctively I knew that she was all wrong for him; he would be putty in the hands of a woman like that.

On the way home that night, Jonny was full of Rita. She had set her cap for him and she had succeeded. He was no match for her. He was completely taken in by her vigorous assault on his ego, by her flattery and admiration. Maybe it was her strength that captured him, or her exuberance. Maybe it was a mother image that he subconsciously needed. I had no way of knowing then and I have no way of knowing now.

"She's a marvellous girl, isn't she, Arnie?" Jonny asked. I mumbled some unintelligible reply. "She's got everything," he continued, "good looks, brains and a terrific personality."

"And all the strength and will of a predator," I added. I could have bitten my tongue off at the look that came over his face.

"What do you mean?" he demanded.

I knew I should keep my mouth shut, but the man who was more than a brother to me was threatened. I was drowning but I opened my mouth and the words spilled out. "She's not for you Jonny," I pleaded. "She may be everything you say she is. But she's much more, that you can't or don't want to see. She's a vampire, Jonny, she'll suck all the blood out of you and leave you dry. She's one of those dominating females. Stay the hell away from her Jonny, for God's sake."

For the first time in our relationship, Jonny looked at me coldly and angrily. "Mind your own business, Arnie," he said, tight-lipped. "I'm not a kid and I'm perfectly capable of deciding for myself who to go out with."

I'm older now than I was then. But I learned something that night that I've never forgotten. It's one of life's truisms. In a situation like this, keep your thoughts to yourself. Never belittle a person with whom a friend of yours has become infatuated. If some day they marry, you may find yourself out on one hell of a long limb. Well, I shot my mouth off, and it was almost a fatal mistake. I resolved then and there never to let it happen again. I might have lost the best friend I'd ever have in my life. "Sorry Jonny," I mumbled. "You're right of course. It's none of my business. It won't happen again."

To my intense relief, Jonny grinned and cuffed me on the shoulder. "Okay Arnie," he said. "And you're wrong about her. She's really a great girl. You'll see."

I nodded but kept quiet. I couldn't speak right then anyway. I wondered about the chill that swept through my body and if I was catching a cold.

There were a number of cases that needed attending to, and Jonny and I were pretty busy in the next weeks. I worked overtime preparing them and was thoroughly absorbed. But Jonny started to date Rita Stern. After each date, he talked about her to me. I knew he was lost. It would only be a matter of time before she had him completely sewed up. But he was happy, so happy that it never occurred to him that he was being had. He had fallen in love with Rita and was blind to everything but his love. I never made the mistake of criticizing her again. It was too late anyway.

Now I'm going to make a confession to you. I've never breathed a word of this to anyone in my life. But it's late now and if I don't get it off my chest once and for all, I'll damn well bust. I'm not proud of what I did and I offer no excuses, except that at the time, I thought I was acting for the best, in the best interests of Jonny. Anyway, you can judge for yourself whether I did right or wrong. Here's the way it was. It was my habit to open all the mail in the office each morning. I would sort it and then distribute it. Well, one fateful morning, I slit an envelope and started to read a letter. It was addressed to Jonny but that in itself wasn't unusual. It happened often at the office. The letter was from Blaze Scotland. It's not important to go into all of it. But one paragraph literally screamed out at me. She wrote, "My dearest, we all make mistakes. Sometimes we're given a second chance. I don't know if that's possible for me. My husband died two months ago, believing that I loved him to the end. I never allowed him to think otherwise. I made him a good wife, I have no regrets about that. And he never knew that I loved another man. It was always you Jonny. Please, let it not be too late. Tell me it's not too late. I love you Jonny."

I stared at that letter for more than half an hour. Can you

imagine what was going through my mind? Can you possibly imagine the struggle that was going on inside of me? If I gave Jonny that letter, all hell might have broken loose. If I didn't, I would be crucifying Blaze. And I loved her too. But Jonny was like my own flesh and blood. I was in a panic. I didn't want his life to get all fouled up. Sensitive, impressionable Jonny, that letter would have torn him in two. That's what I was thinking. I hope you never find yourself in a position like that. It's a terrible, terrible thing to play God, to have to decide people's lives, no matter how much you love or hate them. Blaze was part of Jonny's past; he had accepted that. Now it was Rita he wanted. God forgive me. For Jonny, not Rita, I tore the letter up.

Their engagement was announced. I had expected it, of course, but when it happened the shock was still very great. It's something like watching an elderly loved one die. You know it's inevitable, that it's only a matter of time. You think you're prepared for it. But when it finally happens, there is always the shock of realization that the end has come, finally and irrevocably. All hope is now gone and the sense of loss is infinite. So it was with the announcement. I had to face the fact that my relationship with Jonny could never be the same again. I hoped with all my heart that we would remain friends, notwithstanding Rita, but I was well aware that the old closeness would disappear, that the spirit of our friendship would change. Rita would be most important to him now, and he would share confidences with her that he couldn't share with me. The final jolt came when Jonny asked me to be the best man at his wedding.

We had often talked, as youngsters, about how our weddings would be. Jonny had always said that he would like a big wedding, with all the trimmings. The pomp and ceremony appealed to his sense of the dramatic, a sense that had served him well in the courtroom. The assembled throng, the formal clothes, the solemn walk down the aisle were very theatrical, in his mind, and suited his belief of what was appropriate for one of the most important days in his life. This is what Jonny would have liked. But it wasn't what Rita had in mind at all. She insisted on a quiet wedding with a limited number of invited guests. She selected a hotel in downtown Montreal as the site. She planned the whole thing. The fact that Jonny was unable to invite a number of his colleagues to his own wedding mattered not a bit. Jonny argued mildly but in the end he gave in, as his father had done so many hundreds of times before him. Rita had won the first skirmish.

It was a beautiful day in mid-June, the day of the wedding. As I dressed in my tuxedo trousers and white jacket, I felt washed out and melancholy, not excited and happy for my friend as I should have. But like I said, I was scared stiff for Jonny. God knows I wished him well. But Rita — to me she was like a hovering nemesis, ready to pounce and devour Jonny. Sure I was afraid of what she might do to him. But I was also afraid of what she might do to me, to us. Driving down to the hotel with Jonny, I felt something akin to regret and pity. I felt like I was driving him to his execution rather than his wedding.

Jonny and I were waiting for the bride to appear and come down the tiny aisle that Jonny had insisted be set up in the hotel salon, the only concession that Rita had made to his wishes. As Rita came through the doorway and started down towards us, I had a desperate urge to stop the whole proceedings, strangle her if necessary. At that moment I hated her with a fierce hatred such as I had never felt in my life before. I don't know what Jonny was thinking really, but for some reason, he placed his hand on my shoulder. I took a deep breath and settled down, smiling like an ape. After all, I reasoned, if I was to salvage anything for Temple and Berman out of all this, I had better play it cool, I had better remember that Rita would soon be his wife, whether I liked it or not. As Rita came up to us, she smiled, first at Jonny, then at me. I guess I imagined that her smile was one of victory and triumph.

The wedding breakfast was elegant and subdued, not the sort of ripsnorting affair that Jonny and I had talked about. Jonny was on Rita's right and I on her left. We must have made a cosy threesome sitting there, the bride and groom and the best friend and partner. I sat there smiling until my face ached. I was reasonably sure that after this day my face would wear a permanent smirk.

The bride and groom left on their honeymoon to Hawaii. Long after Jonny's and Rita's parents had left, long after the last guest departed, I still wandered around the salon like a lost child. The hotel staff began to clean up. To them another hotel function was over, another chore was ended. I still moped around until their glaring stares drove me out. As I left the hotel and started for home, a great wave of loneliness washed over me and a great sense of guilt too. Could Blaze Scotland possibly understand? Would she ever forgive me if she found out what I had done? Or would I stand forever guilty of having ruined three lives, well two that mattered anyway?

As I drove, one question kept pounding through my head with insistent repetition. Why did this marriage take place — what in the name of heaven did Rita want with Jonny Temple anyway?

By the way, Jonny was twenty-six years old when he got married.

CHAPTER 2

RITA

I heard the story of Rita's background from her own lips. As a matter of fact, I heard it so often over the years that it began to come out of my ears. One thing about Rita, if she liked a story, particularly about herself, she would repeat it so often that soon her listeners could chorus the phrases with her, without missing a word or even an inflection. She was really something.

Rita's parents came to Canada from England when she was a very small child. Her father was a tall, spare man and very English, from the top of his Derby hat to his oversize sandy moustache to the grey spats he always wore over pebble-grain shoes. He had started his business life as a book-keeper but, fired by an inordinate ambition and a driving will, he had studied accountancy at night. He had become successful in London even before he decided that there was greater opportunity in Canada. He was a taciturn man who believed strongly in self-discipline of mind and body. Nor was he given to bouts of enthusiasm, a feeling that he considered effeminate and plebeian. No, Henry Stern was hardly what you would call a warm person. Even his proposal of marriage to Marion Buckman, a Devonshire girl, was businesslike and almost impersonal. Marion accepted the proposal because she couldn't think of a reason not to. After all, she was twenty-five years old and it was time she married. Henry looked like a real solid citizen, so why not? Strangely enough, it was a good marriage even if it was bloodless. At least it was comfortable and solid. And each in his own way loved the other, albeit unemotionally and often lethargically.

Marion Buckman had left her folks in Devonshire and come to London at the age of twenty-one. She had made the move out of curiosity more than anything else, and although London had failed to fascinate her, she had remained to work as a stenographer in a large exporting firm, of which Henry Stern was the book-keeper. She was a pretty girl in a slow, plumpish sort of way, but because she was inclined to be lazy with a low energy level, she never cared whether she had dates or not. She accepted them occasionally if she wasn't too tired or too disinterested, but her very favourite pastime was curling up on her sofa in her tiny flat and reading. Of all the books she read, she loved cookbooks the best. She probably had more recipes in her head than any woman in London, even if she had never taken the trouble to try them. Henry was a no-nonsense, brusque man and she accepted dates with him because it was easier than defying him. She married him for the same reason. And when Henry decided to study accountancy, she accepted it without comment. It was quite a good arrangement really; it took care of the evenings. Henry studied his textbooks and she read cookbooks. When they had studied and read enough, they went to bed.

There must have been a spark of something in their love, because ten months after their marriage, Rita was born. She was to be an only child. Perhaps the reason lay in the old English joke, "tried it once and didn't like it." As Rita repeated numerous times, she has no recollection of her very early years in London. When she was three, Henry announced to Marion one evening that he had decided they should move to Canada. Marion nodded and then sighed as she began to think about the packing.

Henry had thought of going out west. But when they arrived in Montreal, he decided that he liked the city. So Montreal became their home on a whim as much as for any other reason. Henry set up an office and began practising accountancy. His appearance, his manner, and his English accent suggested competence and he was immediately successful. He found a home for his family in a west Montreal community. And the Stern family of London, England, settled in. They settled in but never became part of it. Henry wasn't interested and Marion couldn't care less. Young Rita was a lonely and introverted little girl. She became more so as she grew older in the calm, sterile, unemotional atmosphere of her parents' home.

Oh yes, one more thing contributed strongly to the growing character of this sad little girl. About a year after their arrival in Canada, Henry sent for his elderly mother who still lived in London. Her coming to live with them diverted what little attention was paid to the child. The matriarch had arrived and was ensconced with ceremony. She became the oracle, consulted and worshipped. The entire household revolved around her. Her comforts and wishes became of paramount importance. The child was left to fend for herself. She practically brought herself up. This Rita admitted even to me, strangely enough without bitterness, without recrimination. Although she denied it, I believe Rita accepted her upbringing as good and right. I think she just didn't know any better.

Rita grew up quickly. What I mean by that is that one moment she was a child and the next a young woman. There was nothing in between. She was so much alone and so largely ignored that she was literally forced to mature quickly, on her own. She took refuge from her loneliness in books and in solitary dreams about her own future. She really had very little, if anything, of the carefree youth and fun-filled growing up that fills the days of most youngsters, secure and loved in the bosom of their families. The fact is Rita was a loner as a child. And like most loners, the youngster who secretly yearned for social intercourse and friendships became self-sufficient and selfish, materialistic and proud. It was only after she married Jonny that her latent social abilities manifested themselves. She liked school. She made few friends but didn't care. Being the top student in her classes, she enveloped herself in an air of lofty arrogance that alienated and at the same time commanded respect. She was a world unto herself at that time. And the outside was to be exploited and turned to account when the time came.

She got one major bequest from her parents and grandmother, in the nature of sound advice. It was drummed into her head that it was just as easy to fall in love with a rich man as a poor one. She was advised constantly to seek marriage with a rich man, even at the expense of love. "You'll learn to love him later," her grandmother said. "You can do without most things, but not money," her mother remarked. "With money you're independent and somebody, without it you're nobody," her father insisted. Rita pondered these pronouncements and found them good. She decided early in life to take this advice. From that moment on, every male she met was judged on the basis of wealth or at least prospects of it.

At college, Rita made a few girl friends, mostly from affluent backgrounds, girls who thought and felt as she did. These girls became her clique. As far as boys were concerned, they dated her, sized her up, and fled, fast and far. She found this amusing for several reasons. First, like so many girls of her type, she felt that what she had to offer was much too good for them. Her folks had drummed into her head that a woman can make or break a man, although it was hardly obvious in her own home. Most of this talk came from her grandmother. "The right woman can raise any man to the heights," she said, "the wrong one will grind him into the dust." Rita's parents nodded silently, in agreement, and the die was cast. Rita now looked upon life with missionary zeal. Her role was to be that of helpmeet and partner to a man on his way up. And because she would be strong and determined, thoughtful and decisive, her man would achieve power and success beyond his wildest dreams. The boys at college weren't worth the effort and she was content to wait. When a man worthy of her came along, she would know it. She would choose him to be the instrument of her dreams. And together, they would conquer the world.

It never occurred to her, for even one small second, that maybe the man should lead and she should follow. It never entered her mind that a man, any man, could have a will of his own and should wish to dominate her. The second reason was her almost holy vow to know only one man. This came not from her mother's teachings nor from a sense of high morals. It went even deeper than that. College boys were out for only one thing. But no one and nothing must interfere with her grand plan. She simply couldn't take the chance of anything diverting her from her pre-planned future. It was just too risky. So she kept those frustrations in check with a steely resolve. Well, now you're beginning to see the kind of girl Rita was, and what I've told you was from her own lips. This is what Jonny fell into, this is the girl he was to marry. You're shaking your head? You haven't heard anything yet.

A married friend of Rita's invited her to a dinner party. She mentioned that Jonathon Temple and Arnold Berman, two up-and-coming young lawyers would be there. "And, my dear, they're both unattached. Who knows, one of them might be just what you're looking for." Get the picture? Rita came to that party to look us over. Like she was on a shopping expedition. Well, she had a good look at the merchandise and she chose Jonny. After that it was easy. Jonny was certainly no match for her. She decided that night she would marry him. And she did. Simple as that.

I missed Jonny very much while he was in Hawaii on his honeymoon. It wasn't only that the work at the office was piling up. But you must understand that for a lot of years I had relied on Jonny being around. I seldom made a decision without consulting him. We had always planned and done things together; our thinking was on the same wave-length. Now that he was away, I felt the loss very deeply. At the same time, I was plenty worried about the future, about what it held for Jonny and me. He sent me a few postcards, two or three lines which said nothing and finally one which announced his arrival home in three days. I was like a kid at the airport, waiting for their plane to arrive, all excited and jumpy inside. When I finally saw them, I breathed a deep sigh of relief. They both looked wonderful, tanned and rested, serene. I wondered, at that moment, whether I'd been all wrong, whether my fears had been completely groundless. Maybe, just maybe, Jonny had found the right key to his marriage. Maybe he would be able to handle Rita. Maybe things would work out a lot better than I had feared. There were a hell of a lot of maybes. But for the moment I believed that the future might be promising and bright.

We plunged into a backlog of work at the office. It was wonderful having Jonny back again. My friend, my brother, my conscience, my security had returned. The office came to life again, things began to hum as we prepared several cases together. As before, I worked on the preparation and Jonny planned the pleading. I felt like I was whole again. In between work, at lunch, and on the way to and from the office, Jonny talked enthusiastically about all the wonderful sights and sounds and smells of Hawaii. He had really gone overboard for that place and claimed repeatedly that he couldn't wait to go back. But the strangest damn thing, he spoke very little about Rita. Well, after all, a man comes back from his honeymoon with his new bride, you'd think he'd be full of her. You'd think that her name would be on his lips constantly — she did this, she said that, she liked it, she didn't, she wore such and such. But he remained amazingly silent about her. About the only thing he did mention was how busy she was house-hunting and the type of furniture she wanted.

Jonny gave up skiing; Rita wasn't at all interested. He gave up golf — she didn't care for that either. He spent his days at the office and his evenings with Rita and with Rita's friends. Quickly and surely all of Jonny's old friends disappeared from their circle. All except me. There could be no get-together, no party, no entertainment, but that I had to be there. On that, Jonny was adamant. And I know why. He wasn't exactly crazy about Rita's old clique. He could barely stomach their bright and brittle conversation, and he loathed the inane, waste-of-time cocktail parties that they threw constantly. I was his bulwark. He could always retreat behind his defences, which were me, by dragging me off to one corner, where we could talk quietly. When his defence was penetrated, he would allow himself to be dragged, reluctantly, back into the thick of the pointless cocktail party chatter. Jonny Temple was becoming a pale carbon copy of his former self in the stifling, empty atmosphere created for them by his wife. I watched and I saw. And I bled a little more each time.

Now no man really knows what goes on inside another man. And certainly no man could possible know what goes on inside a woman. I'm perfectly aware of that. But before you ask me how come I know so much about Jonny's private life with Rita, about his thoughts and hers, let me tell you that I may not know everything, but I know a hell of a lot. After all, Jonny and I couldn't have been any closer. A lot of what I'm going to tell you, I pieced together from chance remarks. Some things I deduced from simple observation. Others I garnered from conversations with family and friends. Anyway these are the things I think and believe. I'll tell you the story as I see it. You be the judge.

Jonny had given in to his wife on just about every matter pertaining to their wedding. I don't think it was plain weakness. He was in love with Rita and simply went along with her wishes, thinking perhaps that, if the arrangements she wanted were that important to her, it just wasn't worth fighting about. Like I said, Jon had been brought up to place women on a pedestal. It just wasn't in his nature to fight with them or to argue or to insist. Giving in to them was part of his heritage; how could it be otherwise? Now as for the honeymoon. Rita wanted desperately to go to Hawaii. There's nothing wrong with Hawaii. So Jonny saw no reason to protest or to suggest any other place. He left the arrangements to her, the flights, the choice of hotel, all the entertainment plans. When Rita announced that she had made reservations at the Hele Mai Hotel near Waikiki Beach on Oahu, Jonny was really quite enthusiastic. Amongst other things, he figured on getting in a lot of golf. In the end, he played only once, but still managed to fall in love with the islands.

Rita arranged sightseeing tours, she arranged swimming parties, she organized the other hotel guests for luaus. She was good at organizing and she certainly had all the qualities that make for a social leader. She was sociable and bright and gay. She was opinionated and strong-minded. She was full of entertaining ideas. And her mouth never stopped. Sometimes people went along with her because it was a damn sight easier to fall in with her plans then to argue with her. The hot Hawaiian sun made her fellow guests lethargic. So, where she led, they followed. Rita was a great success as a leader because she willed it. And even those she led admired her ideas and her energy. They followed her and convinced themselves that they were having a ball.

At first, Jonny enjoyed seeing his wife as the leader of the pack. He chuckled at her enthusiasm, he enjoyed the variety of her plans, he watched proudly as the other guests agreed with her and scurried off to get ready, he admired the efficiency of her schedule. But as the days passed he tired of the constant round of activity and he tired of the incessant proximity of his fellow tourists. He longed to spend a day doing nothing, letting the hours bring what they might, drifting from morning to night aimlessly and effortlessly. He ached to get off by himself for a round of golf. But when he mentioned these things, Rita pouted. Here she was, knocking herself out to make their stay memorable and Jonny didn't appreciate it. As for the golf, didn't Jonny want to spend his time with her? Weren't they on their honeymoon? Wasn't togetherness the name of the game? How could he bear to leave her? Jonny sighed and decided to forget about the golf. What did Rita have planned for them today?

When Jonny and Rita came home from their honeymoon, Jonny convinced himself that he had had a good time, that their honeymoon had been a ball from beginning to end. Incident-ally, don't think for a minute that Rita wasn't great in bed. On that score, she was a perfectly normal, healthy, and somewhat frustrated female. She had waited a long time, in virginal isolat-ion, for marriage and she brought enthusiasm and passion to their marriage bed. No, Jonny had no complaints in that depart-ment. Well, to be quite honest, Jonny had no real, major complaints about his marriage to Rita at all, so far. It was when they got back and Rita started looking for a house and furniture that Jonny made the first of a series of fatal mistakes.

The wedding present from Jonny's folks had been in the nature of a cash gift and it was used for the honeymoon. The gift from Rita's parents was to be the furnishings and equip-ment for their first home. What's wrong with that, you say? Nothing. Nothing at all, provided you realize the implications and consequences. From almost any other family and with almost any other wife, Jonny need never have given it a second thought. But first of all, remember, Rita's folks had hoped that she would marry a rich man, never really expecting that she would settle for one with good prospects only. They gave their gift and it was a generous one. But they gave it with a certain deep-seated resentment and with reluctance. They never got over feeling that had Rita married a man of means, it wouldn't have been quite so necessary. As for Rita herself, somewhere way deep in her mind, was the feeling that she was spending her own money, not Jonny's. It was an indefinable feeling, vague and hidden, but it was there. And because of it, she never really felt that she had to consult her husband on her purchases. Once she had found and rented a duplex in the western part of Montreal, she furnished it according to her taste, equipped it with items of her choosing. Poor Jonny never gave it a thought; he never realized the mistake he had made in accepting the gift so lightly. He had no way of knowing how and when his casual acceptance would come back to haunt him.

I learned to dread the clack of Rita's high heels along the linoleum corridor of our office building. I knew it was her even before she threw open the door to our own offices and swept in, breathless and excited over her latest purchases. No matter what we were doing, no matter how busy we were, no matter who was in the office, Rita blew in like a storm and, heedless of the interruption, proceeded to chatter away about a dozen and one things that couldn't have been less important to us at the moment. She was a near genius at talking trivia for minutes on end without taking a breath. Athletes prayed for the kind of lung-power that was so naturally a part of her. We would sit back and listen — we had damn little choice — until she ran down and, with a blowing of a kiss and a wave, she breezed out, slamming the door behind her.

After she left, the silence in the office was deafening. We would finally recover and, shaking our heads, grin at each other helplessly. Jonny always tried to appear amused by the episode but I could detect something deep in his eyes that was not amusement. Embarrassment maybe? Impatience? Annoyance? I really don't know. One thing I can tell you, I was bloody relieved when the shopping trips were over and she and Jonny were finally settled in their new house. With the end of the shopping came the end of Rita's visits to the office.

Rita became pregnant on her honeymoon. Now this in itself isn't so fantastic; nor, I suppose, is it all that unusual. I guess that happens to a lot of women. Some of you might know about that. Jonny mentioned it to me, kind of sheepishly, shortly after their return. I felt that I had to say something to Rita, so the next time she came into the office, I offered my congratulations and best wishes. She was positively regal as she accepted them. And dramatic. You'd think she was either the first woman in the world to have a baby or that her pregnancy was the most unusual and wonderful thing that had ever happened since the Creation. Having a baby was not a natural event to her; it was earth-shaking. And she was sure that it was equally important to everyone who knew. This was an act of God. The whole world, her world at least, had to be awed by it. After all, how could it be otherwise? And Jonny? Jonny was pleased, joyful I'd say. But I'm pretty sure he was a little stunned by it. I don't think he figured on it happening quite so fast.

Once Jonny and Rita were settled, things really got back to normal at the office, normal in the sense of routine but not in the importance of the case we were working on. This case might well have been the biggest of our careers to date. It started with a long-distance call from Quebec City, seat of the provincial government. The caller was the secretary of the Acting Premier of the province, who asked us to come up to Quebec to discuss a matter of great importance. We agreed on a time for the next afternoon. Jonny and I had a pretty good idea of what the call was all about. The Premier of the province was ailing and after undergoing surgery was recuperating in Bermuda. During his absence, a smart-aleck reporter, allegedly in collusion with a lady of easy virtue, had broken a story of sex and scandal involving a high-ranking cabinet minister.

Now it was common knowledge, not only in Quebec City, but throughout the province, that Monsieur Roland Duceppe had had difficulty for years in keeping his pants zipped. Everyone knew it and everyone joked about it, even the kids in school. But what the hell. The guy had an eye, or something, for the ladies. So what? Who did it hurt? As long as his amatory activities were kept comparatively quiet, people were inclined to shrug and forgive, perhaps with just a tinge of envy thrown in. But this time all hell had broken loose. This time there was a paternity suit. And this time there was a reporter who was determined to make the most of it. This time, too, a gleeful Opposition was only too glad to fan the flames, hoping that a self-righteous and aroused public would help them bring down the government. We knew before it was spelled out for us that it was the paternity suit that we were being called in on. But why us? This we didn't know until we got to Quebec.

The meeting had been arranged for four o'clock and was to take place in a suite at the Chateau Frontenac. It was a delicate matter, this involvement of the government in the case, but it was necessary because Duceppe seldom had a dime to his name. And right now was no time for the newspapers to start bleating about the fact that Duceppe's defence lawyers were being paid by the government. That's why the Chateau was chosen for the meeting instead of the government offices. Immediately after lunch, Jonny and I left by car for Quebec City. That drive was like old times, Jonny and I jabbering eagerly, discussing the case with great animation. I found myself wishing we were driving to California, which would take days, instead of to Quebec, which would take only a few hours.

When we arrived in the city, we drove directly to the Chateau and went up to the suite immediately. The moment we walked in, we knew how seriously the government was taking all this. The Acting Premier was sitting in an easy chair by a desk, waiting for us. He stood as we entered the room and shook hands with us. "Gentlemen, I thank you for coming, it was good of you," he said, "perhaps you would like a drink before we get down to business?" We declined and he motioned us to two chairs which had been placed near the desk. "There's no point in wasting time," he continued. "We wish you to defend Monsieur Duceppe in the paternity suit and to discredit the girl. We trust that your coming here signifies your acceptance of the case."

Jonny nodded and said, "One question sir. Why us? Surely there must be many more prominent lawyers you might have called in."

The Acting Premier smiled. "Perhaps," he agreed, "but we followed, with interest, your handling of the Perrier case. To have secured his release in the face of the overwhelming evidence against him was remarkable. It is imperative that you be as successful for us. You can understand why. And now I must leave you with my secretary, Paul Bergeron, here. He will assist you and arrange for you to see Monsieur Duceppe. Bonne chance." He left and Paul Bergeron set up the meeting with Duceppe for the early evening.

Roland Duceppe was an aging playboy, tall, handsome, and grey-haired. He was elegant and debonair and charming in the French manner. Men were drawn to him, almost as much as women, because he was exceptionally friendly and obliging and because they envied him his joie de vivre and his women. Duceppe was married in name only; he and his wife had long ago decided to live and let live. They went their separate ways and came together only when government protocol forced Roland to ask his wife to act as his hostess for one sort of entertainment or another. For the rest, beautiful women were as necessary to him as the air he breathed. He often said that without them he could not live, only exist. He went through the motions of the days waiting for the nights. And at one thing, he was a positive genius: Former amours turned mistress remained devoted to him even after he had discarded them in favour of a newer, younger, seemingly unobtainable conquest. But it was the thrill of the chase that consumed him, not the conquest in itself. To him, the game was seduction, not surrender. And when he abandoned his current mistress in favour of another, he did so with such grace and charm that she remained his friend forever, certain that the day would come when Roland would come back to her and their romance would attain a storybook ending.

Politics was Roland's second love. He was more than an able politician; he made an excellent cabinet minister, bringing to the cabinet class and distinction and the unquestioned advantages of his vote-getting personality. Love and politics, these were his life. And if the former sometimes threatened the latter, he would shrug with Gallic disdain and leave no doubt as to which one would win over the other. The only other outstanding characteristic about the man was his complete inability to hold onto a dollar. His loves were expensive. This he accepted with grace. After all, what better way to spend one's substance, what better value could he possibly get for his entertainment dollars?

But now he was in big trouble. For the first time in his life, a woman had failed to succumb to his charms. For the first time, a woman not only had no desire to remain friendly, but was actually bringing a paternity suit against him, threatening his political career and his life. Roland was stunned. How could a woman do this to him? Hadn't he devoted his life to making them happy? Hadn't he striven always to entertain them and love them? This was a cruel blow. What's more, it threatened to destroy his whole concept of womanhood. And that would be a disaster, that would drastically alter his way of life, would ruin forever his happiness and contentment. Why? He simply couldn't understand it.

The meeting with Roland Duceppe that night left Jonny and me plenty worried. We certainly wouldn't dare treat the ramifications of the case lightly. I sweated profusely all through the meeting. Winning the case was one thing — it would be a great feather in the caps of Temple and Berman. But losing it. I shuddered to think of our muddied reputations if, God forbid, Duceppe should be found guilty. And Duceppe himself was no help to us at all. For a cabinet minister and a man of the world, he sure took this case casually. He seemed more concerned with the whys and wherefores of women's perfidy than with the implications to his political career and to the government he served. Jonny, trying to build a case, started the questioning. Duceppe had insisted from the start that we call him Roland. Jonny began:

"Roland, a young woman by the name of Lise Aumont has stated to a reporter of *La Presse* that you are the father of her unborn child, a child she expects to give birth to in about six months. She is preparing to sue you for a considerable amount of money, including a stipulated sum for pre-natal care, childbirth, and maintenance afterwards. Now, although *La Presse* has been meticulous in its reporting of the allegations, this case has all the earmarks of blowing up into a full-scale scandal. The Opposition is preparing to make capital out of the whole thing. First, do you admit to knowing the young woman?"

"But of course I know her. I have known her, shall we say intimately, for about three months. And that is what I cannot understand. She is a lovely, sweet child. I cannot believe she wishes to make this trouble for me."

"Alright, you know her. As you say, intimately. Are you planning to testify in court, under cross examination, that you know her . . . intimately?"

"My friend, I don't see how I could deny it. No one would believe me. I pay the rent for her apartment in Montreal. We have been seen together at parties, at nightclubs, and at the theatre many times. Frankly, with my reputation, it would be incredible to suggest that our friendship was platonic."

"Okay, now Mr. Duceppe, I mean Roland. What about the child? Do you believe that you are the father?"

"It is possible, is it not, under the circumstances? Again, would anyone believe that she has been my . . . my amour for some three months and that I am not the father of her child?"

"Roland, this is going to be a damn tough case to win. At this moment, the prosecution has all the cards stacked in its favour. As you yourself said, it's going to be pretty near impossible to whitewash you. But we've got to try. Relax for a few minutes. Pour yourself a drink while I kick a few things around with my partner."

Jonny turned to me and took a long, deep breath. Expelling the air slowly, he said, "Brother this is a toughy. Where do we go from here? I hope to hell you have some good ideas."

"I don't know Jonny," I replied, "we've damn little to hang our hats on. And old Roland here isn't going to be much help. He's just about prepared to admit everything and accept defeat already. I've been thinking about the trying to establish a shadow of a doubt bit, but it hardly seems to apply here. There must be an angle, but I haven't come up with it yet. And the Acting P.M. will have us boiled in oil if we don't move our rear ends pretty fast."

Jonny had been concentrating deeply as I talked. Now he jumped up. "Hold it," he exclaimed, "I think I've got the angle! We were told to defend Roland and discredit the girl. That's it Arnie, that's our angle. Discredit the girl. Cast doubts on her character and reliability. To whitewash Roland, we'll have to smear the girl. It's a stinking thing to do but what choice do we have?"

Roland, who had been listening to our exchange, started to protest but Jonny cut him short. "Look Roland, you're going to have to stop this knight and damsel business if we're to win. Miss Aumont is out for blood, yours and the government's. There's too much at stake to pussyfoot around. A lot of people are counting on your co-operation. Now you sit and talk to Arnie for a few minutes, I have to make some calls." As he left the room and went into the bedroom I couldn't help wondering what had happened to the guy who had always placed women on a pedestal, who dealt with them tenderly, good and bad. I wondered.

Sidney Korvin was a detective who had done some work for us in the past. He now went to work on Lise Aumont. And what he came up with was enough for us to go on. Roland Duceppe had not been the first man in her life. And, luckily for us, Roland's predecessor had left her bed just days before her meeting with him. Now Jonny gambled. He reached Lise Aumont by phone and introduced himself. On the pretext of discussing a settlement, off the record, he got her to agree to see us. She invited us up to her apartment for a friendly drink.

Lise lived in an attractive and luxurious apartment in the heart of downtown Montreal. It was furnished tastefully and comfortably. And the girl, herself, was beautiful, And, believe it or not, innocent looking. I could easily understand what Roland Duceppe had seen in her. You'd have to be made of lead not to find her desirable. And I am not made of lead. She greeted us with cheerful friendliness as she welcomed us to her apartment. In less than five minutes, she showed herself to be as bright as she was beautiful. I began to get uncomfortable as hell and found myself wishing we didn't have to nail her to win our case. Truth to tell, Lise was the kind of girl who invited sympathy and protectiveness. Before long, she had me thinking that Roland was a sonofabitch. Well, dammit, he owed her something. He couldn't keep her as his mistress for months and just walk away at the first sign of trouble. Such was her personality that she was able to induce this kind of dangerous thinking on my part. I could see that Jonny was impressed with her too. He seemed on the point of wavering. And then he remembered why he was there. From then on, the way he handled her was beautiful. He was courteous and charming. He was friendly and sympathetic. He was humble and restrained.

"Miss Aumont . . . . may I call you Lise? Well Lise, this is a messy business. A number of people are going to be hurt, including you, I'm afraid."

"How can I be hurt more than I already have been? We won't talk about my reputation. But I'm going to have a baby now. And Roland is just going to have to pay."

"Of course he is Lise. There's no doubt in my mind that he should pay. I will advise him to pay."

"You will advise him? But you are his lawyer. Oh yes, you did mention a settlement. But I think, Monsieur Temple, that you have in mind a lot less than I."

"The amount is unimportant Lise. I'm sure we can come to an agreement on the amount that will be satisfactory to you."

"Forgive me, Monsieur Temple, if I seem a little suspicious. You are being too smooth, too easy. What do you want of me?"

"Let me put it this way. Mr. Berman and I represent Roland Duceppe. You can well understand what our job is. But we agree that you must be taken care of financially, it is only right. On the other hand, financial arrangements are one thing, scandal that hurts a great many people is another. With your co-operation, we can settle this case happily for everyone. And you will be well looked after."

"What must I do to be well looked after?"

"Don't fight me in contesting the paternity suit."

"And if I do?"

"Well, you know how lawyers are, Lise. I would have to fight back every way I can. For example, I might have to insist on a blood test."

"Which might prove exactly nothing."

"Perhaps. But you understand the implications of my requesting a blood test. Look Lise, right now you're in the position of a wronged woman, a sympathetic position. Roland will not deny his relationship with you. It may not even come to that. But a blood test is something else. It makes things ugly. It implies other men, more than one. And you will gain nothing except a reputation of the worst kind. Do you hate Roland so much that you're willing to risk it?"

"No, it has little to do with hate. And not so much the money. It has to do with my baby."

"Lise, who is Artur Morin?"

"Someone . . . someone I used to know."

"Someone with whom you lived just before you met Roland? Someone with whom you parted just a few days before taking up with Roland? Someone who might just possibly be the father of your child? Come now Lise, you're too smart to get mixed up in all this."

"But not so smart as you, Monsieur. We will discuss the settlement. And then you will tell me what it is you wish me to do."

To say that the public was disappointed is to put it mildly. The case that promised so much in the way of sensationalism turned out to be a pretty mild affair after all. After the first day, even the press played it down, although the firm of Temple and Berman came in for a certain amount of praise for handling a delicate situation with tact and finesse. Duceppe was elated, the government people were elated, everyone including myself was elated. Everyone that is, except Jonny, who had really carried the ball. As had so often happened before, Jonny was listless and apathetic. But this time something else was added. He should have felt that he was sitting on top of the world. But he was sad, immeasurably sad, and I hadn't the faintest idea why.

Jonny had flatly refused to allow Rita to come to court. She was furious. She insisted that it was her right to come to see her husband in action. Rita always was ready and willing to bask in reflected glory. But Jon was adamant. He was equally insistent that her presence would both distract and embarrass him. An unusual situation, wouldn't you say? But now that I come to think of it, in the years that Jonny and I worked together, Rita never once came to court. Whatever the truth of the matter was, Jonny must have had his reasons, but I never did find out.

A few weeks after the case was ended, Rita bore Jonny a son. I guess he was pretty happy about that and for a while the old Jonny reappeared, cheerful and contented. But it didn't last for long. Soon the old sadness was back, stronger than ever. At that time, it was just one more thing I didn't understand. Jonny was reluctant to talk about it. And I might have decided to live with it except that it began to affect his work. It wasn't only that Jonny had no enthusiasm for the cases that poured in on us as an aftermath of the Duceppe case. He was completely uninterested, he couldn't care less. And that scared the hell out of me. I stewed about it but there wasn't a thing I could do.

And then there was the accident. It happened on a warm, summer afternoon on the stretch of highway known to us Montrealers as Route 11, leading up the Laurentian Mountains. Rita had been complaining that her folks were being neglected. It seemed like Jonny, and she too, for that matter, had been so busy first with their home and then with their son, that they hadn't seen Rita's mother and father or grandmother in weeks. Well, Jonny and I had planned to go over a brief one Saturday afternoon, but Jonny begged off, saying that he had promised Rita that they would take the older folks for a drive to the Laurentians. At the last moment our client called and insisted on our working on that brief. It just had to be ready for the Monday morning. Jonny was unhappy about calling the trip off. I guess he knew that Rita would give him a what for. Anyway it was to be postponed for the following week, and Jonny and I worked at the office that whole afternoon. Henry, always stiffnecked and proud, decided that he would drive Marion and his mother up to Ste. Agathe for the afternoon anyway. It was on the return trip, rounding a curve, that the accident occurred. Henry skidded and collided with a truck going in the opposite direction. The truck driver, Henry, and Henry's mother were killed instantly. Marion survived, miraculously with very little injury.

Rita was dangerously calm following the double funeral. And she contained herself very well during the week of mourning. Jonny appeared to be taking it far worse than Rita, and they were Rita's folks. Jonny never said a word to me, and it was years before I learned that, at that time, Rita had insinuated that if Jonny had stuck to his original plan of driving them, the accident might never have happened. And, apparently, she reminded him of it from time to time for years afterward. Guilt feelings? I guess Jonny had them all right, induced by Rita. But damn it all, don't tell me it's natural for a wife to want her husband to suffer like that, and for something that was not of his doing. Anyway, at the end of the week, Rita announced that Marion would be coming to live with them.

Jonny might have had a chance with Rita. Maybe things might have worked out better for them, given half a chance, over a period of time. After all, there was the child, whom they both adored. But when Marion moved in, the chance was lost forever. Perhaps if it had been a large home, just perhaps it might have worked out, although I doubt it. But in the duplex, the togetherness was just too much. There was no more privacy, there were no secrets from Marion. She was always there, especially as she went out very seldom. She was there when Jonny left in the morning, she was there when he returned, she was around when they talked and planned, she was never far when they quarrelled or made love. And she didn't really do anything around the house; she was just underfoot all the time. She read her cookbooks but she never cooked anything. She offered her advice freely, and she had a lot to say about the bringing up of the child. She had always to be considered; her wishes had to be taken into account. And she mustn't be left alone. After all, the child loved her and she loved him, but he could hardly be classified as company for her, especially during the long evenings. Even if they had a large affair to attend, Rita always felt badly about leaving Marion and made damn sure that Jonny felt guilty about it too. Gradually, Marion became the first consideration in the Temple household — whether she liked it, whether it was convenient for her, whether she was up to it, whether it suited her. It was Marion first, the child second. And Jonny? Jonny came last. No matter what it was, everyone else's needs, everyone else's desires and preferences came first.

In all fairness to Rita, I don't think she planned it that way, or even thought about it very much. It's just the way things were. Her devotion to her child and to her mother were one thing; her husband, she just took for granted. It had nothing to do with love. She loved Jonny, in her own way. It's just that some unknown force shaped the formula of their lives, knitted the pattern, produced the fabric of their existence. Neither Jonny nor Rita, nor Marion for that matter, would have dreamed of acknowledging the presence of that force, they simply drifted with it. And since all drifting is aimless, that's what their lives became, aimless.

The spark went out of Jonny Temple. The strong, virile athlete began to slow down. The old sense of humour was kept well beneath the surface. The incentive to win diminished. Getting through each day seemed to be the problem that preoccupied Jonny the most. Where before the accident, he had been unenthusiastic and uninterested for months, now he appeared to be truly suffering. The greatest suffering the world can know is lack of hope. Without hope, there is nothing. I'm sure that Jonny hadn't analyzed his feelings at that time, but he must have begun, then and there, to feel the beginnings of a hopelessness about his daily existence and about his future. Perhaps he sensed the end of his dreams.

I was beside myself. I wanted, desperately, to do something, but I didn't know what. I was very concerned about our practice, but I was more concerned about my friend. I guessed at a lot that was going on inside Jonny and my heart felt like lead inside me, because I was so powerless to do anything about it. I tried to think of ways to get Jonny to snap out of it, but nothing helped. Finally, as a last resort, I asked Jonny to go to New York to do some background work on a case we were working on. Normally that was my job, but I hoped the change would do him some good. I told him my stomach was bothering me and he agreed to go. It's just possible that he looked forward to getting away from the stifling atmosphere at home for a few days.

Jonny flew into New York on a Wednesday afternoon, planning to settle in at the Waldorf and then spend Thursday and Friday working. During dinner that first evening, he was glancing through the *News* when a picture and a name rivetted his attention. It was Blaze Scotland and her latest play had just recently opened on Broadway. Jonny stared at the newspaper picture for a long, long time, oblivious to everyone and everything in the dining room. Then, his mind made up, he left the room and headed down Fiftieth Street to Broadway.

The play was over and after the final curtain call, Jonny made his way backstage. He glimpsed Blaze in the middle of a huge crowd of well-wishers but remained on the fringe of the crowd, with a huge lump in his throat. She was more beautiful than ever. And his mind whirled with chaotic thoughts until he thought it would burst. Blaze was talking animatedly with her admirers when she glanced over and saw Jonny. She broke off in mid-sentence and turned pale. Then she recovered and, plunging through the crowd, caught Jonny's arm and propelled him into her dressing room. She slammed the door and stood facing him, her breath laboured. No sound came from her lips. Jonny, too, stood rooted to the spot, unable to utter a word. Then slowly, dream-like, she moved toward him. Jonny stepped toward her. Like robots, unthinking, unaware, they stretched out their arms toward one another. There was no sound in the room as they came together, enfolding. Jonny held Blaze tightly in his arms, his lips against the softness of her fiery hair. There was no sound. And no room. Only a ghost hovered about. A ghost of things past, a ghost of what might have been.

CHAPTER 3

BLAZE

Anna and Rudolf Kellerman decided that they could no longer live in Germany. There were signs everywhere that a new political party was ascending to power, a party that had no earthly use for Jews. Certainly there could be no future in the New Order for a publisher of a small Yiddish newspaper. Besides, they had no ties, not even a child to be considered. That was the sadness in their lives. They had been married for five years and remained childless. In desperation they had seen doctor after doctor, always to be told the same thing. There was no reason, physical or otherwise, why they should not have as many children as they wished. But no child came year after year. And now things were bad in Germany and would get worse. Why not leave and go to America? A new life. A safe haven. And who knows, maybe the change, maybe life in their new country, maybe something would cause their luck to change. Maybe in America they would find the answer to their five years of prayer and the elusive gift that they so desired, a child. All things considered, this was the time to leave and seek a new life in a new country. It would be good there; a man could breathe and, God willing, bring up his family in open spaces under clear skies. They made their decision, but they never counted on Brooklyn.

Rudolf had a cousin who had emigrated to the United States years before and who had done very well. It was to this cousin that Rudolf addressed himself, seeking information and a promise that the way would be prepared for them. They had their answer very soon. "Come. This is a great country. The opportunities are unlimited. Arrangements have been made for your arrival." And so on a cold winter day, Anna and Rudolf Kellerman left their country, the home of their birth, and travelled to the United States of America. They landed in New York and were met by their cousin, who took them immediately to Brooklyn.

There were few open spaces in Brooklyn. The skies were leaden and grey. And the opportunities that had been promised turned out to be a pushcart on Delancey Street in Manhattan. Delancey Street turned out to be a traumatic experience for Rudolf, who had been well-educated in Germany and who came from a family of journalists. Delancey Street came from nowhere and led to nowhere. It was just a dirty, smelly street where Jewish vendors hawked their wares from pushcarts on the sidewalk. Articles of clothing, piece goods, luggage, umbrellas, food — you name it and you'd find it on the pushcarts. A man could eke out a living there and remain sane, if he didn't think too deeply.

Rudolf's cousin, Ernst, who had Americanized his name to Ernie, was building a fine business. He had progressed from one pushcart and now operated a chain of them, with the help of various relatives. He split the profits with his "managers" and was now semi-retired at the age of thirty-two. His main effort of the day was to stroll down Delancey Street, in his fancy waistcoat and homburg, to inspect his business enterprise. Ernie felt like the rich relation when he offered Rudolf a pushcart on the street. Philosophically, Rudolf determined to make the job a steppingstone. Better things would come to him when he learned more about the ways of his adopted country. Nevertheless, the experience left a lasting impression on him; it was so far removed from what he had expected. And for the first time in his life, money became important to him. The pillars of American society were rooted in money. To be somebody it was necessary to dig down to the well-spring, the source of abundant supply. He worked long hours, he saved his money, he lived for the day when he would publish a newspaper again.

The walkup flat in Brooklyn was old and tired. It was clean only because the immigrant women who lived there spent hours of backbreaking work to keep it so. The brick building in which the flat was situated represented something very special to the new arrivals. There were sixteen flats on four floors. The newest arrivals and the poorest occupied the top floor. As they settled down to the ways of their new country and earned more money, their greatest ambition was to move down a floor. When they reached the bottom floor they had arrived, they joined the aristocracy of the block, they were considered the affluent ones.

Rudolf returned each night and climbed to the top floor. No matter how late it was or how weary he might be, his spirits were revived at the sight of Anna and the smells of the full-course meal that awaited him. He would greet his wife with gentle affection and sit down, ravenous, at the table. Anna hovered over him, bringing one hot dish after another, commenting lightly on the events of the day. But finally, after the strong, dark tea had been served, Rudolf would get up and fetch the bag of peanuts he had brought home with him. Then they would sit together at the kitchen table, shell the peanuts and eat them contentedly. This was the most important time of the day, for now the talk turned to serious things, appraisal and planning for the future. These hours sustained them.

There was still no sign of a child. Still the thing they wanted most to make their lives truly meaningful, eluded them. But one day Rudolf came home early, excited and happy. Yossef Brandt, the man who operated the pushcart next to his, had told him that it was possible in New York to adopt a child. There were numerous orphans who needed a home, survivors of immigrants who, unable to withstand the rigors of the upheaval and the long journey from their homelands, had died soon after reaching America. With a proper introduction and a little palm-greasing, such a thing could be arranged. Anna was beside herself with joy and promised her husband that she would scrimp and save every penny for the palm-greasing. Within a few months the arrangements were made. And the glorious day came when Anna and Rudolf brought an infant boy home to their flat in Brooklyn. They named him Joseph after the man who had given them the suggestion and made the introduction to the right people. Within two months, Anna was pregnant.

It was very hard, bringing up an infant and bearing another. But the Kellermans considered themselves the luckiest people on earth. Their most important dreams had finally come to pass. Anna sang about the house all day. And Rudolf worked very hard, spending long hours at his pushcart. An ambition realized always brings up another. Now they wanted to move down to the third floor because the flat there had an extra small room. Anna gave birth to a daughter, a cherubic little girl who was born with fiery red hair. They called her Andrea after the reigning star of Broadway who also had red hair and whom they were sure she would emulate.

In later years, the girl who had been born Andrea Kellerman looked back with great fondness on her childhood in Brooklyn. There was so much to do around the old neighbourhood, so much to explore, so many friends. And the flat on the third floor, which gave way to the second and then the ground floor was warm and clean and comfortable, and filled with love.

Rudolf got his newspaper, a weekly Yiddish journal which he published and printed in Brooklyn. And even as things got better and more money came into the house, he and Anna never considered moving from the neighbourhood that had brought them so much joy. They were rooted there now; they had found the well-spring there. There was no greater place on earth. Joseph, who never knew he was adopted until he reached adulthood, had a quick mind and a good brain. As a young man, he worked on his father's newspaper and then graduated to the giant dailies in New York. He became a journalist of renown and finally a respected writer of historical novels. Andrea, of the red hair, turned into a beauty and early displayed a great flair for singing and acting. A grade school teacher nicknamed her Blaze and the name stuck with her all through her youth. Blaze Kellerman, beautiful and laughing, became the most popular person in the neighbourhood. Everyone agreed that she would be a star of the theatre some day.

It was a tough climb for the young girl in the theatre world. She was beautiful and she was talented. But beautiful and talented girls were drawn to New York from all over the world. There were many disappointments and equally many frustrations. Broadway, the goal, seemed very elusive in those early days. The chances are, she might never have made it had she not met Arthur Scotland. Now in his fifties, Scotland had had ambitions of being a great dramatic actor. But he decided early in his career that he just didn't have that so-called divine spark that makes a top star of the theatre. He wisely decided that his forte lay in becoming a drama coach. Once he reached that decision, he carved out a rewarding and lucrative career for himself teaching and guiding youngsters who had both the talent and the spark. He became known as the star-maker. To be taught by him was considered the surest road to success in the profession.

Slowly, Blaze Kellerman worked herself up from amateur companies to semi-professional groups who toured the small town circuit. She played everything from Shakespeare to variety revues. She seemed to shine best at musical comedy. But the road shows in which she appeared were a very long way from Broadway. A friend told Arthur Scotland about the beautiful redhead who was appearing in a musical in a theatre barn outside New York. Arthur decided to make the trip to see her. He watched her perform, he was deeply moved by her stunning beauty, he introduced himself to her. And then began one of those collaborations in the theatre that become part of the legend of the art. Arthur molded Blaze, he refined her, he taught her her craft, he guided her. And when the time was ready, he introduced her to the right people. He inserted her carefully and calculatedly into the casts of the road companies of the Broadway shows. And finally, he brought her to the threshold of stardom. He arranged for her to try out for the cast of *Oklahoma,* which was being readied for Broadway. She got the part and Blaze Kellerman became Blaze Scotland.

Well, I told you about the meeting of Blaze and Jonny during the run of *Oklahoma,* and about the love they found for each other at that first meeting. You also know what happened to that love. It was really over before it had gotten half started. As far as Blaze was concerned, the one thing that kept her from mourning at length over her lost love for Jonny was her career. She was kept so busy with it that, although she yearned for the love that might have been, she hardly had time to think, let alone dwell on it. Arthur Scotland arranged for her release from the show when she was offered a starring role in a new musical slated for Broadway. It was a smash success and led to offers to do motion pictures in Hollywood and Europe. It was the day of the big movie musicals, and Blaze was just as successful in California as she had been in New York. Then she was offered a chance to do a dramatic role in a film being made in France and she accepted it. It was there that she met the man who was to become her husband.

Count Louis-Paul de Roberval was the son and grandson of the de Robervals who had made a fortune in the automobile manufacturing industry. Theirs was the largest plant in all France. The family could trace its lineage back to the middle ages and beyond and had served its country in peacetime and in war. The nobility of France was a dying breed, but the de Robervals wore their heritage proudly on their sleeves. Louis-

Paul, born to wealth and position, had considered living the life of a noble-born Parisian playboy. But his enormously high energy level and his driving ambition had made that impossible. So instead of living a life of ease and pleasure, he had devoted himself tirelessly to the family business and had found numerous other interests to consume his time and restlessness. One of his main interests apart from automobiles was the motion picture business. He was the president and chief backer of an independent production company, the company that signed Blaze Scotland as the star of their newest venture. Louis-Paul was present at the reception given for Blaze on her arrival from the States. He looked at her as she entered the hotel salon, he loved her on the instant, and he determined to make her his wife.

The courtship was a stormy one. Blaze was working very hard on the picture against a tight schedule. She was exhausted at night and refused dates with Louis-Paul as often as she accepted them. And although she found him attractive, she was not prepared to fall in love with him. For one thing, he was older than she by a number of years. For a second thing, she thought about Jonny often and in her mind he still symbolized her ideal. And thirdly, she just wasn't particularly interested in marriage. But Louis-Paul was a determined man in love and he set out to woo her by every possible means. He showered her with gifts, he wined and dined her at the best spots in Paris, he offered her his entire studio for her own, he showed her around his enormous plant, he took her for drives around his vast estates and innumerable villas. He wore down her resistance to him by sheer willpower. And at last she consented to marry him.

The wedding took place the night following the completion of the picture. It was a huge gala held at one of the largest and most luxurious hotels in Paris, which had been entirely turned over to them for the occasion. The ceremony was a civil one because Louis-Paul's catholicism was inbred in him and because Blaze would listen to no talk of her converting. It was the social highlight of the season, attended by the diplomatic corps, the wealthy, the famous. Blaze smiled to herself, a little grimly, when she thought of how Anna and Rudolf, unaware in Brooklyn, would have reacted to the wedding of their daughter, the former Andrea Kellerman, now the Countess de Roberval.

It was during their honeymoon that Blaze realized that she had made a mistake in marrying Louis-Paul. At first it was a nagging, indefinable doubt that she was unable to pin down. Louis-Paul was loving and considerate and determined to make their honeymoon an experience that Blaze would never forget. Their trip took them to the capitals of Europe. And everywhere, in Spain and Italy, in Germany and Austria and Switzerland, the name of de Roberval and the de Roberval fortune opened all doors. They were feted and entertained lavishly. Blaze, who had not known these things, attended balls in her honour, occupied the royal box in the theatres and opera houses, even cut the ribbons that marked the opening of new palaces of pleasure. It was a hectic, whirlwind honeymoon that introduced Blaze to the society of European nobility and to the merchant princes of the lands they travelled.

They were a handsome couple, Blaze and Louis-Paul. And if Louis-Paul was honoured and respected, Blaze was loved for her beauty and gaiety. Their honeymoon and their life together should have been perfect in every respect. But a number of things began to destroy the illusion. Blaze could never get used to playing the countess. She came to hate the fawning and subservience; it troubled and embarrassed her. The constant travelling got on her nerves. Always the same routine, the arrival, the bowing and the scraping, the settling in, the round of social engagements that exhausted mind and body.

Gradually Blaze came to a shocking realization. For all his position and power, Louis-Paul was using his honeymoon to show off his latest acquisition. In so many ways, she began to see that her prominence as an actress and her beauty were a sop to Louis-Paul's ego. The man who had everything had now added the beautiful American actress to his list of possessions. Louis-Paul de Roberval had acquired a new plaything. The pride of possession, the admiration and adoration of her public, her beauty and fame, these things were of tremendous importance to him. But no more important than the design of a new car or the success of one of his pictures or the prosperity of any of his ventures. No more important than his plants and his studios and his vast estates. Blaze was part of the picture, the great de Roberval tapestry. She was living proof that there was nothing they could not have or possess. She was to become a detail in the de Roberval legend, to the extent that her own identity would eventually be swallowed up within the framework of that legend. Even her acting, which was her life, would soon be forgotten. And Andrea Kellerman and Blaze Scotland would cease to exist. Only the Countess de Roberval would survive, her legend swallowed up and destroyed in the greater interest of his.

But if Blaze Scotland, born Andrea Kellerman had made a mistake, she was determined to live with it. Her background and her upbringing had given her a strong sense of the importance of marriage and the family. Had not her father and mother stressed that all during her youth? Were separation, divorce, annulment not foreign words to her? Had she not been taught that marriage is a two-way street, in which both partners give and take, and adjust? She would make the best of things, she would give to her marriage all that she possessed, she would even subvert her career for the sake of her husband. She would go more than halfway. She would make her marriage work.

Blaze began to pine for her homeland. She wanted desperately to go back to the United States, even if only for a time. She needed to sort out her thoughts and clear her mind. She wanted to find Andrea Kellerman again, the Andrea who had lost herself, first in Blaze Scotland and then in the Countess de Roberval. She had a deep desire to see her parents again and to roam the streets of Brooklyn where it had all begun. She begged Louis-Paul to allow her to accept an offer of a picture in Hollywood. And he finally agreed.

Blaze was certain that Louis-Paul's varied enterprises would keep him in Paris. And besides, she wanted to go alone; it was important that she have the time to herself. She was shocked and not a little dismayed when her husband announced that he would accompany her. Although it amused her to think of the meeting between him and her parents. Two completely different worlds meeting, two enormously different backgrounds, two different faiths. It should prove to be quite a confrontation.

There was very little evidence of change in Brooklyn. Rudolf had managed to move his family down to the first floor of their apartment building. And Anna had done a thorough job of refurnishing. Their home was cheerful and comfortable and unostentatious. Joseph, who had never married, maintained a bed sitting-room at home but spent most of his time in Manhattan, close to the newspaper on which he worked. And Rudolf's little Yiddish publication had become a bi-monthly magazine with an international circulation. The Kellermans asked nothing more of life. They were healthy and happy. And they had prospered in the new world. They had a wonderful son and daughter, both of whom had become successful in their chosen careers. What more could be asked or expected? And now a letter sat on the kitchen table. Their daughter was coming home. And she was bringing her husband to meet them. They were the envy of all their neighbours.

The meeting between the old immigrant and the young aristocrat was a most remarkable one. Blaze was surprised and gladdened to see the rapport that sprang up between the two men. Generations of behavioural patterns governed the respect and consideration given the old man by his noble-born son-in-law. And as for Rudolf, Louis-Paul was his daughter's husband. He was of his family now. It was as simple as that. Anna had reservations about the marriage, she sensed some of the conflict in her daughter's mind. But she wisely refrained from either showing or discussing her feelings with anyone. And, after all, Rudolf had long ago accepted his daughter's success and absence from his table. She, Anna, never had. She still clung to the hope that Blaze Scotland would tire of her life and return home to become Andrea Kellerman again. Then mother and daughter would draw close and exchange confidences about all the womanly things. And Andrea would forget about the theatre and content herself with becoming a housewife in Brooklyn and with raising a family. She found it difficult to reconcile these dreams with the reality of Louis-Paul's presence. But she smiled benignly and kept her dreams locked deep in her heart.

During their visit, Louis-Paul went into Manhattan on several occasions to look into business matters of his own. But Blaze refused to accompany him. She was adamant about not getting involved in the routine that had marked their arrival in other large cities. She was content to remain in Brooklyn and wander, unrecognised, amongst the scenes of her youth. Alone, she thought about her life and her marriage and came to the same conclusion as before. Only this time she made up her mind that she would give up the theatre. The picture in Hollywood would be her last. When it was finished, she would go back to Paris with her husband and concentrate her efforts on being his wife and perhaps the mother of his children, the future de

Robervals of France. She had made her bed, now she must lie in it. She must forever put Jonny Temple out of her mind. Her future was with Louis-Paul and she would make the best of it, no matter what the outcome might be. She would do her part, their marriage would not fail on account of her.

They flew out to the west coast and slipped into Hollywood unobtrusively. As much as Blaze loved the theatre and motion picture work, she had never learned how to cope with the acclaim, the publicity, and the lack of privacy that comes with stardom. The thought of being greeted by reporters and photographers and crowds of fans sickened her. The first that Hollywood knew she was there was through a report from her agent to the studio, announcing her arrival in the city, and the arranging of makeup and wardrobe tests. Louis-Paul had promised her to remain in the background and he kept his promise. He quietly busied himself with personal business matters and appeared to be content to avoid the gaudier aspects of nightclub and party life. At the end of the day, he and Blaze retired to their hotel suite and spent quiet evenings, allowing Blaze to gather her strength for the following day's shooting. Blaze almost came to believe that their marriage relationship was improving.

The end of the shooting schedule was in sight and Louis-Paul was making arrangements for their return to Paris. He was impatient to get home and back to his businesses. For the last item on his agenda, he had rented a car and driven into Los Angeles to arrange distribution for some of his company's films. Driving back to Hollywood on the freeway, his car hit an oil slick and went out of control. At high speed, he caromed off an embankment and overturned. He died instantly. I guess you'd call it coincidence or irony or maybe even fate that a car crash had such a devastating effect on Jonny's life and also was the instrument by which Blaze's whole life changed so abruptly and conclusively.

Blaze accompanied the body of Louis-Paul to his ancestral home and after a decent interval returned to Hollywood to finish the picture. Then she went home to Brooklyn, once again to ponder her future. She wrote to Jonny once but received no reply. That was the letter that I destroyed. When there was no reply, Blaze decided that Jonny wanted no part of her. She felt she could hardly blame him but she was hurt and saddened.

Now she must pick up the pieces alone. There was no question that she would go on in the theatre — it was the only life left for her now. Wistfully, she had hoped that things might be different, that Jonny might be part of her life again.

But how the hell could that be? A twist of fate had caused me to get the letter from her instead of Jonny. And I, playing God, had ordained that he should not see it. What can I say? That people should learn to mind their own business? That no one has the right to interfere in the affairs of another? Sure, I could say that. But it's too damned pat. It doesn't for one second explain anything about the pattern, the grand scheme of things that seems pre-ordained, the roads our lives take, the influences, the relationships. It explains nothing but that our lives are like leaves in the breeze, that they may blow one way or another, depending on the winds of fate.

Arthur Scotland visited Blaze in Brooklyn and decided instantly that she needed the therapy of work. He contacted producers in New York who were only too glad to consider Blaze for the starring role in their works. Arthur decided that a comedy was what Blaze needed and the arrangements were made. The play was a hit and seemed destined for a long run. And then one night, the inevitable happened. She looked up from a group of people surrounding her backstage and Jonny Temple was standing there.

In the privacy of her dressing room, Jonny held Blaze in his arms for several long minutes. As he did, the months and the years fell away and they were young again. Life hadn't touched them yet and they still had their dreams, shining and inviolate. Pain and embarrassment hadn't come to them yet, nor had violent death found them. There was no past, no husband, no wife, no children. For just the few minutes they forgot. For those minutes there was just the two of them and the love they had found again, never expecting to, never really hoping that it would ever happen again. Nothing really existed outside the walls of that dressing room. But can the past ever be recaptured? Can we ever truly find our youth again? Can we blot out disillusion, despair, unhappiness? Can we possibly start all over again? I guess we know the answers. Blaze sighed deeply and the spell of the moment was broken. She moved in Jonny's arms and looked up at him. Her hand moved up, searching, tentative, and touched his cheek. It moved higher and very gently stroked the first suspicion of grey hairs at his temple. She smiled sadly without self-consciousness into his eyes. Looking down at her, Jonny sucked in his breath in a long, meaningful sigh. Her beauty had never failed to shake him and it didn't now. He stroked the glorious hair and smiled at her.

"You look older Jonny," she said.

"You don't," he replied.

They stood there smiling at each other, hungrily, longingly. "We have so much to talk about, so many things to catch up on," she murmured.

"Yes," he answered.

"Where are you staying Jonny?"

"At the Waldorf. And you?"

"I have a small apartment just a few blocks from here."

"We'll go to your place," Jonny decided. "It wouldn't do for you to be seen coming to my hotel."

"Wonderful, I'll make us some coffee and we can talk as long as we like. Give me five minutes to change."

The fashionable three-room apartment that was Blaze's home in Manhattan was just like her, bright and warm, comforting and gay. Jonny smiled as they entered the living room off the tiny foyer. It was so like Blaze he would have known it was hers under any circumstances, even if she were not there. "Pour yourself a drink and make yourself at home while I change again," Blaze said. "I'll only be a couple of minutes."

She went into the bedroom to change and Jonny called out to her, "Can I fix you one too?"

"Martini," she called back, "very dry."

Jonny nodded and went over to the portable bar. He was just finishing mixing the martinis as Blaze returned in mint-green lounging pyjamas. He paused and stared at her, his eyes widening. His breath caught in his throat as he said, "My God Blaze, you're a beautiful woman. I had almost forgotten how very beautiful you are."

Blaze laughed as she said, "Thank you, Jonny. Sometimes it's a handicap. It's sort of like lots of money. You're never sure of the motivations, particularly where men are concerned." Jonny laughed too as they carried their drinks over to the sofa. They settled into it and turned to each other and raised their glasses in the traditional toast of old friends who had found each other again.

The talk went on for a long time. They had a lot to tell each other about what had happened to them since they'd last seen each other. Jonny started in first. He leaned back and half closed his eyes. Step by step he recreated everything that had transpired. He talked about his work, about his meeting with Rita, his marriage, his child, the death of Rita's father and grandmother, Marion's coming to live with them. Detail by detail he brought Blaze up to date. And then it was her turn. She told him about Louis-Paul and about her decision to remain in the theatre after his death. Both she and Jonny had been very careful not to make any disparaging remarks about their mates or their lives. But somehow, without a word being spoken, way down deep they both sensed that tragedy had touched their lives, not in the sense of loss, but in the sense of things that never were, that might have been. It was late when they had talked themselves out and finished the last of the martinis. Blaze put her hand on Jonny's arm momentarily and got up to make the coffee.

Still later, after the coffee, Blaze leaned very close to Jonny. He put his arm around her and they sat there, musing, for a long time. Finally Blaze stirred and whispered very softly, "Darling, I make no pretense about being a very moral person. Certainly not with you. Would you like to stay here tonight?"

Jonny swallowed hard and his voice, when he spoke, was tight and hoarse. "Yes, I would like that," he choked, "but . . . but . . . I can't stay, Blaze."

"Your wife?"

"Yes, my wife, and my son, and me. You understand?"

"I understand my darling. And you understand me?"

Jonny buried his face in her hair. "I understand, oh I understand, my dearest Blaze."

"Jonny there's a key to the apartment on the little table by the door. Take it with you. I'll be back here after the show tomorrow night. If you should want to come to me, I'll be here. If you don't come, I'll understand. Only Jonny, don't shut me out of your life completely again. Never again. Hear?"

"I hear, Blaze," Jonny mumbled, "and . . . and I'll see you." He left the apartment. As he left, he picked up the key.

There was no sleep for Jonny that night. He paced the floor of his hotel room for hours, thinking, tortured. Finally, at five o'clock in the morning, he dressed and left the hotel in search of an all-night restaurant where he drank innumerable cups of coffee, until it was time to go to work on the job that had brought him to New York in the first place. The day was a total loss. He was incapable of concentrating. Everywhere he looked, in papers, at books, everywhere the face of Blaze Scotland looked back at him, smiling and sad. With an oath, Jonny stumbled out of the newspaper morgue where he had been working and headed for a bar, where he proceeded to drink his dinner. He wandered the streets for hours after dinner and then made his way back to his hotel room. He resumed his pacing. Then with a long, drawn-out groan, he grabbed his coat and fumbled for the key that Blaze had given him.

The apartment was in darkness when Blaze got home. She flicked on the lights as she entered. Jonny was sitting in an overstuffed easy chair, asleep. He looked exhausted and worn but strangely peaceful. Blaze's heart went out to him as she fetched a blanket and covered him tenderly. She left a small, soft light on as she went into the kitchen to make coffee. When it was ready, she took her cup into the living room and sat, watching him. Several hours passed and Blaze got up for another cup of coffee. When she returned to the room, Jonny was staring at her, smiling. She smiled back and, going to him, gently kissed his cheek.

Jonny stood and took her in his arms. "I tried Blaze, I talked to myself, I argued, I cursed. But I couldn't stay away. I don't want to be here now. But I am here. And I'm going to stay. If you'll let me."

"Of course darling. And Jonny, no strings. I think I understand you better than you do yourself. I know this is what it will be like for us. But I'm willing to take this much. And I'll never ask you for anything more. It doesn't matter if this is all we'll have. In a way, it's a second chance. And that's more than most people get."

Jonny could find no more words. He held Blaze closely. It would be enough. It would have to be.

The violence of their lovemaking astonished them both. It was as though a terrible hunger had to be satisfied and they must swallow convulsively without taking even the time to chew. Then, lying beside each other, exhausted and spent, they stared into space, unspeaking, wondering, tranquil. "What are you thinking?" Blaze asked.

Jonny turned to her and raised himself up on one elbow. Searching her eyes he said, "I'm thinking . . . is it possible that a man can love two women at the same time? It surely isn't right, but, somehow, I believe it is possible, under certain circumstances. I do love Rita, Blaze, and my son. I'm sure I do. Perhaps my marriage didn't work out exactly the way I expected. But I do love them. And then I'm with you. And I love you Blaze, more than I know how to say. I don't know if I'm making much sense. But I'm trying in my own way to sort things out in my mind. It's kind of rough."

Blaze smiled up at him. "Poor darling," she said, "perhaps the best thing would be not to think about it too much. Perhaps it's best to feel and not to think. But that's not possible for you, is it Jonny?"

"No," Jonny admitted, "I guess I have a lawyer's mind that requires certain answers. You see, I couldn't ever leave them. And I don't really want to. Somehow, in my mind, Montreal and my family and my work are one part of my life. And you are the other. Somehow, too, both parts are necessary to me. I must be a sonofabitch and selfish too. I want my life at home and I want you too. I need you like you wouldn't believe. But then I know I'm not being fair to anyone. Maybe I can find excuses in my own mind that could justify it. But certainly society frowns on this, a wife and . . . and . . . "

"And a mistress," Blaze interrupted, smiling.

"And another love," Jonny corrected her hastily.

"I think you're right about society," Blaze laughed. But then she became serious again. "I told you before that I know you very well. I know what you're thinking and I know why you're here. I believe that you loved me once and that you love me again. And I know why. You don't have to spell it out for me, ever. And knowing this, can you dismiss society and take things as they are, including me, from time to time?"

"I don't know," Jonny admitted, "I'll have to think about it some more. But Blaze, I do love you. Never think otherwise. I love you."

Blaze smiled and snuggled up to him. The touch of her body drove everything from his mind and he made love to her again, tenderly then passionately. The past had caught up to them, almost too late, but not quite. And yet the past no longer existed, nor did the future, only the immediate, heart-stopping present.

Jonny came to no decision about Blaze in the days that followed. But at least, he was able to work. He threw himself into his work each day, and at night, the lodestar drew him to the theatre, where he picked Blaze up and took her home. Once released, the passion of their love flowed unabated. Talk was kept to a minimum, not because they had nothing to say to each other, but because each sensed the delicate balance of conflict in the other. Jonny loved Blaze. He made love to her yearningly, voraciously. And she responded as though the present had to make up for all time. But there was never one word of the future spoken between them. It was as though the present idyll would never end. But Jonny finished the work that had brought him to New York and it was time for him to return home. Their parting was as casual as they both could make it. One night, Jonny told Blaze he would be leaving the next day. He promised her that he'd be back, in a few weeks if possible. In the morning, he kissed her goodbye and left her smiling cheerfully. He didn't know that she cried most of that day.

Jonny collected his things at the hotel and took a limousine to the airport. He was brooding and heart-heavy. Reality had caught up with him again. With the scent of Blaze still in his nostrils, he was going home. Rita would be waiting for him, and Petey, his son. And Marion would be there too. And, of course, me and the case we still had to win. Reality can be rough. It's like the shocking impact of a cold shower. I can imagine what it was like for Jonny. Leaving New York, more to the point, leaving Blaze, must have shaken him up plenty. He did tell me that on the plane he tried desperately to rouse himself, to get himself back in the pattern that coming home to Montreal represented. But with the rousing came a strong attack of conscience. He made no excuses to himself for Blaze. That was inevitable, that simply had to be. He had not planned it, he had not sought it. But it had happened, it had come to him and he knew that he could no more stop loving her than he could cease to breathe. The trouble on his conscience lay at home. His life would go on. And in his secret, innermost heart, he knew that he would come to compare, that he would, at times, yearn for the unselfish, uncomplicated, comforting love that he had found with Blaze. That Jonny. He even felt sorry for Rita.

I knew that something was bugging Jonny the first day he came to work after returning from New York. He talked about how the research had gone and what he had found that might help our case. But he was as evasive as hell when I questioned him about what he had done for recreation. It's pretty natural to ask someone who returns from New York what shows he'd seen, what restaurants he'd visited and what's doing in the big town. To all of these questions, Jonny mumbled unintelligible responses. Finally I felt I had to worm it out of him. "Come on now Jonny," I insisted, "cut out the bullshit and give. What the hell kept you so busy in New York that you didn't have time to see one show or eat in a decent restaurant?"

Jonny looked at me for a long minute. Then he said, simply, "Blaze is in New York." I must have looked like a fish out of water because he continued, "What the hell's so surprising about that? She's appearing in a new play. That's how I knew. I saw the ads. What's so surprising about her being in New York?"

Of course, Jonny didn't know what was going through my mind. I was thinking of the letter from her that I'd destroyed, so long ago, and I was wondering if she'd mentioned it. She hadn't, of course, and for some reason I'll never really know, she never did.

After that, Jonny went whole hog. He told me everything, every last detail from the moment he met Blaze until he left her. And brother I was scared. I had no way of knowing what might happen in the future. I couldn't begin to guess what might develop from that meeting with Blaze. In my mind's eye, I could see smoke and fire and crashing debris, all leading to the destruction of . . . Jon Temple. Because as much as Jonny talked about Blaze, he never once mentioned Rita or his son, Petey, or anything to do with his home life here in Montreal. Now we all know what a situation like Jonny's can lead to. But the thing that scared me most was that Jonny didn't seem to realize the implications. For all I knew at the time, Jonny may have had the impossible idea that he could go on seeing Blaze from time to time, without it affecting his home life or his way of life altogether. In our relationships with other people, we never fully know what they're really thinking or what ideas may spring into their minds. And I shuddered to think of Rita finding out about Blaze.

For several weeks, I was tempted to bring the matter up with Jonny. I had the strongest feeling that I ought to at least discuss the situation, confront him with the problem, force him to consider a decision, one way or the other. But something in his manner, something deep behind his eyes, made me hold my tongue. Sometimes that's the best thing to do, all things considered.

Our case, which involved the relationship of an American corporation with its subsidiary in Canada, required a few days more work in New York. When I realized it, I brought the matter up with Jonny. Then I said, "One of us has to get down there right away. Do you want to go?"

Jonny considered for several moments. Then he replied, "Yes. Yes, I'll go Arnie. I've got to see Blaze. I have to hold her and love her. And I have to talk to her. And she has to talk to me. There are a few things we have to talk about." Jonny left the next night for New York.

It was about midnight and Jonny stood outside the front door of Blaze's apartment, fingering the key on his ring. He stood motionless for a long time and then he went to the door and listened. There was no sound from inside and he let himself in. The apartment was empty. He wandered around touching the furniture and the knick-knacks in the living room. Then he poured himself a drink and sat down to wait. Blaze's scent was in the room and wherever he looked, he could see Blaze. And she would be looking at him, smiling. He swiped his hand wearily across his eyes and stifled a groan. Then he shook his head violently. Some of the drink spilled.

There was a sound of several people talking and laughing in the outside corridor. Then the door to the apartment opened and Blaze came in, with some of her friends from the cast. No one, not Blaze nor her friends seemed surprised to find Jonny there. The friends greeted Jonny, almost like one of them. Blaze simply smiled her welcome. A look passed from Jonny to her. It said get rid of them. Blaze smiled again and nodded imperceptibly.

The moment they were alone, Jonny took Blaze in his arms. He held her tightly, like a drowning man grasping for his life. They stood like that for several minutes, rocking slightly back and forth. Then Blaze pushed back gently and looked into his eyes. "Jonny, Jonny," she murmured, "oh my darling, you're so troubled and I'm so very upset. But let's not talk just yet. There'll be time for that later. Come." And she led him into the bedroom.

Jonny reached out to her. And the moment his hands touched her lovely body and drew her close to him, his mind cleared and the anxiety went out of him. Now there was nothing on his mind but Blaze, the smell of her, the heat of her body, the smoothness of her skin. With one violent movement, he threw the covering sheet off them and examined Blaze in her nakedness, inch by inch, as if to sear the memory of her, every part of her, forever in his mind. Then, in one motion he pulled the sheet back over them as the tempest broke in all its raging fury and the paroxysms seized him. He threw himself across her, his hands moving, exploring, searching. Lips to lips, tongue to tongue, he held her in a long, lingering kiss. His body moved on her and sank deep into the well-spring of consummate joy and . . . this time he was truly drowning, drowning, drowning.

Blaze stirred and looked at Jonny, asleep with the look of an innocent child on his face. She understood. His need of her at this precise moment in time was so apparent. For this short space, his mind and his body were at rest. In her love, however transient, he could find peace, from himself. She must not allow herself to think of a future where there was no future. Moments like these, whether often or few, were all she and Jonny were ever likely to have. She understood, even if Jonny did not. Tears formed in her eyes and slowly coursed down her drawn face. A haunted look came over her as she reached out her hand and touched her fingertips to Jonny's cheek. Her breath caught in her throat and a great emptiness filled her. Yes, she understood. And she would keep on giving. She would ask for nothing, expect nothing more. Because there was no more. She smiled wanly through her tears. She nodded. She understood very well.

Jonny awoke and reached out for her. She moved into his arms and they lay like that, for a long time, until their heat threatened to consume them both. Then Blaze touched his cheek again and whispered, "Jonny, my darling, you must stop fighting with yourself. We were and are and will be. But only this. Nothing more. Our love, the love we have now, begins and ends in this room. I don't know when or where we will be together again. But if it should be, it will begin again and end again in the same way. If we can accept that, we have a chance to live our lives. And really, my darling, there is no other way possible. I know it and you must know it too."

Jonny thrashed about, fighting, fighting. Then he shouted, "Why Blaze, why? Why does it have to be this way?"

"Because my darling," she said, "there isn't any other. It's not in you to walk away from your family and your responsibilities. And I truly believe you don't entirely want to. You can only practise in your own province, and what else could you do? And the theatre is the only thing I know. There's no place for us except in the worlds we know. You can't come into mine and I can't come into yours. We could run. But where and to what? You must go back Jonny. You must go back to your family and your work. And I must go back to mine. This, tonight, is what we have. It's all we can ever have. In our hearts, we both know that."

Jonny lay like stone, thinking. There were no more words to be spoken. They had been said and their meaning was inevitable. He turned to Blaze and crushed her to him. He held her, in love, and as his lips sought hers, their tears melded together. Blaze and Jonny. And when Jonny told me about that night, my torment matched theirs. How deep was my guilt?

It was a long time before Jonny saw Blaze again. He came home to accept his lot, resignedly. I guess Blaze had gotten through to him, because he pulled himself out of his despair and seemed about to pick up the threads of his life and hold on to them firmly. Blaze never got over Jonny. This I know. She became greater and more famous. But she never married. She clutched the theatre to her heart, as a substitute for Jonny. She was wiser than all of us. Her understanding was so much greater than ours.

Jonny might have made it too. He might have found an acceptable life for himself. He might have been able to work things out for himself except for the goddamnedest mistake of his whole life. He told Rita about Blaze.

CHAPTER 4

PETEY

What made Jonny tell Rita about Blaze Scotland? If you think there's any pat answer to that one, you're sadly mistaken. I guess I knew Jonny better than any man and I've never been sure of the answer to that one myself. Conscience? Maybe. But even that would only be part of the truth. Self-respect? Possibly. But again that doesn't begin to get at the real truth. I remember, at the time the question was plaguing me, writing down all the words that came into my head, seeking some explanation. I wrote words such as pride, honour, consideration, duty, dignity, nobility. And in none of them did I find what I was looking for. I finally decided that the answer lay partly in all these words and wholly in none. The solution lay deep inside Jonny and was not about to be brought to the surface, even for me. In the final analysis, I developed a thesis that might hold the key. I believed that, having made the decision to stay in Montreal with his family, if such a decision had to be made, and having decided to make the best of his life, Jonny felt that he had to start over again with Rita, straight and clean and honest. I believed that Jonny needed to clear the air, relegate the immediate past to the past, start fresh and create new hope for himself. If my thesis was correct, it might have worked — with anyone but Rita, that is. With her, it was a mistake, from beginning to end.

Mind you, the mistake wasn't so apparent in the beginning as it was later on. As I've told you, whatever else Rita was, she was no fool. She knew damn well that if she kicked up a big stink, she would simply drive Jonny right back into Blaze's arms. She was too smart for that. Instead, she adopted the role of the forgiver. She made out like Jonny was a little kid who had sneaked around the corner for a cigarette. Figuratively speaking, she patted him on the head and told him to be a good boy and not to do naughty things again. She didn't bring up the matter again for some time; she buried it, but she kept it in reserve. It became her secret weapon, to be brought out and used only when the battle seemed lost, when a quick victory was needed. And as for Jonny, he had become the kind of guy who wants to buy peace at any price. Well, he paid the price all right. He was so damn relieved at the way Rita took it that he reacted like the kid with the cigarette. He was penitent and grateful; he didn't know what to do to make up. It made me want to puke.

I've already told you how Jonny came in a poor third in Rita's consideration, after Marion and the boy. What about Jonny's relations with Marion and Petey? Well, as far as Marion was concerned, Jonny could take her or leave her. Because he was the kind of guy he was, he saw no great harm in her. He ignored her butting in, her advice, her always being underfoot. He tried to pay no attention to the fact that her wishes and desires always had to be considered first. Actually, I think he kind of liked the old girl, in a passive sort of way. Bloody fool. If it had been me, I'd have gotten her the hell out of my house. I'd have laid down the ultimatum to my wife: Me or her. If it had cost me every penny I had, I'd have seen to it that she moved into her own apartment. It's just no goddam good having a mother-in-law living with you, even if she'd been a hell of a sight better person and less selfish than Marion. But I'm not Jonny, and Jonny wasn't me. He put up with her and suffered in silence, even if he wasn't completely aware that he was suffering.

The boy was a different story. Little Peter Allan Temple was Jonny's joy and pride. He adored his son. And it was he who nicknamed the boy Petey against the objections of his wife and her mother. The name stuck and the boy named Peter was known as Petey the rest of his life. Jonny hadn't had much communication with his own father, a fact which bothered him considerably. So he was determined that it wouldn't happen with his son. He wanted desperately to find a rapport with Petey. Even when the child was very young, he yearned to find the key to dialogue between them. On Sunday mornings, when the weather was fine, he took long walks with Petey. Or they'd go out into the street in front of their house and toss a baseball around. In the wintertime, they built snow forts and went skating. Jonny even made the attempt to teach him to ski. As Petey got a little older, he took him to baseball and hockey games. Petey became an ardent fan. Jonny would have been all right with Petey, if it hadn't been for Rita.

While Petey was young, he adored his father. Naturally, forced to spend so much time with his mother and grandmother, the child had a natural and deep-rooted desire to escape into the world of men. The boy was dark and tall and wiry like his father. From Jonny, he inherited a lively personality and a fondness for athletics. You could say that the boy really looked up to his father in those days. On their many outings, during attendance at various athletic events, their conversation was serious. Jonny never talked down to his son, never lost patience, never tired of answering the childish questions. Petey would ask and Jonny would answer, thoughtfully and thoroughly. He made the boy feel that they were equals, co-holders of certain knowledge, partners in a man's world. In those days, Jonny was happiest when spending time with Petey.

Of course, you have to remember that in those days, the world was different. Parental relationships were different. The thing then was for mothers and daughters and fathers and sons to be pals, buddies. The generation gap and the credibility gap weren't discussed so vehemently or so often, if at all. Discipline was imposed by the parents, based on their own experiences and accepted by the younger generation as right and just, if not always completely understood. Of course, there were minor rebellions, but the point is, they were minor. Sure the kids had their own music and their own dances. A certain freedom from the influences of the parents was beginning. Sure every genera-tion reaches the point where it feels that the older one is old-fashioned and not with it. But what I'm trying to say is that it didn't amount to anything in those days. It was still possible for moms and dads to keep their kids in line and remain friends to all intents and purposes. For God's sake, our biggest crime as youngsters was to sneak around the corner for a cigarette or occasionally to visit what we lovingly referred to as a cat house. And the girls didn't even do that. We also had the odd booze. But that was just about it. The hang-ups of today didn't exist as such. There wasn't so much openness in talk and action about sex and drugs and violence. There wasn't such an obvious widening of the generation gap. There was no student revolu-tion. There wasn't the same deadly serious conflict between the hippies, the yippies, and the establishment. Remaking the world wasn't the scene. Education and the search for success was. So the relationship between Jonny and his son was a happy and healthy one. But only for a time. It might have remained that way for all time but, like I said, there was Rita to contend with.

There's no doubt in my mind that it was Rita, and she alone who was responsible, from the outset, of alienating Petey's affection for his father. Perhaps not deliberately. She may not have even realized what she was doing. But one thing is certain, she was determined to dominate the boy's youth. And that brought about the ultimate destruction of the rapport between father and son. You see, it was the very type of person Rita was that made the end result inevitable. She was so damn strong and dominant, egotistic and self-righteous that Jonny never had a chance.

Another thing about Rita, she had delusions of grandeur. Everything she had and everything she did was the best, the finest, the cleverest, the most-planned. At home, she complained and nagged. Jonny wasn't strong enough, Jonny wasn't rich enough, Jonny wasn't considerate. He was this, he was that. No matter what he did or didn't do, it was never right. But, secretly, I'm convinced she relished her role of thinker, planner, and sergeant-major. She made goddam sure that the whole household revolved around her. She paid lip service to Jonny and Petey and her mother, she tried to make her family feel that everything she did and planned was for them. But it was for her. Everything was said and done and thought and schemed for her. It was always her; she came first, even if she made a hell of a pretence at being the self-sacrificing martyr.

And what about Jonny in all this? I don't know. I've thought about it a hell of a lot. Was he weak? Was he too spineless to stand up to Rita? Had he reached a point where he didn't give a damn? I don't really know. Because to me, Jonny was the greatest guy who ever lived, the perfect partner, the true friend, the gay companion. Socially and in our work, people liked him. They trusted him, they found strength in his counsel, they took comfort from his support, they admired his athletic prowess, they enjoyed his humour and his personality. So your judgement of him is as good as anyone's, your estimation as sound as anybody else's. But to get back to my story . . . .

In spite of all Jonny wanted to do and to be to his son, the atmosphere in the home was all wrong. As happens in so many families, most of Petey's time when he was very small was spent with his mother and, to an extent, with his grandmother. Naturally, when he was an infant, he was asleep when Jonny got

home at night, and seen for only a few minutes before Jonny
left in the morning. As the boy got a little older, Jonny did
make the effort to get close to him on weekends, as I mentioned. But even that was limited by the amount of time that
Jonny could spend away from his homework. There were always briefs to be read and preparations to be made for court
appearances. Jonny consoled himself with the belief that when
Petey reached school age, they could become real friends and
companions. And like I said, it might have worked. If Rita
hadn't taken over so completely.

It was she who made certain that Petey did his homework.
It was she who did his lessons with him. She selected his
clothes, she conferred on his extra-curricular activities, she
checked on his friends. Alright, but like a lot of women, she had
the goddamndest way of suggesting to the child that daddy
didn't understand, that daddy was too busy, that she knew best.
It was only suggestion, but it worked, slowly and surely. Petey
got into the habit of asking his mother, of checking with her on
all things. In his child's mind, Rita became number one. And
Jonny became the visitor, the man who was around the house
occasionally. And slowly but just as surely, Jonny began to
accept it all. He left all the decision making, as far as the boy
was concerned, to Rita. Perhaps he excused himself on the basis
of preoccupation with his law career. Perhaps he just gave up
trying to cope with Rita's little strategies. The whole situation
mightn't be so devastating in other families, but in Jonny's it
was murder.

Whenever an argument came up, whether it had to do with
Petey's upbringing or anything else that went on in the Temple
household, Rita invariably won. Jonny just couldn't match his
wife in her rages, her womanly logic or her martyred righteous-
ness. He couldn't match her denunciations or her invective. He
didn't even try. And Rita had the ultimate weapon, the one
weapon that would bring hostilities to an immediate halt. She
had Blaze Scotland, and her invoking of that name had all the
power of an atom blast.

When Rita trained that atomic cannon, the fight was over,
the victory won. At a given point, Rita, having decided to
deliver the knockout punch, would create the armistice by
saying, "I suppose things would be different if you had married
Blaze Scotland," or, "I bet you wish you were with Blaze

Scotland right now," or, "Why don't you go to Blaze Scotland, she'd understand you much better." At this point, Jonny would simply throw up his hands and walk away from it. He had no answer. There was nothing further for him to say. He would admit defeat and look to retreat. He was beaten and he knew it, beaten by the power of words that cut. And by the final, conclusive argument of a woman. All these things Petey saw and heard.

Now don't think for a minute that Jonny gave up on his son. In spite of everything, he fought for the love and respect of his boy. After all, he reasoned, to Petey he would represent fun and relaxation from discipline, male companionship and all the things between men from which women are excluded. Jonny would be fun and dreams to Rita's realities. She could be paramount in the things that are, or should be, important. Jonny would be the weekend crony, the comrade of diversion, Rita the weekday taskmaster, the shaper of manhood. Noble thoughts but they didn't work, although Jonny continued to cling to his son, wanting desperately to pour out on him all the love and affection and frustration that was crying for release. It's more than a tragedy that Jonny, while never giving up, began to accept the inevitable. It's a crime against humanity that he, realizing the battle was lost, still fought on. I should qualify that. Realizing is not the right word. Maybe if he had realized all that was going on, things might have turned out differently, he might still have had a chance. No, in the business of day-to-day living, Jonny simply got lost. He lost out to a superior will and determination, a scheming woman of whom he was not, could never be the equal. He just got buried in an avalanche of living force.

In a situation like that, something had to give. And what finally gave in the end was the rapport, the empathy between Jonny and his son. Damn her, Rita would have denied any complicity. Jonny was unwilling to face the shocking truth. And Petey, when he was old enough to understand, would never know what had brought it about. Perhaps only Marion, had she wished, would have been able to speak the ugly truth.

One of the saddest things in the world is to watch anything disintegrate. It's even sadder to watch and not to be able to do anything about it. Well, I watched the gradual disintegration of a man. It was very slow, very gradual, but there was no question of its inevitability, the disintegration of Jonny Temple, of his household, of his marriage and of his relationship with his son. I watched and I squirmed and I screamed inside, and there was nothing I could do to prevent or stop it, or even slow down its course. I guess we've all felt helplessness at one time or another, but to feel the helplessness of despair is the very worst kind. And to have to stand by and watch it all happen to a dear and close friend is an experience we could all live without. We stand, screamingly helpless and we watch. We want to run and yell and clutch and hold. We want to claw and fight and scratch and tear. We want to curse and cry and hurt and maul. We are outraged. We are furious. And what do we do? We do nothing. And why do we do nothing? Because we are impotent. Because society, the society in which we live, dictates that we must not interfere, we mustn't butt into the life, the problems, the grief, or the afflictions of another man, no matter how close he may be to us. We must gnash our teeth, we must remain silent. We may chomp at the bit, we may strain against the ropes. But we must hold our tongues. And after all, if we should shout and scream and shrill and howl, who is there to listen, who is there to hear? No, my friends, we can only weep silently, despairingly. There is nothing to be done. We are silent. We are a mask.

Now when I mentioned the disintegration of Jonny's marriage a few minutes ago, you mustn't think for a minute that it was anything sudden or dramatic. And it was not a dissolution. Rather it was an erosion. It took a long time. The deterioration factor, caused by many other factors, developed over a period of years. But erosion is not easily discernible, not unless you're really looking for it. I saw it, as an interested bystander. But neither Jonny nor Rita saw it. They would even have denied the very existence of it. You see, neither one of them would have accepted the possibility that it even could exist. The words divorce and separation, when brought up about others, actually filled them with horror. I'm sure it never entered their minds that there was anything so unusual with their marriage. I'm equally sure that they both believed that the way they lived was the way everybody lived.

What was it then? Well, I've always believed that in really rough situations, the traumatic ones, a man can take just so much. And then he loses something. Under terrific punishment, something has to be lost. A little bit of spirit maybe, or a certain amount of will. They say a cat has nine lives. It's just possible that we humans, too, have several lives. Perhaps that's what we lose, one of our lives. Sure enough, we go on living. But with each loss, we have one life less. As to how many we can afford to lose before there's nothing left, I think it varies with each one of us. And Jonny was pretty strong, as far as lives go.

As I look back, it was really pitiful to watch the blight come over the carefully nurtured bloom of Jonny's affinity with his son. I saw it wane from week to week, month to month, year to year. I'm sure that the puzzlement in Petey's mind matched the sorrow in Jonny's heart. A young boy, growing up, is vulnerable to all sorts of pressures, suggestions, conflicts. Imagine a situation where a boy loves his father and admires him but whose feelings first turn to doubt and then to condemnation and finally to contempt. The pressure that brought these things to bear was less subtle later than at first. But it was a steady, persistent pressure, a pressure that only a woman like Rita could bring to bear.

I remember the look of pain in Jonny's eyes the day he recounted an incident that concerned Petey. Apparently it was one of the times that Rita dredged up the memory of Blaze Scotland. She and Jonny had gotten into one of their endless discussions concerning the fitness of things and Rita had ended it, in a fit of rage, with the remark, "As far as that goes, this sort of thing would never have happened with Blaze Scotland, would it?"

Jonny blew his top. "Goddamit Rita," he shouted, "Leave her out of this. And stop dragging her name up. It's been a hell of a long time. You have nothing to gain by continually mentioning her."

Well, Petey overheard the whole conversation. And some time later, when he and Jonny happened to be alone, he asked, "Daddy, what's a Blaze Scotland?"

Jonny was plenty startled but, realizing what was up, he knew he had to come up with some fast answers. He sat down with Petey and, painfully, conjured up an explanation. "Petey," he began, "Blaze Scotland is not a what, she's a lady that I knew a long time ago. She doesn't live here in Montreal or even in Canada. She lives mostly in the United States, although she travels about the world a lot. You see, she's an actress in motion pictures and on the stage so she has to go where her work takes her. She was a friend of mine years ago and I haven't seen her since except once in a while in a movie."

"Does Mommy know her too?" Petey asked.

"No Petey," Jonny replied, "Mommy doesn't know her. She just knows about her."

"Well, if she doesn't know her, why doesn't she like her?" Petey demanded.

Jonny had to think about that one. "She doesn't dislike her Petey," he said, "it's pretty hard to dislike someone if you've never even met them. But women don't think exactly the same way us men do. It's kind of hard to explain. But a wife doesn't usually think too much of a woman her husband used to know. She feels kind of superior because, after all, she was the one that the man married. But she sometimes feels a little jealous, too — jealous of anyone her husband knew before they were married. Do you understand what I'm talking about?"

"I think so," Petey answered, "but if that's all, why did you get so mad? Are you developing a temper like Mommy says?"

Jonny passed his hand through his hair wearily. "Petey," he pleaded, "try to understand. When we get older, we get a little tired. And when we're tired we get impatient sometimes. You know, when we're impatient, we talk a little louder, yell sometimes. But it doesn't mean much. It just means we're tired that's all. You can understand that, can't you?"

"Yes," Petey admitted, "except Mommy told me that a man should never yell or shout at a lady. It isn't nice."

Jonny nodded and groaned inwardly. How much more can you explain to a young boy, especially if it's his mother you're talking about? "Your mother's right," Jonny stated solemnly, "us men should control ourselves. We're supposed to be strong. I guess that's a good thing to think about."

Petey nodded, as solemn as his father.

By the time Petey reached high school, the thing that he and Jonny had had for each other was just about gone. Petey had long since ceased to confide in Jonny. If he had any confidences to discuss he discussed them with Rita. Actually he talked very little with his father. To Jonny the boy had become reticent, almost mute. By God, that Rita had done her work well. Jonny never talked about it though, even to me. But I knew him so well. I sensed what was happening because Jonny seldom talked about Petey now. And I saw the look that came into his eyes whenever the boy was mentioned. It was a look that spoke of love and joy and, at the same time, pain and sorrow.

To tell the truth, I wondered what was going on in Jonny's mind at the time. If a man doesn't talk, you don't know; you can only guess. And I guessed that Jonny's heart was breaking for love of his son. But, after all, Jon was an intelligent man. Whatever he may have known, whatever he may have felt, why in the name of God didn't he talk, shout, cry out, attempt to communicate? Why, at home, did he crawl into a shell and turn to silence too? Why indeed! Have you ever known a woman like Rita? Need I say more?

Jonny made one heroic attempt with Petey at about that time. A boy in high school has to think of the future. At the very least, he has to think about his further education, even if he's undecided about what he wants to do with the rest of his life. Yet Petey had said nothing, discussed nothing concerning the matter. I remember, it was during the Christmas holidays and Petey had about seventeen days off from school. Jonny, probably hoping that Petey might evidence some interest in law, suggested that he spend the holiday with us at the office. He even enlisted my help, making me promise that, should Petey accept, I would show him the routine, acquaint him with the files, the library, the investigations and the hundred and one other details that are part of a law office.

For once, Rita agreed with Jonny and convinced the boy that the idea was a good one. I don't know why she agreed but if she hadn't, sure as hell Petey wouldn't have come. Anyway he did come and I was more than passing excited about it. You see, I wanted to observe the boy at close hand. I wanted to find out a lot more about him than I knew. I hoped that being with him so much for several weeks might help me solve the mystery of the lost rapport between my friend Jonny and his son.

The day that Petey came to work for us, I pretty near blew my cool. Jonny came in with him that morning, proud and happy. Knowing what I did, I found his parental joy touching and a little pathetic as he introduced his son to one and all. Jonny was positively beaming. But Petey was reserved and wary, almost to the point of being sullen. I wanted to grab that kid by his shoulders and shake him till his teeth rattled. I wanted to hit him. I wanted to shout at him till his eardrums burst. But more than anything else, I wanted to tell him off, but good.

I wanted to say, "What the hell's with you kid? This is Jonny. This is your father. This is the greatest guy who ever lived. This is gentle, loyal, clever, humourous Jonny. This is my friend you're treating this way, the kind of friend a man could die for. So what the hell is it with you? Maybe he's not good enough for you? Maybe you have such a hell of a lot more to offer? Or maybe it's your mother. Maybe she's the one who's brought all this about. Well, smarten up boy. Neither you nor your mother is fit to lick the boots he walks in. Neither of you could ever hope to hold a candle to him for character. He's ten feet tall and the two of you are little, little people. Don't you ever patronize or freeze my friend Jonny again or, so help me God, I'll knock your goddam block off."

That's what I wanted to say but, of course, I said nothing. I just stood there and grinned like an ape until all the introductions were over. Then, while Jonny went into his own office to look over some work I had prepared for him, I took the youngster in tow. We toured the offices and as a first lesson, I explained the filing system to him. Amongst other things, he was to fill in for the filing clerk, who was away ill. Afterwards, we went into my office and helped ourselves to coffee from the electric percolator that ran continuously from morning to night.

"Ever see your dad in action, in a courtroom I mean?"

At my question, the look of wariness that had almost gone from Petey's eyes returned double-fold. "No, Uncle Arnold," he admitted, "I guess I never have."

"Well, wait till you do," I said, "you'll get quite an eye-opener. He's great in a courtroom, sharp, incisive, brilliant. I'm the detail man. I do the preparation of the cases we get. I'm what you might call the library man. But in court, he's top dog. He's the greatest. Wait till you see."

Petey nodded and then yawned. "Sorry 'bout that," he grinned, "even in school I never wake up till the last period." He completely ignored what I had been saying about Jonny. I gritted my teeth. More than ever I wanted to bust him one. Maybe at that point I would have, but we were interrupted by Jonny coming into my office.

"This has all the earmarks of being a toughy as cases go,"

Jonny was saying. "Is this guy Ladouceur part of the old Perrier gang?"

"No, I don't think so," I answered. "As far as I can tell, he's either a lone wolf or maybe has a partner stashed away someplace the police don't know about. Anyway, the police haven't been able to get him to admit he has a partner or partners. Why do you ask?"

"Oh, I don't know," Jonny replied, "this whole case sort of reminds me of when we were just starting out and the kind of work we used to do for the Perriers. And they're getting older. I figured this guy might be of the new generation of punks but somehow connected with them."

"Not as far as I know," I said.

For the first time since Jonny came into my office, Petey spoke. And for the first time since he had come in that morning, he was showing a semblance of interest. "Who's Ladouceur? Who's the Perrier gang?" he asked.

Well, I told him about the Perrier brothers, our first important clients, and then I filled him in on Ladouceur, our latest. Yvon Ladouceur, I explained, was a professional political activist. Actually he belonged to no party but was available for hire by any dissident group that had the money to pay him. He specialized in terror. He was an expert in the construction of home-made bombs and he wasn't too fussy where he planted them.

Only this time he had made a slight error in judgement. He had set one of his bombs to go off in the home of an important member of the Montreal city council. But the timer was faulty, and the bomb had gone off while Ladouceur was preparing to leave the scene. He was injured and was still lying there when the police arrived. At the hospital, under guard, he demanded that the police contact his lawyers. When asked who his lawyers were, he named Temple and Berman. Must have remembered us from the old Perrier days, or maybe he kept our name in his mental file should he ever need the services of lawyers.

Petey was puzzled. "What I don't understand," he said, "is what he thinks you can do for him. If the police know he put the bomb there and caught him right on the spot, he's going to jail and there's nothing you or anybody else can do about it."

"Not exactly," Jonny said, "that's what lawyers are for. It's up to your Uncle Arnie and me to build a case for his defence. It's our job to defend his innocence."

"Even if you already know he's guilty?" Petey demanded.

"Under our law," Jonny explained patiently, "he's innocent until he's proven guilty. So that's a good start for the defence. We start by presuming he's innocent. It's up to the crown to prove he's guilty. It's what we call the burden of proof. Part of our defence is convincing the jury that the crown hasn't sufficient proof of his guilt or at least that there's sufficient doubt that he actually committed the crime for which he's been charged."

Petey turned to me. "But Uncle Arnie," he insisted, "you seem to know all about this guy. So must the police. So must everybody else. Everyone in that courtroom is going to know he's guilty. And you know he's guilty. So why waste the time and money defending a creep like that?"

"Well Petey, everyone, no matter who or what he is, is entitled to a defence. It's one of the advantages and rights of being a citizen of this country. The way our laws work, even a known criminal has his rights."

"Well our laws are stupid," Petey burst out. "If you get him off, he's going to head right home and start building bombs again. What if someone gets killed the next time? There's something wrong if people like you and Dad keep getting people like Ladouceur freed every time. How can you do it anyway?"

Jonny interrupted to say, "First Uncle Arnie prepares the case. He examines, as much as possible, all the evidence for and against. He studies similar cases that have come up before. He goes over points of law that may help us. He tries to outguess the opposition. And then, one way or another, he builds us a defence. Then when all that's done, I plead the case in court. And right along we try to pick holes in the prosecution's case. Occasionally we win by a fluke, a technicality in law that wraps up the case for us. I know what you're thinking Petey, but wherever you have a democratic or at least a free way of life, that's the system. It's not perfect, but it's the best we've been able to develop so far. And it keeps getting better all the time."

"Well, I think it stinks," Petey muttered, "and I don't think it's getting better. And I think you and Dad should be trying to make it better instead of just going along with the establishment and accepting things the way they are."

I was beginning to get embarrassed for Jonny. And I didn't

think any good purpose would be served by continuing to argue with Petey. So I tried to be funny and lighten the conversation. "We're too old for that," I said. "I guess we'll have to leave it to your generation to make all the good changes. In the meantime, it's a living, if nothing else."

From the look that Petey gave me, I knew that I'd laid an egg with the wisecracks. I wished, at that moment, that I'd kept my big mouth shut. Old folks shouldn't get smart with young ones. They'll nail you every time. In the end, you're the one who feels stupid.

I turned to Jonny. "One simple fact," I said, "there are no witnesses. No one actually saw Ladouceur enter the house or place the bomb. Circumstantial evidence. Naturally the police put two and two together. A bomb goes off in the home of a municipal politician. A known criminal is found at the scene, injured. Circumstantial evidence says that the known criminal, Ladouceur, planted the bomb. But that's all. No witness. No actual proof beyond the obvious facts. Maybe it's as good a place as any to start. Anyway, I called Sidney Korvin. You remember him, the private detective who worked with us on the Duceppe-Aumont case. He'll be here soon. Maybe he can dig up some stuff for us; maybe he can even establish an alibi for our client, although I doubt that. But it's worth a try, wouldn't you say?"

Jonny nodded agreement. "Maybe we'll have to try to make a deal with the crown prosecutor," he mused, "maybe we can get him to reduce the charges in return for a guilty plea. It's an angle we may have to consider. Think about it anyway."

Petey snorted and walked out of my office. I looked at Jonny and he looked at me. Why the hell we should have been discomfited I'll never know. Perhaps that's part of the system too. It's one that ought to be changed damn quick.

Life is full of contradictions, they say. While I was working to prepare the Ladouceur case, Petey studiously avoided me. It was pretty obvious that he wanted neither to be involved in the preparation nor to discuss the case. He continued to come to the office. He did the filing, straightened out the library, and looked after the mail. But whenever Jonny or I asked him to lunch, he always seemed to have just eaten or he wasn't hungry. His general air of disapproval infuriated me. I caught myself looking at him and then at Jonny for reaction. But Jonny seemed to have developed a poker face and I could tell nothing. So I kept my mouth shut. But I couldn't help the way I felt. I was pretty heartsick for Jonny.

However, things changed, considerably for the better, when we got into court. First of all, Petey was fascinated by Sidney Korvin. And the detective liked the boy from the start. They spent a good deal of time together once Korvin got going on our case. Petey asked a million questions and Korvin never tired of recounting the many cases he had worked on. Whether or not Petey approved of Korvin I never did get to know. But it didn't seem to matter.

Anyhow, once we got into court and Jonny took over, the relationship between him and Petey seemed to improve. As I've said before, Jonny was a tremendous trial lawyer and never looked better than when he was pleading a case. And every time he objected to some procedure and the judge sustained the objection, Petey almost glowed with satisfaction. Did I detect the beginnings of a growing admiration for his father? I certainly hoped so, more fervently than anybody could possibly imagine. Petey even came to lunch with Jonny and me and seemed to enjoy our discussion of the case. I had pretty high hopes for the two of them.

The prosecution had prepared its case carefully. They were fully aware that circumstantial evidence was about all they had to go on. And they were determined to take no chances with Jonny's famous courtroom tricks. They did everything possible to avoid putting themselves in the position where Jonny could capitalize on the slightest slip or breach of the law. Their case was pretty airtight.

Korvin's help hadn't amounted to much and Jonny tried to build a case of persecution. He admitted his client's past but insisted that he had reformed. He tried to infer that the police were carrying out a personal vendetta against poor old Yvon Ladouceur who only wanted to go straight and live in peace. And what was his client doing at the scene of the crime? How was it that he happened to be there and been injured when the bomb blew? Why, ladies and gentlemen of the jury, Yvon Ladouceur had broken with his former associates. He had determined never to get involved with bombs or bombings again. But the associates were not giving up that easily. They could literally kill two birds with one stone. They could get rid of a hated politician and teach Ladouceur a lesson at the same time. But Ladouceur had tried to outsmart them. Not wishing to be tapped for the crime, he had actually gone to that house with the sole intention of dismantling the bomb. After all, he was the expert when it came to bombs. Was it likely that he would have been so careless as to allow his own bomb to blow up on him? Not likely, ladies and gentlemen, not likely. And before this case is over, we hope to prove that it was Yvon Ladouceur's former associates who planted the bomb and not the defendant, our client.

The defendant, our client, Yvon Ladouceur did precious little to help our case. He was surly and unsmiling. When he wasn't glaring at the police witnesses or the jury, he sat in his place, uninterested or doodling on the pad of paper in front of him. All through the pre-trial period, Jonny and I had hammered at him. We were certain that he had had help in both the making of the bomb and the planting of it. No matter what we said or did, we couldn't seem to convince him of the seriousness of the situation. And we couldn't get him to name anyone else involved. He didn't try to make us believe there had been no one else. He simply refused to implicate anyone.

Right up to the time of the trial, Jonny and I had pinned our hopes of winning on our ability to get through to him. We knew damn well we'd have a better chance if we could involve others. And the crown prosecutor had implied that if Ladouceur would talk and make possible the arrest of others, he would be willing to take it easy on our client and perhaps even consider the reduction of the charges. But now, Jonny had made his little speech to the jury and Ladouceur still hadn't talked. Things were not going well.

Even Petey seemed to get more jittery as the trial progressed. Whatever he may have thought or was thinking, he seemed very anxious for Jonny to win. Now I'm no psychiatrist, but I believe that Petey needed desperately for Jonny to win that case. I think that, secretly or subconsciously, he yearned to find a reason to admire his father. Maybe, in his young mind, he would have been glad of the opportunity to find Rita wrong. I'm sure it's not natural for a youngster to grow up without a feeling of pride and respect and love for his father. And I believe that Petey was hoping to regain these feelings through this trial. Had we won, Petey's hopes and dreams would have been vindicated.

Knowing this, can you imagine how I wanted us to win? And can you imagine that when I thought of the possibility of our losing, I also thought how ironic life can be, when the win or loss of this particular case could make all the difference in the world in the future relationship of a man and his son, my friend and my adopted nephew?

Well, Ladouceur didn't spill, and the jury became more and more hostile towards him. I worked like a bastard behind the scenes; Jonny was absolutely heroic in the courtroom. Apart from anything else, he could have won an academy award for acting. Behind his jitteriness, Petey was cheerful and encouraging. But no matter what we did, no matter how we tried, nothing seemed to be working for us.

The final blow came when the judge gave his summation to the jury. Even though he liked and admired Jonny, he was determined to throw the book at Ladouceur this time. His charge to the jury was a masterpiece of controlled fury and vindictiveness. By the time he got through with them, he had them so fired up about their duty to protect the public, that there wasn't much doubt of the outcome. From experience, there was little question left in my mind what the verdict would be.

Jonny tried to let Petey down easily. While the jury was out, we went across the street from the courthouse for coffee. "Look Petey," Jonny said, "you can't win them all. I don't say we've lost. You never know till the jury gives its verdict. Now if we've won, fine. But if we do lose, it doesn't mean that we're discredited or that our reputation is immeasurably damaged. That's how it is with the law. You win some cases, you lose others. Just as long as we've done everything possible for our client. Just as long as we prepared our case carefully and did everything we could from a legal point of view, there's been no harm done. We've defended a man, we've given him every opportunity under due process of law. But he has, in the final analysis, to be judged by a jury of his peers. And that judgement is the final one, unless we appeal. But whatever the judgement, the case for our democratic system has been served. A man gets a fair trial; he must abide by the final verdict."

"But what about Yvon Ladouceur?" Petey objected. "You may be satisfied that you've done all you can, but he's the one going to prison."

I broke in. "We all knew he was guilty, Petey. But your Dad and I have nothing to reproach ourselves for. We worked to the very best of our ability and experience on the case. And, when you come right down to it, he helped convict himself, if he's convicted. He sure did everything possible to screw himself in front of the judge and jury. And by refusing to at least talk to us, he made it very tough for us to defend him. I'd like to say this, though. Only your father could have taken us to even this point, where the possibility that the jury will find in our favour exists at all."

Petey grinned at me mirthlessly. "Must be the whole bourgeois society that's to blame," he said, "the society that brings about the reasons for things like this happening, that creates the need for men like Ladouceur in the first place." He continued to grin at me as we made our way back to the courthouse. If I could have clobbered him then, just once, I wouldn't have cared so much whether we won or lost.

Sitting and waiting for the jury to make its appearance, I was very aware of Jonny's concentrated gaze on his son. To the dozens and dozens of times we had waited like this, one other thing had been added. This time Jonny wanted to win for Petey. Winning this case meant winning his son back. I think if the jury had known how much was at stake this time they would have brought in a verdict of not guilty. But they didn't know and the verdict was — guilty.

The moment the word was spoken, Petey walked out of the courtroom. Jonny rose as if to follow, but I restrained him. If he had followed Petey out of the room, what good would it have done? Losing the case was bad enough. Jonny didn't need the added humiliation of a rebuff from his son at this time. The final irony was when the crown prosecutor came over to shake hands with us. "A hell of a good job as always," he said to Jonny, "and if it weren't unethical, I would like to thank your client for winning this case for me. It was easy to beat even you with him on my side." It wasn't the first time in my life that I felt like throwing up in public.

Well, that did it as far as Jonny and Petey were concerned. I can't say I was surprised. I knew it would be just like that. But I guess I'd been hoping for some sort of miracle to occur. But miracles don't occur, do they? I know that I've lived long enough and experienced enough to not believe in miracles. But you know something? I'm sorry for people who don't believe in them. I'm sorry for people who go through their whole lives being completely practical and down to earth. Oh I agree that you can't live with your head in the clouds. But dammit, dreams are the essence of living. And miracles are part of those dreams. I'm sure I'd rather be like me, believing in dreams and miracles, than believing in nothing. In spite of all that happened, in spite of all the lousy things in this world, I'll cling to my dreams and my miracles. Without them, I don't think my life would be worth a damn. At the very least, they bring a measure of beauty into a dull and ugly world.

Petey refused to discuss the case with Jonny. He had lost all interest in it and in its outcome. I know now that, in Petey's mind, Jonny had let him down. Like in athletics, instead of being a hero to a boy, Jonny was a bum. In our society, we're geared for wins, not losses. The spirit of competition has been so drummed into our heads that it's no longer how you play the game, but winning that counts. It takes a special kind of orientation to accept losing. There are still some people who can take a loss gracefully. But not Jonny's son and not Jonny's family. I can just imagine Rita's reaction. I'm bloody sure she took it as a personal affront. And I can imagine the discussions between her and Petey.

Whatever was said, the results were there to be seen. That little something, that little ray of hope, that glimmer of understanding and rapport between Jonny and his son died aborning. It died with our hopes of winning the Ladouceur case. It died for lack of effort. It died for lack of direction and understanding. For all these reasons, it died. And it was buried. And after the death and the burial? The aftermath was a particular tragedy as far as I'm concerned. According to my theory, with the loss of his son, Jon Temple lost the second of his lives. Or was it the third? No matter. What scared the living hell out of me was figuring how many there were left.

CHAPTER 5

MARION

By now you're beginning to see what was going on in Jonny's house. I think you'd agree that between Rita and Petey, it was no picnic for him. Now what about the fourth member of the household? Don't forget Jonny's mother-in-law, Marion. Naturally, living with him, she played an important part in his life. As to what her contribution actually was, you'll see very shortly. As I mentioned, in the beginning Jonny didn't think too much about her, one way or the other. He tried to ignore her and pay as little attention to her as possible. But in the long run, Marion was not an easy person to ignore. There must have been times when, in spite of himself and his original passive liking for her, he would have cheerfully strangled her or at the very least, wished her out of his house. And what about Marion herself?

After the car accident which took the lives of her husband and her husband's mother, Marion's first reaction was panic. It superseded her grief over the loss of her husband. The abrupt change that would have to come about in her way of living was of critical importance to her. Remember, she had been the passive partner in her marriage. She had left all the important decisions to her husband. Plumpish and inclined to be lazy, she had taken whatever Henry had to offer to their marriage and had contributed very little. And because Henry had been strong, her life was easy, contented and undemanding. All in all, she had felt sheltered and protected. Then suddenly, Henry was no longer there. In one crashing instant, her sheltered protection was no more. So her first reaction was that of panic, an enormous concern over her future way of life.

Marion was hardly the type of person to take the bull by the horns and make a new life for herself. The idea of independence and self-sufficiency would never have entered her mind. You can imagine the relief of a woman like that when her daughter suggested that she move in with her and her family. Now when I say relief, I don't mean gratitude or thankfulness or anything like that. As far as Marion was concerned it was her due, it was coming to her. Rita was her daughter. And now that Henry, who had always looked after her, was gone, it was Rita's duty to take over the responsibility. It was part of her obligation as a daughter. It had never occurred to Marion, for one minute, to consider her obligations as a mother.

I've often wondered what it is that happens to people as they grow older. I've seen it happen so often that men and women who were once contented and happy, unselfish and extroverted, kind and considerate change completely as old age approaches. I've never been sure whether or not it's illness and approaching death that causes the change or some other reasons entirely. But whatever it is, the change is remarkable. Contented, happy people become miserable and querulous. Unselfish extroverts suddenly become introverted and immensely selfish. Kind and considerate people turn thoughtless and bitchy.

Suddenly, too, there aren't enough of the good things in the world to go around. These older folks become mean and grasping. They want the most and they want the best. Nothing is too good for them, nothing is too much. They live with miserliness. They live for comfort and acquisitions. Other people need nothing, they need everything. Other people can do without, they must have. They are lonelier, sicker, poorer, older than almost anyone else. They are more neglected, unwanted, uncared for, and abandoned than their neighbours. They have been forgotten and their lives have become a hell on earth. Nobody cares what happens to them, no one cares if they have enough. And envious. Why should others have more, why should others have better? Other people's children are much more concerned, they cater far more to their parents. Their children couldn't care less what happens to them. But they need, they want, they must have. And why not? How much time have they left to enjoy?

Some medical men hold to the theory that as people get old and sick, they lose all their inhibitions. All the things they've always felt deprived of they now want. All the frustrations and anger and bitterness and disappointment can now be brought out into the light and aired. Why? Because there's not much time left, the end is approaching, illness has taken hold. Let those who will survive know what they're going to miss, let them feel guilty for their neglect, let them feel anguish for all the things they should have done and didn't. Now, quick, before it's too late. Before it's too late let them know all these things and try to atone. Now, right now, before it's too late.

Marion Buckman Stern didn't wait until she became an old lady to develop many of the unpleasant traits usually reserved for the aged. She was selfish and inconsiderate to begin with. From her childhood through her marriage with Henry, she had put her comforts and her feelings before anything else. She believed that the whole world — her world — owed her respect and consideration. Most people, she couldn't care less what they thought or did. Rita owed her because she was her daughter. Jonny owed her because he was her son-in-law. And Petey owed her because he was her grandson. They all owed her. But she owed nothing. She demanded but she gave nothing in return except a lot of unwanted advice. Her position as the matriarch of the family entitled her to every consideration. But she had to consider no one except herself.

One other thing about Marion. Somewhere along the line she had convinced herself that she was smarter and knew more than anyone else. She would argue about things she knew nothing about. Well, argue isn't exactly the right word. She would make declarations, statements of fact, and no matter how erroneous they were, the conversation ended there. There was no use arguing with her, her strength lay in her certainty that she was right. So plump, unlined, untouched Marion was often the catalyst that provided the explosions in the Temple household.

I remember Jonny telling me about an incident with Marion that made it very clear to me what he had to contend with. It came about immediately after we lost the Ladouceur case. Whatever Rita and Petey had talked about, whatever they may have thought, they kept quiet about it. If you think it's unusual for a family to avoid discussing a matter of such great importance, you know by now how it could come about with the Temples. But Marion was not about to let the matter drop. It started one evening right after dinner. It started on a low key and built up out of all proportions. It must have been a beaut.

Rita had started to clear the dishes and Petey had gotten up to help her. Jonny was concentrating on getting his pipe started. With deceptive innocence Marion made her opening remark.

"You haven't said anything, Jon," she murmured, "but I see by the papers that you didn't win the Ladouceur case."

With equal innocence Jon answered her. "No, that's right. The verdict went against us."

"You never should have accepted the case," Marion declared.

"What?"

"You shouldn't have accepted the case," she repeated.

Jonny stared at her for a moment. Then he put his pipe down and resigned himself to the discussion that he knew lay ahead. "I'm a lawyer, Mother," he began, "but I wouldn't be much of one if I turned down every case I thought I might possibly lose. Everyone is entitled to a defence. We take on a case and we do the very best we can. There's never a guarantee that we'll win every one. There are often extenuating circumstances that may swing a verdict either way. The important thing is, win or lose, to put up the best defence possible and to give the defendant every available opportunity under the law. That's what lawyers are for, not to perform miracles."

Marion sniffed. "Well I just don't think it's good business to take on a case if you don't think you can win it."

Jonny made a tremendous effort to remain patient. "We don't take cases with the intention of losing them. We know that some are going to be tougher to win than others. But we do our homework and we fight with all the weapons at our command. And like I said, the verdict can go either way. We could win the case, no matter how tough it might be."

"But the chances are you could lose, too."

"Of course we could lose. But I never heard of a lawyer that won every case he ever tried."

"Well, you're not any lawyer. Anyway, I don't want to belabour the point. I just think you ought to be more selective, that's all."

Jonny was beginning to feel that he'd blow up any minute, lose control. It took a herculean effort to remain calm. "Marion, please," he said, "let's drop the subject, shall we?"

Marion sniffed again. "Of course, if you don't want to talk about it. But seeing Petey was with you, it would have been better to take on a case you could win. It would have made a much better impression on the boy."

Jonny simply stared at her, unable to believe his own ears. His impulse was to shout, "What the hell has it got to do with Petey?" But then he shrugged mentally. It was just no use going on like this with Marion. This was one argument he was going to lose, no matter what. Marion, self-righteous as always, stubborn and opinionated, had already decided the outcome of the conversation. Jonny got up and left the room. Neither Rita nor Petey had said one word in all this time. It seemed they were content to let Marion carry the ball.

There were many times, while Petey was growing up, that Jonny felt the need to discipline the boy. Rita, with Marion's backing, was quite prepared to take a very permissive attitude toward her son. This was the new thing to do, backed by child psychologists and adult psychiatrists. This new hypothesis held that a child should be free to seek his own level, unfettered by parental discipline and established codes of behaviour. If it seemed right and natural to the child, he should be allowed to do as he wished and how he wished it. He should not be bound by ancient behaviour patterns and outmoded ethical premises. He should be free and unfettered. It sounds fine, but the danger is that you're liable to bring up a little monster in the process.

Jonny refused to buy that theory entirely. He objected strongly to Petey calling his parents and grandmother by their first names. He refused to allow the youngster to do anything he damn well liked. In spite of Rita and Marion, he tried to communicate with his son, to teach him a sense of morals and old-fashioned values. In spite of Rita and Marion, he spanked the child on occasion, yelled at him frequently and disciplined him continually. Not to a fault, you understand, but when the occasion warranted it. Jonny had his own ideas as to how to bring up his son to be a man.

Invariably, after a disciplining session, even if Rita held her tongue, Marion would take the boy's part. She would comfort and cajole him and, in a few short minutes, undo all that Jonny had hoped to achieve. Petey learned at a very early age to run to his grandmother whenever his father got rough. And there wasn't a hell of a lot that Jonny could do about it. He could glare and gnash his teeth and . . . hold his peace. His impotence in the face of all the odds hung heavily on him.

Jonny tried. He'd say, "Marion, please." Or he'd say, quietly and in private, "Marion would you please let me discipline my son, and in my own way." Marion's answer did nothing more than drive him up a wall. He got nowhere with her and nowhere with Petey either.

As time went on, the problem with Marion got worse. Not

only did she just sit and sit, becoming less active all the time, but now she indulged in long periods of sulking, when her misery and the misery she created hung over the household like a poisonous cloud. And a new element entered the situation.

Up till now, I've had very little to say about Jonny's parents, Rose and David Temple, since his marriage. You see, in the beginning, Rose made elaborate speeches about not interfering in the children's married lives. What David thought or felt, no one ever knew. He was the weak, silent type. But Rose couldn't cut the apron strings. She absolutely insisted that Jonny phone her every night, resorting to bitter recriminations whenever he missed. On the other hand, she and Rita had very little use for each other, so the get-togethers between the Temples, senior and junior, were kept to a minimum and usually reserved for special occasions. After the birth of their grandson, the excuse of coming to see the child became one type of special occasion. Usually their visits were short, confined to Sunday afternoons.

But then, for a while, they became close to Marion. Older folks, with very little to do, often are drawn to each other. Jonny's folks and Marion got into the habit of playing cards together. They played gin rummy and the winner of each two-handed game played the third. Sometimes Rita or Jonny would get roped in to making a fourth, so they could play partners.

At first these card games weren't too bad. Rita put up with them because they kept Marion occupied and reasonably quiet and contented. And Jonny was glad to see his parents in his home, friendly with Marion and happy in their relationship with their grandson. It was usually peaceful and quiet in his house during those games. But, as the novelty began to wear off and the games became a routine, the bickering began. The quiet of the house was shattered.

Marion invariably started the trouble by making a snide remark, or by involving Petey in the discussions. Sometimes she complained about Jonny's "heavy-handed" methods in bringing up the boy. Other times she bragged about the youngster's accomplishments to the point of embarrassment. And often she'd ask Petey directly, in the presence of the others, who his favourite grandparent was. She'd needle and bait him into admitting it was she and she'd get a perverse pleasure from the pained reaction of the others. Well, what the hell was the big deal? She lived with Petey. Certainly she was closer to him than Jonny's folks. And what was with the measuring, the big yard-stick? It even began to bother Petey after a while. And it drove Jonny crazy.

The card game sessions came to an end. The senior Temples had other friends and they didn't need the crap that Marion was always throwing against the walls. So in the end, Marion was the loser. She sat by herself and vegetated, without company, without friends. The visits from his folks became less and less frequent. Jonny felt lousy about it but there was sweet bugger all that he could do.

Marion got worse and worse. From an opinionated person, she became an oracle. Her pronouncements took on all the fervour of the ten commandments. Her advice was more fre-quently given. Her desire, her need to know everything going on, no matter how intimate, between her daughter and her son-in-law reached the point of no return. In short, she became a pesty, interfering, argumentative old woman.

Jonny brought the subject up several times with Rita, but got nowhere. Rita took Marion's part, at least to the extent of excusing her mother. "She's all alone," she would say, "and she's interested. She means well. Anyway there's nothing to be done but put up with it. And she's often right you know." I was about to say that things couldn't have been worse. But the worst was yet to come, and soon.

Marion took sick. It was nothing too serious, or terminal, or anything like that. She had an ulcer. How the hell anyone as cow-like as she could come down with a thing like that I'll never know. I've never known anyone who took better care of herself.

Now I'm not suggesting for one minute that an ulcer is either pleasant or painless. It can cause a great deal of pain and discomfort. I'm not, in any way, trying to minimize it. But most people I know who discover they have an ulcer learn to live with it. They are given a bland diet, anti-spasmodic pills, tranquilizers and other forms of medication, and they learn to cope without driving everyone around them completely nuts. There is a claim that ulcers come about not through what you eat but what eats you. Most ulcer patients accept this theory and adjust their living to it.

Not Marion. She played the scene for all it was worth. At

the first sign of an attack, she'd press the panic button. She'd take to her bed, the doctor would be summoned again, the medical prescriptions refilled. And the whining would commence. No one had ever had such miserable, upsetting, painful, serious ulcer attacks. Hers were far, far worse than anyone else's. The whole house was on wheels. Everyone was pressed into service. Marion was catered to, cajoled, comforted, sympathized with. The running was constant, to and from Marion's room.

Marion and her condition became the sole consideration, not only in the house, but outside it as well. Rita was tied down, her mother had an ulcer attack going. All appointments were cancelled, all her friends were advised that she was incommunicado until her mother was feeling better again. Petey had to tell his school friends that he was required home immediately after school in case he was needed to run messages to the drugstore or what have you. And Jonny had to mention it to us to explain his exhaustion and his depression. It became a catch-phrase at the time. Jonny's state of mind was summed up in the remark, "My mother-in-law is having one of her attacks again."

If anything, Marion became more unbearable than ever. Not only did she talk incessantly, about herself, but her complaining took on a whining, self-pitying quality that had been absent before. And critical. She criticized everything and everyone. Nothing done in the house was done right. Nothing said was said right. And everyone — family, friends and acquaintances — came in for their share of criticism. This one didn't dress right, that one didn't speak right. So and so was just an old gossip. His wife is stupid, her husband is a big-mouth, their kids are always looking for trouble. That's the way it went, day and night.

Was everything calm and serene after an attack? The hell it was. Marion never did shut her mouth. As if that wasn't bad enough, she became thoroughly sloppy in her dress. Formerly quite clothes-conscious and meticulous in appearance, she became, not only sloppy, but downright dirty. There were always stains on her clothing. She spilled on herself and then continued to wear the same clothes for days, until, in desperation, Rita gathered them up and sent them to the cleaners. Marion stopped wearing make-up and her hair was in a constant state of disarray. I don't know about Rita, but Jonny was scared to death to have anyone over to his house, lest the apparition of his mother-in-law make an appearance.

Jonny began to crack. I watched it begin slowly, then gather momentum. There isn't a man alive who could live with what he had to live with and not be affected. As far as gentle, sensitive Jonny was concerned, the wear and tear began to show, more and more obviously. And finally it began to affect his work. I, more than anyone, of course, knew what a tremendous effort he made not to allow this to happen. It was almost physical the way he tried to force himself to concentrate on his work at the office and in the courtroom. For God's sake, it's inhuman to expect that a man could live in the environment of Rita and Marion and suffer such disappointment in his son and remain whole.

Chronologically, I equate many of the parts and pieces of Jonny's life to cases that we worked on. After all, Jonny, in the courtroom, was alive and vibrant and often brilliant. He would rise to the occasion demanded of him while pleading a case and I'm sure there wasn't a better criminal lawyer in Montreal at the time. What went on at home was one thing, his social life was another. But in our offices and in court, Jonny was the greatest thing I'd ever seen. But now, while we were working on our latest case, I saw the signs of the crack in the dike. And I worried myself sick about it, keeping my thoughts to myself for the time being.

The first sign was a matter of frequent preoccupation on Jonny's part. I might be talking to him, discussing a point of law or some aspect of the case, and suddenly Jonny wasn't listening to me. He had one of those faraway looks in his eyes and he'd be doodling on a scratch pad in front of him. I'm positive if I'd passed a hand across his eyes, he wouldn't have blinked an eyelid. What he was thinking about I didn't know. As a matter of fact, I had realized that it was quite often lately that I hadn't the foggiest notion of what was passing through Jonny's mind. It was damn scary, because for many years we were like one in thought as well as action. I just wasn't used to not knowing what Jonny was thinking, and it bothered me to the point where I began to lose sleep over it. But whenever I snapped my fingers or called out, "Here Jonny, come on back here," he would look at me and, as his eyes cleared, grin and immediately launch into the problem at hand. I sensed that this was only the beginning.

Now this case we were preparing was a comparatively simple one and, at the outset, there had been no doubt in our minds that we could win it hands down. Basically it was a divorce case. We would have never come into the picture except that the man involved, our client, had been accused by his wife of attempted murder. The prosecution's whole case seemed to rest on the testimony of one witness, the wife's sister. We didn't figure to have much trouble discrediting her testimony and we also thought we could build a good case for our man by proving collusion between the two sisters. So this was one case I was willing to bet money on our winning.

One of the first things I did was to reach Sidney Korvin, who is the best private detective in Montreal. I went over the facts of the case with him and got him going. It was imperative to our case that he dig into every detail of the activities of the husband and wife and the wife's sister.

His report was almost classic in its simplicity. What he dug up was this. Erica and Mai Persson were two beautiful Scandinavian girls, sisters who had left their native country and emigrated to Canada. Soon after their arrival in Montreal, they had both been hired by one of the top model agencies and had begun their careers as fashion models. Their blond beauty and old-world charm were soon in demand by all the major fashion houses in the city, for showings and for photographic sessions.

Now Arthur Dryer owned one of the larger sportswear firms in town, and the girls began to do a lot of work for him, sometimes one, sometimes the other. Arthur, a bachelor, began to date Mai from time to time. He took her to dinner and to the theatre. It was nothing serious on Arthur's part. He just enjoyed the company of this lovely girl and liked to show her off. But one day, when Erica was working his showroom, he asked her to dinner. She was the one he married. Mai took it very well and all seemed blissful for a while. But the marriage disintegrated and the next thing, Erica was suing Arthur for divorce. What's more, she claimed that Arthur had tried to kill her, an accusation corroborated by Mai.

But Sidney Korvin was used to digging under the surface of things and he came up with facts that shed a completely new light on the whole case. He interviewed the three principals, as only he can interview, and came up with the theory on which we intended to base our case. First, Arthur Dryer was incapable of murder. Second, Erica didn't love him, never had. She loved only his money and position. Third, Mai did love him. And it was her jealous spite that had triggered the whole thing, including the murder bit.

As I said, I didn't anticipate any trouble at all in winning this case. Even our client, Arthur, seemed to think the whole thing was a macabre joke. He was absolutely certain that he would beat the murder rap and win the divorce case as well.

As a lawyer, I've always deplored the part the press plays in cases of this type. The job of the press, to be sure, is to report the facts of the case and acquaint the public with the details concerning it. Fine. I have no quarrel with that. It's the embellishing that bugs me. Granted, the public appetite demands details as lurid and erotic as possible. But when the reporters and particularly the sob sisters get hold of a case like this, they play up the gory details to such an extent that the case is prejudged by the public, the members of the jury, and sometimes even the judge himself. After all, the judge and jury are human. And the prejudgement may be subconscious. But the implications are there, and many an innocent defendant had been judged guilty because of the overwhelming attitude of the press. I've often thought that the press ought to be acquainted with the facts of the case only after it is over and the judgement handed down.

Lawyers sometimes find themselves in the position of having to fight public opinion and the press, as well as the prejudgement I've mentioned. In this particular case, Jonny got more than an earful at home. Rita and Marion were in absolute sympathy with the women and, as far as they were concerned, Arthur Dryer was as guilty as hell on all counts. First Rita, then Marion insisted on discussing the merits of the case. They pretty near drove Jonny crazy, giving him their opinions and advising him how to conduct the case. They sniped at him day and night, at the breakfast table, at the dinner table and in the evenings. If Jonny didn't go off his rocker at that time, it was the miracle of all time. And that was the frame of mind in which Jonny commenced his plea in court as the case got underway.

I knew immediately that things were not going well for us. That first day, as the prosecution stated its case, Jonny was preoccupied and lethargic. He just wasn't his usual on-the-ball self. He failed to object when he should have, and when he did, he failed to press his point. On cross-examination he was less than brilliant. He seemed unable to deal with the flippancy of both Erica and Mai. And on several occasions when the court-room rocked with laughter, he peered around as though he couldn't understand what it was all about.

I could feel the sweat oozing from every pore in my body. In desperation, I got Jonny to request a recess, which was granted. I needed the time to try to get Jonny back on the beam. Something was wrong, radically wrong. Jonny had never been like this before, never this bad. The case was one thing but this situation was shaping up as something far more degener-ative, certainly as far as Jonny was concerned.

We were sitting in an anteroom and Jonny was shaking his head. "I don't know what's wrong with me, Arnie," he was saying, "I just can't seem to concentrate. My mind keeps wandering. You've prepared a good case and I'm mucking it up. Maybe you'd better take over."

I groaned inwardly. I had been thinking the same thing, for the sake of our client. And I felt like I was being torn apart. I knew I should take over, but I just couldn't do that to Jonny. If I did take over, I was damn sure that something catastrophic would happen to him. On the other hand, Arthur Dryer deser-ved a hell of a lot better defence than we were offering so far. It was really a brain buster of a problem.

I opted to go along with Jonny. And I tried to talk to him like a dutch uncle. "Now look, Jonny," I begged, "you've always handled the courtroom routine. That's the way it has always been with us. I prepare, you plead. Changing things around now isn't fair to anyone. Now for God's sake get hold of yourself. Put everything and everyone out of your mind. Don't think about anything except the case. We can win this one. But a lot's going to depend on what you do with the witnesses. Come on now, Jonny. You can do it. And Jon, it's important."

"I know," Jonny whispered, "I know how important it is Arnie. If you think . . . I'll try. Arnie I'm going to try like hell."

We didn't lose the case. We didn't exactly win it, either. I mean we managed to get the murder charge dropped for lack of evidence. But the divorce was granted and Erica got one hell of a settlement. For the first time in our careers, the prosecution was able to make it look easy. And Temple and Berman lost on a series of fumbles and errors. I felt pretty bad about the case. But I was thoroughly alarmed about Jonny. He took it really badly. Of course he blamed himself. And it had the effect of dropping his morale to an all-time low.

The press didn't help matters much. According to the papers, Arthur Dryer should never have beaten the murder rap. According to them too, he was not only guilty as charged but got off too easy on the divorce settlement. But it wasn't because his lawyers handled the case well. It was because the prosecution failed in it's presentation of the case. Either way we lost. And we sure didn't look too good in print. However, it wasn't nearly so disastrous for our firm as Jonny made out. We certainly could have weathered that little storm. But Jonny seemed bent on making a federal case out of it, and nothing I could say or do was apparently going to stop it.

I guess Rita didn't ride Jonny too much about the case. But I gather that Marion was smugly satisfied that her predictions and convictions had been justified. And that as much as anything else contributed to Jonny's attitude about the whole thing. I was trying to prepare myself for all eventualities, because I couldn't for the life of me figure out what Jonny was thinking or planning. The one thing I wasn't prepared for was the bombshell that Jonny dropped in our office three days after the end of the trial.

I knew something was brewing the moment Jonny walked into my office that morning. He had a kind of wild look in his eyes, a sort of desperation that I'd never seen before. He dropped into the chair in front of my desk, his eyes burning. I braced myself for the onslaught. But when it came, it wasn't anything like what I had bargained for. Nor was it an onslaught. It was a quiet and simple statement. And like all such statements it had the effect of a sledgehammer.

Jonny simply said, "Arnie, if I don't get away, if I don't leave Montreal for a while, I'm going to crack up completely. And, Arnie, I don't mean for a few days. I mean for an extended period."

I just sat there and stared. My brain was racing with a thousand conclusions and a thousand questions. But I wasn't able to say anything. I just sat like I'd been pole-axed, which I had been.

"Arnie, you know. You know that I have to get away from

here, away from my family, away from this office, away from everything. I've weighed the consequences carefully. I know the implications. I know how tough it's going to be to just take off. But I also know that if I don't, something real bad is going to happen to me. You do understand, Arnie, don't you?"

"I understand, Jonny, believe me I understand. And don't for one damn moment worry about me. I'll manage just fine. I'll get a couple of juniors in here and I'll manage. But what about you? What will you do? Where will you go?"

"I haven't thought that far ahead," Jonny replied thoughtfully, "but I'll come up with something. You know, Arnie, this is one thing I never would have thought possible, leaving my practice, even temporarily. But . . . well I don't have to spell it out, do I? You know."

I nodded. "What about your family?" I asked.

Jonny smiled grimly. "That's going to be a pip," he said, "but I'll have to face it and get the hell out as quickly as possible. They'll be fine financially. And I can't think beyond that. I have to think of me now, Arnie, before it's too late."

I nodded again in silent agreement. Then I said, "Okay, Jonny, let me know if there's any way I can help. And if you want me to know where you're going, fine. If not, that's okay too. This office will be here when you come back. By the way, is Marion the straw that broke the camel's back?"

Jonny considered for a minute. Then he said, "Could be, Arnie, could be."

For a couple of days Jonny wandered in and out of the office. I could see that things were weighing heavily on his mind. I decided the best way I could help would be to keep my mouth shut and wait for Jonny to come to me. When he finally did, he seemed almost relieved. He walked into my office, half grinning. "You should have been at my house this morning," he said. "It was like a three-ring circus. The noise, the shouting, the recriminations. It was like out of a dime novel. But what had to be said has been said. I'm a prize bastard and a low-down sonofabitch. But I'm free to go now. And that's the important thing. You'll never know how important. I've moved into the Windsor Hotel for a day or two while I decide where to go."

"Anything you want me to do Jonny?" I asked.

"Just be my friend," he replied.

Two days later Jonny came to me again. "I talked to Blaze

last night," he announced. "I'm going to her, Arnie." I must have looked very surprised because he continued hurriedly, "I've thought about it and, in one way, I know it's the wrong thing to do. But I also know that I need her desperately right now. She's the only one who can help me. I guess this is going to sound corny, but she's the only one who can make me whole again, who can make me feel like a man again." Somehow, in the light of all that had happened, it didn't sound at all corny to me.

"I talked to her for a long time last night," Jonny went on. "I tried to explain everything to her. I also tried to give her every chance to refuse me. But she didn't. So, I'm flying out to California tonight to meet her. I can't tell whether you approve or not, Arnie."

"Who the hell am I to approve or disapprove?" I answered. "If it's right for you and for her that's all there is to it. It's nobody else's business anyway. You're a lucky guy to have her Jonny. What else can I say except good luck?"

"You know," Jonny mused, "when I left her the last time, I didn't ever expect to see her again. That's the basis on which we both parted. The last thing in the world I wanted was for her to become a part-time mistress. I just couldn't do that to her, assuming she was willing to accept that sort of relationship. But I don't feel that way about her at all. I just know I have to be with her now. And I'm grateful, very grateful." He didn't say anything else. I guess I imagined him saying, "It's a matter of life or death."

It was weeks before I heard from Jonny. And it was a lot longer than that before I was able to piece together the subsequent events. But eventually the jigsaw pieces of Jonny's life fitted together, and I was able to keep the chronological order straight.

Jonny flew out to New York that night and made connections with a plane for California. In a matter of a few hours, the plane was circling Burbank airport preparatory to landing. During the trip, he had forced his mind to follow a flight plan much as the pilot had done. He had refused to allow his thinking to dwell on what he had done to himself and his family. Like a drowning man, he had only one thing in mind. And that was self-preservation. He reached out for something solid to grasp, to keep him from going under. That something was Blaze. The

thought, deep in the recesses of his mind, that he was going to
her, sustained him and kept him afloat. And he wasn't afraid.
He knew that when he reached her, his safe harbour, all would
be well. He would be saved and he would be safe.

The plane landed and taxied to a stop. As he stepped out
onto the ramp and saw her waiting for him behind the steel
fence, he breathed very deeply, drawing the air down, down
into his lungs. The weight had been suddenly lifted. He had
been right to come. Blaze was there, waiting for him. And that
was right too. Nothing between them could ever be anything
but right. He ran down the steps, toward the fence. He didn't
stop running until he reached her.

As he folded her into his arms and buried his face in the
fragrance of her red hair, he breathed deeply again and his
whole body trembled with joy. He was safe at last. He was
where he belonged. He loved and was loved, unselfishly, un-
demandingly. He would find peace again. In Blaze's arms his
bruised mind and body would be healed. He smiled down into
her eyes and the tears came.

Blaze moved her fingertips along the side of Jonny's face.
As she examined him, it took all her experience as an actress
not to show her concern. He had changed. Deep lines that
hadn't been there before now etched his face. There was a lot
more grey in his hair. And his eyes — hollow and black-ringed —
blazed like live coals. He looked as though he was recovering
from a long illness. She fought the tears back from her own eyes
and smiled brightly at him. She would start right now nursing
him back to health. It would be a bigger job than she had
thought.

"My darling," Jonny murmured, "you haven't changed one
little bit. If anything you're more beautiful than ever. You
don't know what it means to me to be with you again. Thank
you, thank you my dearest."

Blaze kept her voice well controlled. "I'm glad you're here
Jonny," she said simply.

What she was thinking, what she wanted to scream out was,
"I've missed you so much, I've wanted you so. There were so
many times when I didn't want to go on living without you.
Nothing has been worthwhile, nothing has seemed important
because you weren't here with me. I'd give it all up in one
minute to be with you. I'd do anything with you, live anywhere

with you, be anything you want me to be. If only we could be together always." Instead, she smiled radiantly and took his arm. "Let's get out of here, Jonny," she whispered. "We'll go to my place and make plans."

They were having an early breakfast in the kitchen of Blaze's home in Beverly Hills and Jonny was wolfing down the food as though it were going out of style. He smiled as he thought that he hadn't eaten like this in a very long time. He looked up into Blaze's eyes and smiled happily. Then he laughed.

"First we feed the furnace and get a real good fire going," he said, "then I'm going to love you as you've never been loved before. Deal?"

Blaze laughed too, joyously. "Deal," she said, "and by the way, darling, I've decided that it's best if you stay here. You're going to be my own sweet house guest. You can't argue with me, because I simply won't come to visit you in a hotel. Besides, there'll be lots of talk if the employees see me leaving in the mornings. It will be more convenient, more comfortable and safer here. How do you like that for an argument?"

Jonny moved to her and took her in his arms. He kissed her long and hard. "Mmmm," he said, "you'd make a hell of a lawyer."

Blaze grinned at him wickedly. "I made a lawyer a long time ago, in New York," she said. Then she squealed as Jonny whooped and chased her through the kitchen and through the the house toward her bedroom.

She tripped near her bed and fell across it heavily. Jonny, trying to stop his forward progress, tripped also and fell across her. They wrestled for a minute or two and then Jonny caught her to him in a tight embrace. They kissed passionately, the tips of their tongues searching each other out. Then desire took hold of them, welling up until they thought they would burst. Convulsively, feverishly they began to pull at each other's clothes, each trying to help the other, until all their clothes lay in a crumpled heap on the floor beside the bed. They looked down the length of each other and then melted together and became as one. There was no sound in the room except that of their breathing and the sounds of their love. The spasms shook them time after time, until they fell back spent and exhausted.

Then the only sound in the room was their breathing as

they slept. And even as they slept, Jonny started up the road to fullness again. The cure of mind and body had started. It had needed only the catalyst of Blaze's love. The heat of her flesh, the response of her passion, the rapture of her enveloping desire provided the medicine for the cure. No other medication was needed, no other hands were required. Blaze was doctor and nurse; her home was hospital and clinic. Jonny had found the road back, the road leading directly to Blaze.

In just a few days the change that came over Jonny was remarkable. His face filled out and the deeply etched lines were far less noticeable. The black rings around his eyes faded and the hollowness was no longer apparent. And his eyes were bright and happy. The haunted look disappeared and was replaced by the look of the love of a man for a woman. Jonny looked like his old self again.

Blaze watched the change with joy in her heart. But she said nothing. She would never ever let Jonny know of the terror that she had felt as she met him at the airport. It didn't matter now. She had her Jonny back and he was getting well again. For as long as it would be, for as long as she could hold him, she would make the most of it. For as long as Jonny stayed with her this time, she would pour out the fountain of her love to him. She would cherish these days while they lasted. And she would not think about the future. There would be no future and no past. There was no place in her heart for the pain of the past or the future. There would only be now, today and tomorrow. She would love Jonny today and tomorrow and for as many tomorrows as there would be. There was nothing beyond that that she cared to think about.

Jonny had awakened early and slipped out of bed quietly so as not to disturb a soundly sleeping Blaze. Slipping on a robe, he had padded softly through the quiet house and out into the garden. The day held promise of being glorious, filled with sunshine in a cloudless sky. Jonny breathed deeply of the fragrant tropical air and smiled up into the heavens. He frowned momentarily as a fleeting thought of Montreal wafted across his consciousness. But he forced the thought out and concentrated on the image of Blaze lying in the bed with her red hair fanning across the white pillow. He continued to smile upwards and he nodded. There was no question of right or wrong. He had to be here. He was alive again. Drowning, he had stretched out his hand. And when he had clasped the hand of the red-haired girl called Blaze, he had known he was saved. He laughed aloud now and shook his finger at the heavens. Then he made his way back into the house. He had to awaken Blaze. He had to tell her how good it was to be alive.

CHAPTER 6

THE SWEET LIFE

Jonny stood silently in the bedroom of the home in Beverly Hills and looked down at the sleeping girl. The expression on his face was at once tender and contemplative. He allowed his mind free rein as his thoughts ranged from Montreal to Hollywood, from his law office to this house in Beverly Hills. This one time, he decided, he would allow himself to think back over the past, back over the events that had led to his being here, in this place, at this time.

For years now, Jon Temple had worked at self-control. But to him self-control meant primarily the control of his mind and his thoughts. He had developed a defence mechanism which had kept him going through some of his most difficult times. Part of the instinct of self-preservation, this control of his thoughts had allowed him to put difficulties, troubles, heartaches out of his mind temporarily and concentrate on pleasant, happy thoughts. Without this disciplined control, without this ability to channel his thinking along lines of his own choosing, Jonny would long ago have sunk into the depths of despondency and hopelessness. The discipline of his mind had been a high barricade to him; the armour of his control had held the outside world at bay. He was entrenched, the enemy was repulsed, he was invulnerable.

But now, standing in this room, this fortress of love and peace, he thought back. He thought about his youth and the high hopes he had had. He smiled tenderly as he thought about his first meeting with Blaze. And in the next fleeting moment pain clouded his eyes as he thought about his family back home, the trial of his marriage, the loss of his practice. But then he thought fondly of his law partner and lovingly of the girl sleeping so peacefully below him. What exactly happened? Where had it all gone wrong? Why was he here, miles from his home and his work, here with this girl who was not his wife but who was truly the love of his life? Where had he failed? Where had he been failed? If the answers did not come readily to him, it was because he was not now ready to accept them. He needed more time, time to think, time to recover his balance, time to heal.

There was a rustling sound and his eyes swung down to the girl in the bed. Blaze had turned over and the covering sheet had fallen away from her. She was naked and again his breath caught in his throat as his eyes took in the exquisite perfection of her body. His fingertips touched the freckles on her shoulders and traced the outline of her firm, pink-tinted flesh. This was reality, this was here, now. He needed to think only of her now. The scent of her intruded into his consciousness; the warmth of her flowed up through his fingertips and suffused his whole body. The heat in his loins rose and the excitement shortened his breath. He slipped off his robe and lay down beside her. He reached out to her and, still sleeping, she came into his arms. At the touch of the length of her body against his, she awakened and smiled. His embrace tightened. He crushed her to him. And in a moment there were no thoughts, and the past never was. There was immediacy and urgency. The mind was shut off. Only the senses were alive.

Jonny lived the days that followed in a dream world. And he would allow no intrusions. His mind, his thoughts and his feelings were only for Blaze. He lived each hour of each day and thought of nothing beyond it. But the hour itself was filled with Blaze, the thought of her, the scent of her, the feel of her. There was gaiety and laughter, peace and contentment. There were immediate plans to be made and there were immediate dreams to be followed. There was the therapeutic touch of the hot California sun. And there was love, physical and spiritual, love that was the cure-all, the be-all, the end-all. The wounds were healed, the body strengthened. All care, all worry, all guilt were purged by love. It was a tangible, pulsing force. It was the fountain of youth. It was the giver of life.

Blaze had finished working on a picture just before Jonny's arrival, and although she had to stay close to home in case retakes were needed, she was actually free to do as she pleased. It would be at least a month before her next picture was to start filming. She arranged with the studio to give her two days' warning should they require her on the set and promised to leave a forwarding address and phone number should she be away overnight.

"Jonny darling, I want to show you Southern California. There are so many beautiful places. There are old missions, lush gardens and wide, sandy beaches. Let's be gypsies and live out of the station wagon for awhile." Blaze was so excited and animated, it was contagious. Jonny, who had never been much of a sightseeing enthusiast, found himself responding to Blaze's inspiration. And the idea of days filled with driving about the countryside with Blaze constantly at his side was an intoxicating one. The nights alone with her in different places, far from friends and acquaintances, alone and unknown, was even more stimulating.

"Sounds great," Jonny agreed. "When can we get started?"

"What's wrong with this afternoon?" Blaze replied. "I can't think of any reason why we shouldn't leave right away."

"Neither can I," Jonny grinned as he caught her to him and held her close.

What he would never know, what Blaze would keep secret to her grave, was that although it was just a fun trip to him, to Blaze it was her honeymoon trip. There would be no wedding, no marriage. But no one could ever take this honeymoon away from her. It was hers, to share with no one, not even Jonny. It was a deeply personal secret that she would keep forever locked in her heart. It was her confidential payment for love freely offered and joyfully given. The balance would be struck, the account would be squared — her love for this honeymoon. It would be repayment in full and she would ask no more.

The picnic lunch was prepared, the station wagon packed up, and they were on their way. There was no set plan, no definite itinerary. They would just go where their fancy took them and when. Blaze, with almost no make-up and wearing slacks and blouse, a kerchief on her head, was unrecognizable as the internationally known film actress. She was just a girl, obviously in love, out with her man. Blaze Scotland, actress, was left behind in Beverly Hills. The girl in the station wagon was Andrea Kellerman from Brooklyn. The years were rolled back. The future lay ahead. A young, unsophisticated girl was in love for the first time and she was on her honeymoon.

The boy beside her was not Jonathon Temple, criminal

lawyer and family man from Montreal. That Jonathon Temple had remained in Canada. The boy at the wheel was young Jonny Temple, carefree and unmindful of the future. He, too, was in love with his first girl and they were on a trip together, a trip to the unknown, where past, present and future melded into now. Nothing mattered except that the two of them, the young girl and the carefree boy were here, now, in love and fancy-free. This now would last forever; it had to, it was too beautiful for it to be otherwise.

They drove out of Beverly Hills, through Pacific Palisades to Malibu. It was a glorious day and, as they parked at the beach, they both knew, intuitively, that they would stay at the edge of the sea for a day or two. As they walked, no words were spoken. It was as if they could read each other's minds. Jonny had his arm around Blaze's shoulders, her head rested against his. The sound of the surf crashing against the shore and then washing out to sea again provided a symphony of peaceful solitude that found its echo in their light hearts. Again an unspoken word was sounded and they stopped and removed shoes and stockings. Then they continued their walk, this time wading through the shallow waters. The sun beat down from a cloudless sky, the sand was hot and the blue Pacific waters cool against their legs. They were lost in the timelessness of torpor, innocents in a guilty world, more sinned against than sinful. It was hours before fatigue and hunger forced them to retrieve their shoes and stockings and head for the car and the picnic basket.

The sea and the air had made them drowsy and that first night in the motel room, they fell asleep instantly, wrapped in each other's arms, the sleep of innocence, unthinking, unknowing. It was after midnight when they awakened, refreshed and searching for each other. And then even their lovemaking was innocent, without violence. There were only soft caresses and murmured endearments. They stroked and they kissed, they touched and they felt, but it was as if it had never happened before, as though they were alone in the world and had discovered each other, and had discovered the wonder of love. And finally as the ultimate act of love welded them together, they opened their eyes and looked deep into each other. And the wonder grew. And the joyfulness and the peacefulness grew. And the heavens smiled.

They languished at the beach for several days, two love children, wandering through time, wrapped up in the beauty of perfect nature and each other. They lazed in the sun. They ate and drank and waded and swam. And they lay in the sun again. And at night they made love. They made love until they discovered each other completely, perfectly and unashamedly. And in the consummation they were fulfilled.

They laughed and they joked. They teased and they grinned. Only two subjects were taboo. By tacit agreement, neither the past nor the future was to be mentioned. This perfect idyll was not to be marred by remembrances of pain and loss and mistakes and might-have-beens. As for the future, if indeed there were any sort of future for them, it was filled with uncertainty and the promise of more pain. This was a time for joy, not suffering. So neither subject was considered fit for conversation. Blaze tried very hard not to think about them. And Jonny forced them entirely out of his mind. They would live in the present only, together, loving and laughing. This was time out of context, for now there must be nothing more.

Giggling and shouting, hand in hand they were running along the hot sand of the beach. Blaze tripped and Jonny caught her as she fell. The two of them dropped heavily to the sand, still giggling and thrashing about like playful puppies. Jonny began to tickle her and Blaze screamed and threw sand at him. He caught her hands and threw himself across her. As his weight pressed down on her, she struggled mightily, gasping with laughter. Then she was still, looking up at him. Jonny relaxed and bent to kiss her.

With a whoop, she struggled free and ran into the water, Jonny in hot pursuit. This time when he caught her, he held her tight and forced a long, lingering kiss on her salty lips. Blaze returned the kiss with passion and, for just a moment, her eyes filmed with tears of unrestrained joy. She clung to Jonny, there in the water, and yearned for this time to never end. But she wouldn't voice the thought aloud. Nothing, certainly no word of hers, must spoil this moment. It was perfection and must remain so. Her eyes shone brightly again and she wriggled free and threw herself back into the water. She splashed upward and caught Jonny with a cascade of water. The shock of it in his face and in his eyes caused him to stagger back until he fell into the water too. He recovered and began to splash water at the giggling girl. Then the two of them were laughing and shouting and splashing water mightily until the area around them resembled a whirlpool. People on the beach looked out at them and smiled tolerantly. From the distance it appeared that two youngsters, innocent and untouched by human cares, were having the time of their young lives. The people smiled enviously and wished that they might be so carefree.

Jonny and Blaze exhausted themselves and wearily, hand in hand, made their way back to the beach. Still giggling, they lay down on the hot sand, the length of their bodies, still cool from the water, touching. Then, as lassitude overtook them, they slept. They awoke when hunger nudged them and Jonny ran up the beach to the station wagon to fetch the picnic hamper.

They drove into town that evening for an early dinner, and afterwards a Brigitte Bardot movie. Then, tired out from the and the sea, they returned to the motel early. Slipping into pyjamas and dressing gowns, they sipped cool drinks and watched television for an hour. Blaze had difficulty keeping her eyes open and kept nodding off. Finally she forced herself to her feet. "I'm completely bushed, darling," she said to Jonny, "could I interest you in bed?"

Jonny grinned up at her. "Best invitation I've had all day," he exclaimed, "and from such a beautiful girl. Who could resist?"

He got to his feet and, putting his arm around Blaze's shoulders, led her over to the bed. Slipping under the topsheet, they came into each other's arms, lying quietly for a few minutes until their warmth and the contact of their bodies produced a stirring of the flesh. As the heat came up inside them, they kissed, long and passionately. Their lovemaking became wild and abandoned. Lips to lips, hands searching, bodies meshing, they fought against climax, wanting only to savour the moment, wanting desperately for it to last forever. But then Blaze clutched Jonny convulsively. "Now darling, now," she gasped, "oh please, now." And as they entered Canaan, the angels were singing. That and their laboured breathing were the only sounds in the room.

Jonny was lying, hands intertwined under his head, staring up at the network of tiny cracks in the motel-room ceiling. He was praying silently, offering thanks for the girl beside him. Blaze had turned on her side, facing him, and her fingers moved

gently through his hair, exploring the patches of grey that were
to belie his otherwise youthful appearance. Now she spoke
tentatively.

"Darling, I have an idea. Tell me what you think of it."

Jonny turned to her smiling, inquiring.

"Well," she continued, "since you've come, we've lived in
my house and now here in the motel. Wouldn't it be great fun if
we could have a house of our own for a while, one that really
belongs to both of us?"

Jonny asked her tenderly, "Where did you have in mind?"

"I thought perhaps Santa Barbara," she answered. "It's
lovely there and maybe we could rent a little house overlooking
the ocean. It's not very far."

"My darling," Jonny responded, "you could talk me into
going to the ends of the earth, however far that might be. And
it would be lovely if you were there. We'll go to Santa Barbara
tomorrow and look for our little love nest. Deal?"

"Deal," she sighed happily and promptly went to sleep in
his arms.

Santa Barbara is an old Spanish mission town, built along
the shores of the Pacific, about a hundred miles northwest of
Los Angeles. Founded by Father Junipero Serra and Captain
José Francisco de Ortega in 1782, it has preserved much of the
architecture and atmosphere of its Spanish heritage, and its
mission is called the Queen of the Missions. It was drowsing in
the mid-morning sun as Blaze and Jonny drove into it and took
the road along the ocean-front.

Luck really smiled on them because they had only driven a
few miles when they found "their" house. A "for rent" sign had
caused them to stop and they fell in love with the house
immediately and for all time. It was made of stone, with a red
Spanish tile roof, and perched on a cliff overlooking the ocean.
It was built to overhang the water, and the waves, lapping on
the beach below, came up under the house. The eternal sound
of the waves was to be their song of love during their stay.

The house was built in two parts. A small, square reception
room was connected to the main house by a long, narrow, open
passageway, parallel to the ocean-front. The passageway, like a
monastery walkway with its balustrades and open, Spanish-style
windows overlooking the water, led directly to the main door.
Neither Blaze nor Jonny could wait to get in and see the main

house. The rent sign read, "Apply to Santa Barbara Mission," and gave a phone number and a name, Father Molino. Jonny drove along to a service station and called the Mission. Father Molino asked them to wait by the house, where he would meet them in fifteen minutes. They spent the fifteen minutes walking around the house, exclaiming with delight at the lush shrubbery and the exquisite flowers that surrounded the building on three sides.

Father Molino was an exceptionally tall man, about six foot four. His steel-grey hair topped a thin face of which a hawk nose was the most prominent feature. Old-fashioned pince-nez glasses perched precariously on the magnificent nose. His spare frame was indefinable under the loose, flowing robes of his habit. Slim, sandalled feet completed the picture of a monk who, in appearance at least, had been born about one hundred and fifty years too late. And his eyes did nothing to dispel the image. All-wise, all-seeing, their kindliness blazed forth a welcome that was tangible without words.

He came towards Blaze and Jonny with his hands outstretched and smiled a greeting that enveloped them in its warmth. "Welcome to Santa Barbara," he said in a soft, musical voice, "I hope you will be happy here. You wish to rent the house?"

"Yes Father," Jonny replied, "but only for a month, if that would be alright."

Father Molino looked doubtful for an instant and searched the faces of the two facing him. Whatever he saw there, he answered, "That will be alright. Come and I will show you through. We call this place the Hermitage. It is a place of solitude but not of loneliness. There are the flowers and the sea for company. The surf will sing you to sleep at night and be waiting to awaken you in the morning. The scent of the flowers will surround you like a fragrant cloak. And the sun will warm you and caress you. Nature will never allow this house to be lonely. I'm sure it must have been built with young lovers in mind." His smile was sublime. It gave the sense of a choir, soft and invisible.

As they entered the reception hall and took in the heavy, Spanish furniture, intricately carved and solid, they sniffed appreciatively at the odour of old wood and dark leather. It was charmingly antique, yet extremely comfortable. Father Molino opened the door to the passageway and a new odour intruded itself. It was the odour of the sea, distinctive and invigorating, an odour which, through the centuries, had beckoned to many men and women the world over.

Walking through the passage, they all stopped momentarily to look over the blue waters and the whitecaps closer in. Father Molino pointed to some markers bobbing in the water about a hundred feet from shore. "Lobster traps," he said. "I come over here most mornings and I have never been disappointed in the catch. You will find the lobsters have no claws, only flippers. Actually they are crayfish. But delicious, simply delicious. They belong to you while you are here."

They continued to the end of the passage and stood before the massive wooden door of the main house. Father Molino unlocked it and threw it wide. And now a third odour assailed their nostrils, that of a banked wood fire. As they entered the great main hall or living room as it is now called, they saw the reason why. One entire wall, to their left as they entered, was a huge stone fireplace. Six-foot logs were stacked beside it, awaiting placement and the touch of a match to give forth cheery, warm, intoxicating comfort.

The room itself was huge, with high beamed ceilings. The furnishings were a mixture of Spanish antique and Spanish modern, massive and comfortably inviting. An enormous bear-skin rug, in front of the fireplace, dominated the room's furnishings.

Blaze squealed with delight and ran across the room and up the short staircase to inspect the kitchens and bedrooms. She was back in an instant, her arms wide and her eyes shining. "It's perfect," she beamed, "it's the perfect dream house. I've never seen anything like it."

The two men smiled at each other, the smile of the male indulging a loved female or the innocence of a small child. "Good, it's settled then," Father Molino said.

Jonny turned to him, grinning broadly. "It's settled. And Father, we would both appreciate it if you could find the time to visit us."

Father Molino nodded. "I will," he promised, "and I hope you will visit our Mission. It's very old, very beautiful."

Blaze and Jonny agreed and accompanied the old man to the door. Blaze put out her hand to shake hands and then pulled it back abruptly. She gave a little curtsy instead. The

boiling in them, then went out to the passageway and watched the men's progress. Jonny was at the oars and, as they came up alongside the markers, Father Molino leaned over the side and began to raise the traps. There were four of them and they contained fifteen lobsters, for a total of about twenty-three pounds. Jonny whooped and signalled to Blaze. He held up his hands and waggled his fingers at her, ten, ten, and three. Then he began to row furiously for shore.

Father Molino cooked the fifteen lobsters and when they were done, he carefully shelled them. The kitchen table was soon heaped with a mouth-watering mound of lobster meat.

"Couldn't be much fresher," the Father remarked. "Now my dear if you will fetch tomato ketchup, mayonnaise, and relish, I will prepare a dressing, California Russian, that will be a fit complement to our beautiful lobsters." He cubed the lobster meat and added the dressing, which Blaze had helped him prepare. When all was done, the enormous lobster salad was placed in the fridge to chill for lunch.

"Of course you'll stay Father, we absolutely insist," Blaze said.

Father Molino sighed deeply. His eyes twinkled as he replied, "I thought you'd never ask. But I do feel that it is my solemn duty to stay if only to make certain that not one ounce of that celestial dish is wasted."

They were seated in the living room after lunch. In spite of the warmth of the afternoon, Jonny had insisted on lighting a small fire in the huge fireplace. Now they were completely relaxed in their chairs, staring into the flickering flames, each lost in his own thoughts. For perhaps ten minutes they sat in complete silence. Father Molino was the first to stir. He turned and contemplated Blaze with a broad, warm smile. She felt his gaze upon her and turned to him, returning the smile with a matching warmth.

When he spoke, the Father's voice was low and dreamy. "I'm sure," he began, "please forgive me, but I'm quite certain I've seen you before. Have you ever been to Santa Barbara, have you been to our Mission?"

There was a moment's hesitation and a shadow darkened Blaze's eyes. Then she answered very softly, "No, I've not been here before, Father. I'm a motion picture actress, perhaps that is where you've seen me."

Father Molino shook his head negatively. "I do not think so. You see, I do not go to the movies. I never seem to have the time." He frowned. "And yet, your face is familiar to me." He continued to frown as he searched his memory. "Aha, I have it," he exclaimed triumphantly, "magazines. I have seen your face on magazine covers. Yes, that's it. You are very well known in your profession." He hesitated. "I'm sorry, I think you would have been grateful had I not recognized you or, at least, had I not mentioned it."

Blaze shook her head, rather sadly. "That's true," she admitted, "but I know that it's impossible."

Father Molino turned to Jonny, who had been listening to the exchange intently. "And you, my son, do you work in pictures also?"

"No, Father," Jonny replied steadily, "I'm a lawyer by profession."

There was a long silence then, finally broken by a long-drawn sigh from Father Molino. "Forgive an old man's curiosity, my children," he said, "I should have known better than to ask questions like that. I should have sensed your reluctance to talk about yourselves. I cannot even use my age as an excuse. It was insensitive of me. I ask you to forgive my lack of tact."

The old man looked so miserable that Blaze and Jonny, in spite of themselves, hastened to reassure him. "It's quite all right Father," Blaze insisted, "and perfectly natural. Please don't give it another thought."

"That's right," Jonny added, "no harm done. As a matter of fact, perhaps it's just as well. You've been wonderfully kind to us since our arrival, Father. And we both value your friendship. There are things you ought to know." He looked over at Blaze for confirmation and she nodded. Turning back to Father Molino, he continued, "Would it embarrass you very much to know, Father, that we are not married?"

Father Molino held up his hand. "Just a moment," he said, "confession is not a prerequisite to friendship. I want you to understand that. We will remain friends whether or not we continue this conversation. You must understand that, too. And you must tell me only what you wish to tell me, that is if you wish to tell me anything at all. I will listen to you, of course, but only if you think it necessary and desirable. And to answer your question first. No, it does not embarrass me. I knew yesterday that you are not married and I am here today. So perhaps you would prefer to drop this conversation now."

At their look of astonishment, he smiled gently. "I would not have mentioned it, had you not brought it up. Oh, perhaps when I was a young priest I would have felt it my duty to lecture you on morals and ethics. But I am no longer a young priest and I have an old man's sense of duty now which does not permit of rebuke or censure. I'm not so old that I do not know that the world is changing rapidly. Life is changing and values are changing with it. The very speed of change makes it so. What's more, you are both intelligent and mature. Whatever your reasons for being here in this place, at this time, they are valid ones I'm sure. I wish to accept them as such and I have no wish to judge them."

Jonny sat still, amazement written all over his face. But Blaze jumped up and ran over to Father Molino. She was about to kiss him when she stopped short in embarrassment. Perhaps, she was uncertain, but perhaps the elderly priest would not welcome such a show of emotion. Perhaps he would be embarrassed. Perhaps it was not the thing to do with a priest.

The Father noted her confusion and smiled up at her. He pointed to his cheek and said, "Please don't stop now. This is a very great compliment to an old man. I will keep it to myself but I will always remember that once Blaze Scotland kissed me."

Blaze kissed the old man's cheek and hugged him. "You're wonderful," she breathed, "isn't he wonderful, Jonny?"

Jonny nodded and came over to join them. "You're quite a guy, Father," he said, "and there's something else you should know, if you don't already. We, Blaze and I, are not of your faith. Does that make any difference?"

Father Molino chuckled. "What is the expression . . . a wise-acre? I don't mean to sound like one but I gathered you are not Catholics. We priests have little ways of determining that quite quickly. So now that you know that I know you are neither Catholic nor married, there can be no bars to our friendship. We are even. We must take each other at face value . . . as human beings. I think that is almost all we have in common." He laughed merrily at his own witticism and Blaze and Jonny joined him wholeheartedly.

"I have a few things to do," Blaze said, "you men stay and talk. I'll be back in a few minutes."

As she left the room, Father Molino smiled at Jonny and said, "She is a very beautiful young woman. And good, which is far more important."

"And smart," Jonny laughed, "smart enough to leave us to men's talk for a few minutes." He turned serious as he faced Father Molino directly. "I don't want to plead my own case," he said, "but I've been forcing myself not to think too much since I got here, to California I mean. Perhaps this is the time to talk and to think, to you. Perhaps in the telling I'll gain new perspectives. You won't be bored?"

Father Molino shook his head and waved his hand. "No, no," he said, "please go on."

Jonny plunged into his story. In quick, broad strokes he sketched the events of his past life, leading up to his arrival, with Blaze, at the Hermitage. He spoke quietly and dispassionately, trying hard not to colour the narrative, trying to simply present facts. When he came to speak of Rita and his home life, he was particularly careful to keep bitterness and rancour out of his voice. Not out of a desire to protect Rita and Marion, but because he didn't want to becloud the issues for Father Molino.

He concluded with, "I make no excuses and no plea, Father. I'm here because I have to be here. I accept no guilt, either for myself or for Blaze, especially not for Blaze. She's the most innocent of all. I don't know if there are any answers. I don't know that I want any answers yet. Maybe they'll come in time. There is always time, later, for answers."

It was completely silent in the room as both men stared moodily into the fireplace, and Blaze returned.

Father Molino looked up at Blaze as she crossed the room to take her chair. He looked over at Jonny, seemingly mesmerized by the fire. He cleared his throat. "I was not born a priest," he began, "and I was not a very young man when I became one. My grandparents came to this country from Italy, my parents were born here in California. My father and his father before him managed a small vineyard not far from here. I was brought up with all the advantages and all the disadvantages of youth in this bountiful state. I was neither rich nor poor. I was obscurely blended into the great middle class. I knew love. All would have been well; I might have become a contented vineyard manager, but for an enormous restlessness and a compelling urge that seized me, shook me and would not let go.

"I felt that I was trapped, caught up in a prosaic life of sheer boredom. I was convinced that I was really born to be an artist, although I wasn't sure which art I should follow. But I knew that I desired to live excitingly, a life of glamour in a world of glamour. I felt a deep need for fame and wealth. I thought I'd go out of my mind if I didn't achieve these things. I really didn't want to live without them.

"I won't bore you with the details of my search for the sweet life. But I did search. And it eluded me, completely and irrevocably. In my desperation and my anguish, I turned to my religion. I turned my back, finally, on the secular life. And I found solace. The meaning and the purpose of my life was revealed to me. Becoming a priest was almost secondary. It simply enabled me to extend the purpose which I had found."

Eyes twinkling, Blaze exclaimed, "Surely, Father, you're not suggesting that Jonny become a priest and I a nun?"

Father Molino laughed uproariously. Then he said, "In the way of a metaphor, I am suggesting just that. As I told you before, I cannot be judge or arbiter of your lives. But I can advise you to seek the purpose and the meaning of your lives. I can hope that you will find comfort and happiness in the answers when they are revealed to you. I can pray that your way, when you find it will bring you lasting peace. You know, in pagan times, a priest was one who officiated at the altar or performed the rites of sacrifice. The ancient rabbis did exactly the same things. Someday you both will find an altar upon which to offer your lives. And then your lives will be complete.

"As to the rites of sacrifice, everyone in this life sacrifices something or someone. And in the sacrificing, one has a chance to be reborn and fulfilled. Provided the sacrificing is done with humility and generosity. I hope I have not disappointed you in what you were seeking from me."

Jonny was looking thoughtfully at Blaze as Father Molino stopped speaking. He turned and said, "You're a wise and profound man, Father. Blaze and I, we're both grateful for your friendship."

"And I for yours," the priest replied. "But now I must leave. I do not wish to wear out my welcome and I must get back to the Mission. I walked over this morning. Perhaps you wouldn't mind driving me back."

"Of course not, Father," Jonny exclaimed. He got up and

moved over to Blaze. Kissing her, he said, "I'll be back in a few minutes. Why don't you get into your swimsuit, darling? We can have a nice, long swim and then I'll take you out to dinner. Good deal?"

"Good deal," Blaze agreed joyously.

On the way back to the Mission, and still feeling the effects of what Father Molino had said to him, Jonny watched the old priest out of the corner of his eye. The Father was looking straight ahead, his eyes clear and bright and calm. Smiling grimly to himself, Jonny broke the silence in the car.

"Just what is life all about, Father?" he asked. "I mean, we're born as infants and soon we become children. But just as soon, we forget our childhood. And whether it was a happy or unhappy childhood doesn't much seem to matter. Because then we're grown up and have become adults. We marry, have children of our own and seek ways to earn a living for our family. We look for small diversions, small happinesses. But the frustrations, even the agonies are always there. We're not consulted, when we're being conceived, as to whether or not we wish to be born. We're simply placed here on this earth and told to make the best of it. Our parents bring us into a lousy, dog-eat-dog world and then leave us to flounder for the rest of our frustrated, impotent lives. Oh, I was listening while you were talking back at the house. But tell me, Father, how does the rat get out of the trap?"

Father Molino sighed deeply. "I think the answer to that one lies in the very words you've just spoken," he said. "If, as you mentioned a moment ago, we're born into a lousy, dog-eat-dog world, should not our purpose be to try to improve on things as they are? Should not the altar and the rites of sacrifice be one and the same with making the world less lousy and less dog-eat-dog for your children and theirs?"

Now it was Jonny's turn to sigh. "Sounds wonderful," he agreed, "except for one thing. The rat in the trap is not free to improve his lot or anyone else's. Maybe someday, someone will figure out how to get rid of the trap. That, at least, will be a beginning. Will you come to us again soon, Father?"

"Yes," Father Molino replied, "and in the meantime, I'll do some thinking and some praying."

Jonny returned to the Hermitage to find Blaze still dressed, completely unmindful of the swim they had planned. She had been crying and her eyes were red-rimmed and swollen. There was no need for explanations — he knew her feelings. His were entirely the same. Taking her into his arms and holding her close to him, Jonny said, "Forgive me darling. I shouldn't have started all this. We're not ready to look for altars or to think about rites of sacrifice. There will be plenty of time for that later, much later. Right now, I want us to concentrate on us. We're going to forget about this afternoon's conversation, forget about everything except now and us, and having fun. Deal?"

"Deal," she said through fresh tears.

Jonny moved suddenly and picked her up in his arms. "I know one sure way of concentrating on us," he grinned as he started up the stairs to the bedroom.

There was no more talk of the past or the future. Both subjects were studiously avoided. Father Molino, on his frequent, much-welcomed visits, made sure to keep the conversation light and airy. There were days of swimming and sunning. There were evenings of dinners and cruising the countryside. And there were nights of quiet and love. No evil thoughts were allowed to intrude, no word was spoken to mar the perfection of their idyll. Only once did Jonny wink and say, "This is the altar. This is the purpose. I think I'll spend the rest of my life making love to you. And, at this rate, it is going to be a short life and a merry one."

Blaze had gasped in mock horror and buried her face in her pillow. "Any more talk like this, Jonny Temple," she choked, "and I'll take the matter up with Father Molino." That was the only reference; otherwise all was tranquility.

They were lucky at that. There had been no call from Hollywood for retakes. But now the month was up and it was time to leave the Hermitage. The last few days had been hard on both of them. Each tried to spare the other's feelings, each tried not to show the ache in his heart.

On the morning of the last day, Blaze insisted on driving into the town by herself. She told Jonny she wanted to pick up some groceries and things to take back. She asked him to finish closing up the house and to wait there for her return. Slightly puzzled, he agreed to do as she asked. But as she drove off, he hated the thought of closing up by himself. He dreaded having to lock in the ghosts, lock them in a house that had so terribly quickly taken on the atmosphere of disuse.

Blaze returned, all smiles and cheerful. Jonny was astounded and studied her carefully. "You okay?" he asked cautiously.

"I'm fine darling, just fine," Blaze answered. "By the way, we have to wait here for Father Molino. He's coming to say goodbye."

"How do you know that?" Jonny demanded suspiciously.

"Oh, I met him in town. He said to wait. He'll be here in a little while. He thought it would be better to say goodbye here rather than at the Mission. He'll be here soon. Let's sit down by the beach and wait for him."

Johnny shrugged his shoulders. "I still don't get it," he muttered, "but if you say so, we'll wait."

It was an hour before Father Molino drove up. As he got out of his car and descended the steps to the beach, he, too, was all smiles.

"Has everybody gone nuts?" Jonny burst out. "I'm damned if I know why everone's so cheerful. Is the end of the world in sight?"

Father Molino laughed as he handed Blaze a large, brown envelope. "The end of nothing is in sight," he grinned wickedly.

Blaze took the envelope and went over to put her arms around Jonny. Smiling, she said, "Father Molino has been one busy priest this morning. He had to work real fast. Jonny darling, I just couldn't stand it. . . . I got the idea last night. . . . I had to convince him. . . . oh, my darling, I've bought the Hermitage."

Jonny stood transfixed, his mouth agape. He mouthed several words, but no sound came. Then he closed his eyes and nodded his head several times. He crushed Blaze to him as he whispered, "Of course you did. I should have known."

"It's ours, it always will be," Blaze declared fiercely. "Oh, Jonny, no matter what happens, it will always be here waiting for us. I'll never come back here without you. And if. . . If we should not come back together, it will stay locked till the end of time, till it crumbles and falls into the sea, along with our dreams." "We'll be back together," Jonny promised her solemnly.

To avoid the pain of a lengthy farewell, the parting from Father Molino was made swift and with a false gaiety that fooled no one. Blaze and Jonny drove off down the road to Los Angeles. The old priest drove off on the road that led to the Queen of Missions.

CHAPTER 7

HEAVEN AND EARTH

It was one night, long after his return to Montreal, that Jonny told me more of the story, the part that took place after Santa Barbara, the part that took place in Beverly Hills and Hollywood. If only they had been able to stay at the Hermitage, if they had been able to live, shut off from the rest of the world, with only Father Molino as their outside contact, it would have been a different story indeed.

But we do not, we cannot live alone. Try as we would wish, walking the narrow pathway between life and death, we must constantly come back into the world. For better or for worse, we walk the earth with others. The good Lord might have done things differently. He might have arranged the order of things in such a way that His children would have lived their lives as they would wish to, with freedom of action and thought and deed. To be free, completely free, can you imagine it?

But we are not free. We co-habit, we conform, we rely, we compete, we accede. So often, we do what 'they' want, not what we want. From the time we are born, others tell us what we must do, and how we must do it. First our parents, then our teachers, then our friends and family. Even when we are not told, we are shackled with the chains that society places upon us. We can do this, but not that. We can behave in such a way, but not that way. This is acceptable, that is not. Do it 'our' way or forever remain beyond the pale. And like children, all our lives, we worry, fear and consider what 'they' think we ought to do and be. Just so that we may belong.

For Jonny and Blaze, freedom lasted for a few, short weeks. As near as I can remember, these are the details of the events that followed. They returned to Beverly Hills and almost immediately the honeymoon, if you want to call it that, was over. The dream of Santa Barbara and the Hermitage became just that, a dream. And like all dreams, it quickly became something fuzzy and half-remembered, something joyful to be locked away in the deep recesses of the heart and mind, some-thing to be thought of as the time of happiness and contentment. But the dream was without detail, without real definition. It became part of something past and had to be relegated to the past.

Only occasionally, one or the other of them would say, "Remember that lobster feed? Never tasted anything better." Or, "Remember Father Molino's thoughts on that subject?" Or, "Remember the sound of the waves as they came up under the Hermitage?" Then each would search his own memories and try to conjure up the details, the thoughts and feelings and emotions of that moment in time. But the dream had become tenuous and, gossamer-like, had floated off in wispy spirals. And the details became more and more elusive. Finally, because of the sadness it invoked, the dream was mentioned less and less often. Perhaps the yearning, deep inside, never left them. But . . . Jonny and Blaze came back, back from their Shangri La, which was the Hermitage, back to hard and cold reality.

Within hours of their return, it seemed, Blaze had to report to her studio for a script conference on her new picture. It was to be a musical based rather loosely on the early years of the life of Queen Elizabeth the First. And like all historical films, there followed day after interminable day of costume fittings and make-up tests. Now only the nights were left to her and Jonny. The dark hours were doubly precious because, once shooting started, there would be no let-up. And also because they had become used to spending all their waking hours together. This being apart, this spending so many hours of each day away from each other was something new to them, a reality they had not had to face before. The adjustment was difficult, the misery great. The situation became intolerable and built toward the explosion that was bound to come sooner or later. It came, sooner rather than later.

It was in the middle of the second week after their return that Blaze burst through the front door of the home in Beverly, screaming for Jonny. As he rushed to meet her, she fell into his arms, sobbing.

"It's no good, Jonny darling," she wailed, "no good at all. I can't stand it another day." And she lapsed into a torrent of sobs that racked her body from head to toe.

Holding her tightly, uncomprehending, and with an alarm bordering on panic, Jonny tried to calm her. As the sobs subsided somewhat he cradled her face in his two hands. Searching her eyes for clues, he shook her gently. "Blaze honey, Blaze stop it," he entreated, "for God's sake tell me what's wrong. Calm down and talk to me. What happened? Something at the studio?"

Blaze shook her head and fought to get herself under control. There was a moment or two of silence and then, like a dam breaking up, the words poured forth in a great tidal wave. "Oh my darling," she cried, "this whole situation is no good . . . this being away from each other day and evening . . . I think about you all the time and I can't concentrate . . . I worry so about your being bored and unhappy . . . I start sweating and I can't breathe when I think that maybe you'll get tired of this and want to leave me . . . Jonny, I want to quit . . . I want to break my contract, tell them I'm sick or something . . . I want to get away from here, with you . . . Jonny let's go away somewhere, anywhere, for good . . . please darling, let's get away before everything we have together is lost . . . don't you see Jonny, Hollywood is not a good place for people who love each other . . . something bad happens here . . . please, please let's get away before it's too late."

Jonny's hands slipped from Blaze's face to her waist. "Whoa, honey, whoa," he cautioned, "calm down so we can talk. Come, I'll fix you a drink. Then we'll talk this out properly." With his arm about her waist he led her into the living room and settled her on the sofa. She sat silent, waiting.

Jonny took the time while mixing the drinks to collect his own thoughts. For the truth of the matter was that the past ten days had been a drain on his nerves too. The novelty of the return to Hollywood had worn off very quickly. Then the days became endless. Blaze would leave for the studio very early in the morning and return when the evening was almost over. Jonny would spend the day prowling the house, fixing himself snacks, reading and watching television. It had become a real drag. Only his great love for Blaze had kept down the mounting frustration.

But lately another match was being held over the powder-keg. Blaze was coming home exhausted. After looking forward all day to her return, daydreaming about a night of companion-ship and lovemaking, he had had to content himself with watching her fall, prostrate, on her bed and sleep the sleep of the drained until morning. He would lie awake, watching her, touching her gently, feeling the warmth of her body until his own body writhed with the torture of nerve ends exposed and inflamed.

Looking at the beautiful girl sleeping so soundly beside him, he knew that he loved her deeply, emotionally and mentally. But he also knew that the strong physical attraction between them was a reaction of chemistry that bound them together. It was the chemistry that was in danger. He had been wrestling with the problem himself and now Blaze had touched the match to the powder-keg and the explosion was rocking the very foundation of their love. He knew that what he would say to her now was of the very greatest importance. He knew that he must choose his words carefully. He must be very, very careful.

Jonny turned, with the drinks in his hands, to find Blaze staring at him, dejectedly. He summoned up a broad grin as he crossed to her. "Now come on, girl," he said, as he tousled her hair, "what kind of talk is this? Drink your drink, it'll make you feel better. No, drink first and then we'll talk."

Blaze sipped at her drink silently, waiting for Jonny to continue, her eyes never leaving his for an instant. When she had finished most of her drink, Jonny put his down.

"Blaze, honey, you're very tired," he began softly, "and that's depressing in itself. But the shooting schedule won't last forever."

"Only several more months," Blaze inserted passionately.

"Well, and then you'll demand a nice, long vacation," Jonny countered, "and we'll go away, perhaps back to the Hermitage."

"And you?" Blaze questioned, "can you hold out that long, Jonny? Can you go on living like this for several more months? Can you, without climbing the walls?"

"Yes," Jonny replied, but he didn't sound convincing, even to himself. "Look honey, we've talked about this before. Right now we're both thinking about the Hermitage, about how, for a little while, we were completely carefree and happy. It's natural that we should want to recapture that time of peace and joy. But we also know that it doesn't work that way. We knew at the time it couldn't go on forever, that someday we'd have to leave our Eden and come back to the world. And, although I hate to say it, for financial reasons if for no other. That's something I have to start thinking about one of these days. But not right now."

Blaze started to interrupt him but Jonny stopped her. "No, my darling, I don't want to get into a discussion of that right now. I know only one thing. I love you, body and mind. I refuse to think about the future, except that I know you mustn't ruin your career. We'll simply have to wait out the end of the picture. Running away now will solve nothing and it might bring on other complications. There was never a running away that was any good, with one exception. And that was when I ran to you. And we're here, together, now. So, let's hold on for a bit. The moment you're through work we'll go. Deal?"

Blaze moved into his arms and snuggled close. "Deal," she murmured, "if you say so darling. It's not me I was worried about. I can finish the picture, tired or not. It's you. I panic when I think of your leaving me, for any reason. But if you say it's alright, then it's alright. And if you don't want to talk about the future, that's alright too. Just keep loving me as I love you. And think only of reasons for staying with me. Think of nothing else. Hear?"

"I hear," Jonny replied solemnly. Blaze's words had no basis in prophecy. Jonny, at that moment, had no inclination to be prophetic either.

It was quiet in the room. Blaze lay, unmoving, snuggled in Jonny's arms. Their unspoken thoughts were much the same, Blaze wondering if she could possibly hold on to Jonny forever. How and where? She wished she could be sure. Jonny heard Blaze's earlier words echoing in his mind . . . please darling, let's get away before everything we have together is lost . . . could that possibly happen? Could events, thoughts, feelings conspire to separate them? Could what they had together ever be lost? He wished he was positive that they couldn't.

Blaze stirred. She had thought of one solution, albeit only an immediate one. "Darling," she whispered, "I'm not tired now."

Jonny smiled down at her and kissed the flaming red hair. Chemistry. The age-old answer to so many of the vicissitudes of life. His hand moved gently across her back and over her shoulder. Now he noticed the heat of her body through the silk blouse. His hand slipped down and cradled her breast. He squeezed and the heat rose in him, chokingly. Desperately he tugged at the glass buttons that held the blouse. They gave and his hand moved to unhook her bra. The warm pink flesh was exposed and he bent to kiss the rosy tips. At the same time he pressed the hardness of his body against her yielding softness. She gasped and moaned, "Now, darling, come to me now." Then all was commotion and fury as clothes flew in all directions, until their bodies melded by heat and passion into one.

They lay together a long time while the fury of their emotions spent itself. Just as they were drifting off, out of this world, Blaze whispered, "I know one way to hold you, Jonny Temple. I just mustn't ever be too tired."

Jonny kissed her forehead in affirmation. "Chemistry," he mumbled. And fell into a deep sleep. Blaze slept too, a happy smile on her lips. They remained that way, locked together in a fierce embrace, unconscious, until the morning.

Things were better, for a while, after that night. Jonny thought up a hundred and one ways to keep himself busy during the day, even making it a point to get away from the house. He joined a golf club and renewed his acquaintance with that sport. He managed to convince himself he was reasonably content. Blaze, unknown to Jonny, had armed herself with pep pills, reasoning that it was only for the duration of the picture, after which she would be able to relax and regain her natural energy. Their mutual effort and the physical contact at night kept things on an even keel. But although neither would have been willing to admit it something had indeed been lost, had been left behind in Santa Barbara.

We cannot recapture something past, we cannot go back. Circumstances change, we change with them. What had been left behind was spontaneity. Now they were consciously working at maintaining their relationship. The Hermitage was all gaiety and abandon with an endless future of love. And it was part of the first flush of their togetherness. The love was still very much there. But it was no longer quite so spontaneous. Worldly things had intruded. And wordly things are always threatening. No, we do not go back, we cannot live in or for the past. We must live in the present and hope for the future. If we are lucky enough to have our Hermitage once in our lifetime, it may have to suffice. If we are so fortunate as to find it again, we are twice blessed. It is a hope not to be abandoned.

Montreal, July 12th.

Dear Jon:
Things are well here, as far as I know. I have not seen your

family but I have made inquiries and they seem to be managing adequately. Petey is at a boys' camp in the Laurentians for the summer and is apparently well and reasonably happy. Rita refuses to be drawn into conversation about you with anyone but, I'm told, she looks well enough.

Business is good at Temple and Berman. I've engaged a junior and have taken over most of the pleading myself. I'm not the ham you are but I manage.

I've been making regular deposits for you, both in your joint account and your personal one. Rita has been withdrawing as she needs it and your own account is quite respectable. No problems there.

Jonny, I hope all is well with you. Give my very best to Blaze and write me when you feel like it.

> As always,
>
> Arnie

> Beverly Hills, July 18th.

Dear Arnie:

Thank you. Thank you for everything. Thank you for your letter, your tact, your looking after things. Above all, thank you for your consideration.

I'm in a far, far better frame of mind than when I left. I believe I am thinking straighter, more normally than before. I don't have to tell you how wonderful Blaze is and how wonderful she has been for me. Right now she's working on a picture, which poses some little difficulties, but we're looking forward to the end of the shooting schedule.

I don't allow myself to think much about the future, I know I'm not ready for that yet. But I also know that I'll have to face up to it one of these days. And I can't let you carry the ball indefinitely. Do you know how much I appreciate your patience?

I plan to write you in far greater detail very soon. Blaze sends her love.

> As ever,
>
> Jon.

P.S. I'm playing a hell of a golf game these days.

My letter to Jonny and his reply to me were the first pieces of correspondence exchanged between us since he left Montreal. Maybe the letters should have said more. Maybe they should have said less. I don't know. It was only later, in retrospect, that I realized the importance and the repercussions of that seemingly innocent exchange.

Jonny showed my letter to Blaze. He also showed her his reply before he mailed it off to me. I know now that the letters had the same effect that a pail of cold water splashed over a sunbather would have. It was the cold shock of reality, the sobering factor that intruded itself on an already precarious situation. Figure it this way. Jonny and Blaze were fighting for their lives together. And the fates were not being kind. Try as they would, clinging desperately to their love for each other, they were wrestling with themselves and, at the same time, struggling to stem the onrushing encroachment of the outside world.

We might wish to create an island unto ourselves, we may try mightily to cut off contact with undesirable elements, we can lock the doors and bolt the chains. But we cannot win that battle. Our defences must, in the end, be pierced by the battering rams of intruding thoughts and interloping forces. The walls are scaled, the fortifications come tumbling down, the sanctuary is entered. The locks and bolts are ground into the dust. And our island, penetrated and conquered, stripped and violated, falls easy prey to the forces that were bent on destroying it. We cannot live alone, we are not permitted to dwell in our Edens. We are accountable.

My letter and Jon's reply struck Blaze with all the force of a sharp blow. Her plans, her hopes, her dreams were going down the drain with those letters. And she didn't know what to do about it. She became convinced that she would be unable to hold Jonny. She felt that she was losing him, that he was slipping away from her. She experienced the tightening of the arms of a vice around her heart, the vice of naked fear. When? When and how would the end come? What would the rest of her life be without Jonny? For just a little while he had been entirely hers. She had possessed him as he had possessed her. In Jonny's arms, in the enveloping cloak of his love, she had been a whole woman. Now, if half of her were torn away, could she survive as a half-woman? These and other questions staggered her imagination. Her brain numbed, her feelings dulled. She went through the motions but she was only partly alive.

The realization came slowly to Jonny, slowly because he willed it away. In his mind nagging doubts became bitter realities. A decision had to be made; he would have to make it. I couldn't help him. Blaze certainly couldn't. No one but he himself could make any kind of decision. But what? What must he decide, what must he do? To leave Blaze was unthinkable, to return to Montreal and try to forget her, impossible. The law practice, the family back home, the responsibilities were like spears poised at his heart. Only Blaze stood between him and the spears. She was the shield. But he knew that he could not long hold her in front of him to bear the brunt. He knew that the time would come when he must step out from behind her. And then, mercifully, one of the spears would pierce him. Perhaps then he could offer what was left of his torn heart to Blaze.

It's a remarkable thing, is it not, that two people, so much in love and so close in spirit, could keep their terrifying thoughts and their soul-wrenching feelings to themselves. Often it is those who are closest who cannot communicate with each other. Of course, the reason is understandable. It is because of mutual love and great tenderness that neither can bear the thought of causing grief or hurt to the other. At the very moment when they should speak, when they should reach out to each other, when a few words would clear the air, they are silent. The silence is born of fear and they walk hand in hand together. But we live with fear and therefore we remain silent.

Neither Blaze nor Jonny was in any way ready to face the issue head on. In desperation they kept their thoughts and their feelings hidden from each other. At least for the time being, at least until they could summon up the moral courage to think in terms of the inevitable. Like so many of us, they were only too glad to push the sweepings under the rug. Tomorrow would be soon enough. Yes, they would think about it tomorrow.

Blaze fought valiantly to blot any thought of the future from her mind. She strove with all her might to live each day as it came. She forced herself to concentrate on her work at the studio. And at night, with the aid of her pep pills, she enticed Jonny into making love to her. Love and fear, in magnified proportions, made her own lovemaking so frenzied and abandoned that she almost succeeded in returning their lives to a state of comparative normalcy. Poor Jonny never knew that, unconsciously, she was groping for fulfillment, seeking for the immediate all that she might lose in the future, straining to condense into a short period of time all that the millennium might have had to offer.

He willingly gave himself up to the tidal wave that threatened to engulf him, he yearned to drown himself in the sea of her love, he was almost happy. But like the children of the storm they were, the edge of the precipice was approaching, and the next lightning bolt might cause them to stumble over it. At the bottom, their fate was sealed. But they could not read it. For now the winds of the tempest were too strong. And they could not see.

Jonny knew that he must write to me again. Two sentences from his first letter ran through his mind like a never-ending refrain, "But I also know that I'll have to face up to it one of these days. And I can't let you carry the ball indefinitely." There you have it in a nutshell, the two sides of the coin. Blaze or Rita, life in California or in Montreal. Decision required. The law practice and me carrying the load. Decision required. But there's never been any doubt in my mind that Jonny was incapable of making such decisions at that precise moment. And I'll tell you something else. There isn't anything in this whole world that would have made me want to trade for the kind of hell he was going through. It shouldn't happen to my worst enemy. And here it was happening to Jonny Temple, my dearest friend.

The letter didn't get written, for the time being anyway. There had to be one more convulsive effort to avert the destruction of their hopes and their dreams. The effort came from Blaze. It was a clutching at straws, but the plan she devised had to be attempted. She decided to try to build a social life for themselves, particularly for Jonny. Perhaps not being alone so much during the day might help. In the company of others, with new and different interests, maybe, just maybe, Jonny would stop dwelling on thoughts of the future, of decisions that had to be made. It was worth the try.

"Jonny darling, I'd like to introduce you to some of my friends and acquaintances. Not all of them are busy every day. Some are between pictures, others are standing by for retakes. Darling, perhaps we've been alone too much. Being with other people, doing different things, changing our conversations might give us an entirely new perspective. Would you let me try?"

Jonny's first reaction to Blaze's suggestion was to say no. To agree with her meant unbarring the doors, letting the outside world in, opening their own lives to public scrutiny. As long as the doors remained barred, the world beyond could only guess, could only assume their relationship. But, as he looked at Blaze and saw the eager anticipation in her eyes, he knew of the difficulty he would have in refusing her. He would make a simple try and then give in.

"Blaze, honey, I understand what you're trying to do. And it might work out alright. But is it worth it? You do belong to the public, you know. Everything you do and say, everything you wear is food for gossip and criticism. Why should you make it easier for them? Why should you subject yourself to the whispers and the slanders? Let's face it my darling, we're living together with all that it implies. As long as we keep to ourselves, our lives are not open to curious scrutiny. But if we let them in, we're asking for headlines. You say we don't care? It's none of their business? That's all very true. But there will be pain and hurt and suffering along with the scandal. Honey, what do you need it for?"

Now he had said it, now his words had brought out into the open some of their very private thoughts, thoughts that they had been refusing to admit, even to themselves. It made him sick. The lurking, nauseating currents of self-examination were threatening to turn from abstractions to hateful realities. And should they become recurring themes, their existence, their dreams, their very lives would come tumbling down like the walls of ancient Jericho. And in the end all would be dust. He wished the subject had never come up.

"I don't care, Jonny. I just don't care. I won't let it reach me. And no matter what, it's worth the try. What we have, what we are to each other is more important than all of them. What will be for us is of more concern to me than all of their sick, morbid curiosities. I only care about us, my darling. They don't matter at all, not really. Not now or later. Never, never."

Jonny groaned inwardly. He knew that Blaze was deluding herself. The "they" she referred to were lying in wait. The hawks were circling, waiting to pounce. Their talons were sharp, ready to rip and tear. The torment of their victims only made them more vulnerable prey. It was the old story all over again, old as creation. The victor and the vanquished, the strong and the weak, the bird of prey and the nestling. The sophisticated and the naive, the guilty and the innocent, the powerful and the meek. Man's inhumanity to man.

Well, alright. If there's to be a fight made of it, let's get started. Let's face them down. Stand up and be counted. Fight for our rights. Give them their comeuppance. Don't give up. Fight back. He owed Blaze that much. He had come to her in desperation, sick and worn. And she had opened her arms to him and had nursed him with all the love in her heart, unselfishly. She had asked for nothing in return except his love and his strength. Yes, he owed her. They would try it her way. He couldn't say no to her. It might even work.

The effort was doomed from the beginning; the experiment never had a chance. Blaze arranged a succession of get-togethers with fellow actors and actresses, producers, and directors. Some of them were even decent, intelligent people. But the circumstances in which they met together made dialogue and communication impossible. There were nightly wild drinking bouts, there were forays to the glittering night spots along the Strip, there were weekends in the country. Blaze's friends were ready, more than ready, to accept Jonny as one of them. The phone never stopped ringing. But the new friendships were without substance; they had been founded on the wrong premise. The gaiety was false, the chatter idle. There has to be more than a constant pleasure seeking. Solid structures cannot be built on rotten foundations. It didn't take very long for Blaze and Jonny to find that out.

Drinking heavily, making small talk, indulging in inane conversations only heightened the awareness of their inner struggles. There was never a moment when they could forget why this was all happening. In their minds, the background of the seriousness of their position only caused the false gaiety to grate on their nerves, until they were left raw and bleeding and exposed. Blaze had made the try. The effort had failed. Now they had to close the doors of the sanctuary again. The bolts and the chains had to be put up. The outside was to be locked out once more, the enemies repulsed. But are we not our own worst enemies? How in the name of heaven do we fight ourselves? What weapons of defence can we find to combat our private wars from within? None. For we are bent on self-destruction.

Fifteen minutes after Blaze left for the studio that morning, the phone rang. Frowning heavily at the intrusion, Jonny picked it up.

"Hello?"

"Hello, Jonny. How are you?"

"Oh no, it can't be. Father Molino?"

"The very same. Surprised to hear from me, Jonny?"

"Surprised is not the word, Father. Mental telepathy or a cry of need would be more like it. How could you possibly know how much I needed to hear your voice?"

"I didn't hear from you. I was concerned. I had to know how things are."

"Father, Blaze and I, we were coming down to visit you this weekend."

"That's wonderful. But I've come to visit you first. I'm here at the bus terminal in Los Angeles."

"Father, you're enough to almost make a man change his religion. Stay right there. I'm coming down to get you."

With something akin to exaltation, Jonny ran from the house to the station wagon parked in front. Father Molino. Thank God! Things would be better now. A way would be found. The Father would know what to advise. For the moment, Jonny was very happy. He had found another straw to clutch.

Father Molino had not changed one bit. As Jonny looked into the wise old eyes, he smiled contentedly. For the first time since the return from Santa Barbara, his heart lifted. Looking at the priest, his mind conjured up the past. Carefree days and nights. Love and peace. The Hermitage.

He didn't let it show on his face, or in his eyes, but Father Molino was greatly disturbed. Jonny had indeed changed. There was pain in the eyes. Frown lines creased the forehead. The face was drawn and pale. The man in front of him was at war with himself. A mighty battle was being fought. The hour of decision was close at hand. Father Molino closed his eyes and fingered his rosary. He gave thanks for the inspiration that had brought him here this day.

It was decided that the visit should be kept secret from Blaze, a surprise until her return that evening. Guiltily, Jonny realized that he was looking forward to having Father Molino to himself for the day. He needed this day. He craved private conversation with the understanding old man. With Blaze away, perhaps he could find in their talk the key that would unlock the fetters of his mind. A man needs to talk to another man sometimes. It is different from talking to a woman or to a child. It is the rapport of two of a kind.

With coffee in front of them at the kitchen table, the two men settled back, awaiting the starting gun. There was some reluctance on the part of both men to start the conversation. Each knew that once there was a break in the dam, the waters would flow unchecked, that the tide might engulf them, that whether they drowned or not, they might never be quite the same again.

There was a long sigh from Jonny. It had to come. He might as well get going. He began at the beginning, immediately after their return to Beverly. He told Father Molino of Blaze's fears of their remaining in the film capital and his own fear of being the means of ruining her career. He told him about the golf club. And then he told him about the letter from me and the reply, and the consequent repercussions. He finished with the abortive attempt at the social life. He did not mention the most important thing of all, the decision that was being forced upon him, the decision that was beginning to occupy his every waking moment, the resolution of which would shape their lives for all time. He knew he should, but he couldn't bring himself to talk about it, not even to Father Molino, who was his friend and his confessor.

Father Molino was puzzled. Instinctively he knew that Jonny was holding something back. But he didn't know what or why. Actually he could have anticipated all that Jonny had told him. It was nothing if not normal according to the circumstances in which Jonny and Blaze were living. He thought back over what Jonny had told him. What was the real crux of the matter? In which part of the story did the true questions and answers lie? The exchange of letters. Of course. That had to be it. Guilt. A decision to be made. Stay or go back. Rita or Blaze. Shocked, Father Molino now held the key. He would willingly have dropped it. For what to say, he didn't know.

"It is very difficult for me to speak," he began. "I know what you and Blaze would want me to say. I know, too, what I would like to be able to say to you. But everything that I have been and everything that I am allows me to speak in only one way. I have to advise you to go back to your home, my son. As a priest, I have no choice but to side with the wife and mother.

The church is specific in these matters. And although you are not of my faith, I know that your own church embraces the same teachings in these cases. There are no miracles any more, my son, only duty and priority obligations. It is hard, only great courage and sacrifice will enable you to do what is right and just. But only you can know if you have enough moral courage. That is what I must say to you. I pray to God that I have spoken wisely."

Jonny stared at the priest with horror. He was finally able to speak, but with enormous difficulty. "But what about us, Father," he whispered, "what about me and Blaze? How could I possibly hurt her so? With all that she has given me, am I simply to break her heart and slink away? You ask too much of me, Father, you ask too much."

" I ask nothing, Jonny," Father Molino replied, "only that you and Blaze search your own souls and do what is the morally right thing to do. When you have decided, come to me again and I will move heaven and earth to find comfort for you."

Jonny nodded slowly. The decision was still his to make. He thought for some minutes and then he looked up at Father Molino. His eyes were bright with unshed tears. "I must think some more," he said, "and I must talk to Blaze. But Father, I believe I know now what my decision will be."

Blaze was delighted to find Father Molino there when she got home. But something in the manner of the two men changed her delight to apprehension. However, keeping her voice light and gay, she said, "I do believe that you two have been deciding my fate."

Jonny, his voice matching hers, smiled. "No, my darling, just mine."

Nothing Blaze or Jonny could say would entice the old priest into staying for dinner. Whether true or not, he stated that he must get back to the Mission that night. He insisted that they call a cab. As he was leaving, he kissed Blaze lightly on the cheek. Then he turned to Jonny. Clasping his hand in a surprisingly firm handshake, he looked directly into his eyes. "Whatever you decide," he murmured, "it will be a decision from your heart. And that is the very best kind. God bless you my son."

He released Jonny's hand and as he turned away he lifted his own again. The gesture was slight. But it was unmistakably a blessing and a benediction.

With his arm about Blaze's waist, Jonny closed the door and led her back into the living room. He put his arms about her and held her close. With his lips against her hair, he began to talk. "Blaze darling, there are some things I must say to you." As she stirred and made as if to move back from him, he tightened his hold and said, "No darling, don't move. Let me talk to you like this. It might make it a little easier."

With his lips deep in her hair, he continued. "Do you remember, a long time ago, in New York, the first time I made love to you? I told you then I could never leave my wife and my son permanently. I also told you that both parts of my life were necessary to me. I've been doing a lot of thinking about those words recently; I guess we both have. I've been saying to myself, 'where do we go from here?' And I've decided what had to be decided. Blaze darling, I could no more leave you than I could stop breathing. If I had to leave you, I'd want to stop. I'm going home and ask Rita to divorce me. Then I'm coming back here and marrying you. It has to be like that, Blaze. There's no other way possible for me."

A strangled sob broke from Blaze's lips and she went limp in his arms. Alarmed, Jonny eased her into a chair and crouched down beside her. But Blaze was recovering. She even managed a weak smile. "Oh Jonny, my darling," she gasped, "I thought I was going to die when you started talking. I was so sure that you had decided to leave me and go back to your home. My heart almost stopped."

Jonny smiled back in great relief. Stroking her hair, he began to talk rapidly. "Listen to me, Blaze honey, I've a lot of arrangements to make. First, there's the question of the divorce and the settlement. Then I have to look into the question of my practising law here in California. I don't know what the requirements will be, but they shouldn't be insurmountable. Then we have to talk about your career and mine and how we'll make them both work. And then, then, my darling, we'll take a long honeymoon vacation at the Hermitage. How does it all sound?"

"Sounds wonderful," she breathed, "almost too wonderful to come true. Oh Jonny, do you really believe all this is possible for us? Do you really think we could ever have such happiness?"

"I believe it," Jonny affirmed solemnly, "and you'd better believe it too."

Fifteen minutes before takeoff, outside the airport departure room, Jonny held Blaze tightly in his arms. "I'll be back as soon as I possibly can," he was saying, "probably before you've finished the picture. I'll phone you several times a week to let you know how things are going. It won't be long, Blaze honey. And when I come back we'll never be apart again. Deal?"

"Deal," Blaze replied, smiling brightly.

They entered the departure room, beyond which Blaze could not go. She clutched Jonny's arm. "Darling," she pleaded, "can you really go through with it? Can you Jonny? Will you have the strength?"

Jonny's face was grim as he replied, "I don't truly know darling. I hope so. I think so. I must."

The plane took off. Blaze remained motionless for a long time, her face pressed against the glass of the window. At times like these, she was thinking, there are always things left unsaid. Perhaps better so. A cold shiver shook her body. She remembered her last thoughts as she watched Jonny mount the steps of the aircraft before he disappeared inside. She remembered the fear and the choking sensation in her throat while she held her tongue. She was afraid for Jonny. An intuition that sprang from the depths of her being screamed inside her, told her that something terrible would happen to Jonny if he went back. Was it a childish fear? Was it born of the loneliness she already felt, moments after he had left her? Another spasm shook her and she moaned softly. Her brain reeled as the thought pounded its sides, unchecked. Could it happen . . . that she would never see Jonny again?

. The lonely figure remained at the window, but the eyes were unseeing. Once before she had written, "We all make mistakes. Sometimes we're given a second chance." Had she muffed the second chance? She willed her eyes to focus on the aircraft. She would run to it. She would hold Jonny back. She wouldn't let him leave her, now or ever.

But the plane was airborne. It was getting smaller and smaller in the sky. Then it could be seen no more. The figure slumped against the glass, the eyes became blank again. The heart broke and fell in pieces upon the ground. And as the beautiful girl watched remotely, a pagan priest gathered it up tenderly and carried it to the altar. Slowly, gently he held his hands over it as he performed the ancient . . . rites of sacrifice.

CHAPTER 8

THE DEVEL

I got to the airport about an hour before Jonny's plane was due to land. Thinking back on it, I don't remember what made me decide to go out there so early. I do recall that I was very nervous. Sitting in the coffeeshop, consuming one cup of coffee after another, I kept fingering the telegram in my pocket, although I had memorized it letter perfect. Let's face it, I knew that Jonny would write to me again sooner or later. But that telegram, so unexpected, had put me into a mild case of shock.

"Arriving Montreal tomorrow 5 p.m. Please meet me. Have much to discuss." Alright, so Jonny had decided to come home. Nothing so remarkable in that. But in the back of my mind, the suddenness of that decision was somehow ominous. I knew Jonny as well as any man, and I was sure that he had reached a crossroads. Which direction he would take now was going to cause repercussions which would seriously affect his future, that of his family, and of the firm of Temple and Berman. I didn't really give a damn about any of the others, including myself. But I was worried sick about my friend.

I tried to imagine what decision he had taken. But no matter how I figured it, it didn't come out well for Jonny. I had the feeling way deep in my guts that things were drawing to an inevitable conclusion, sad and calamitous. And if impending tragedy weren't enough to torment me, the feeling of impotence was driving me up a wall. By the time the plane landed I was close to being a blithering idiot.

The taxiing plane came to a complete stop at the arrival gate. The ramp moved into position, the door opened, and a few people descended the steps. Then I saw him. I could have bawled my head off . . . with relief. As a smiling, tanned, healthy-looking Jonny waved and started towards me, I felt the anxiety drain away. And I felt foolish to have subjected myself to all that mental anguish for nothing. Jonny had obviously made his decision, and whatever it was, Jonny looked fine for having made it. I decided then and there that I'd been stupid. Tragedy, smagedy. Things would be okay. Jonny would handle them. And I'd help him. Everything was going to be great.

"Arnie, you old sonofabitch, you look wonderful." Pumping my hand, Jonny was grinning like in the old days. I was grinning too, fighting the impulse to take this man in my arms, this man who was my brother. Fleetingly I realized that he had looked better from far away. The deep tan almost hid the lines in his face, particularly around the eyes. And the hair was greyer than I had remembered. But I put all evil thoughts out of my mind. Jonny was back. And in pretty good shape, considering.

"You look okay too, Jonny. California must have agreed with you."

"Tell you about it later, old buddy. Now drive me to your place. I'm staying with you tonight. Lots to talk about."

I kept my face blank, wondering if Rita knew he was back. I began to sweat. How would she react when she found out?

That first night, Jonny didn't go into all the details of California. That was to come later. But one of the first things he did say hit me like a dash of cold water in the face.

"I came back to ask Rita to divorce me, Arnie. It was the only decision I could make. Look, our marriage has failed. I'm not sure why or how. But I am sure that, whatever years I have left, I want to spend them with Blaze. She is my life, Arnie. What do you say?"

I was gulping like the proverbial fish. And like the fish I was thrashing around, trying to get back into safe waters. I couldn't think of a damn thing to say. Not that the idea of a divorce surprised me so much. But my brain was exploding with a hundred possibilities that involved Rita. And every one of them was bad for Jonny. I had no doubt she'd make things as tough as possible for him. For goddam sure, it was going to be rough. A long time ago, when I tore up the letter from Blaze, I was trying to keep him from being pulled to pieces. Maybe that was my fatal mistake. It looked like he was going to be torn apart now anyway. Maybe then . . . but Jonny was staring at me.

I pulled myself together, I had a lot of thinking to do. "I don't know what in the hell to say, Jonny," I mumbled. "You've got to give me time to figure a few things out, time to think. I can't say anything so damn fast. I need a little time." Then, I forced a grin. "Brother," I said, "you sure as hell know how to give a man a heart attack."

The witticism escaped Jonny. He remained deadly serious. "Arnie, listen to me," he began. "I'm going to say things to you that I've never admitted to anyone, not to Blaze, not even to myself, until very recently. But maybe after I've told you, you'll understand." He stood and went over to the window. Standing there, with his back to me, he continued in a monotone.

"I'm entitled to live, Arnie. I decided that. If I should die, a few people, my folks, you, Blaze would mourn me for a little while. But the pain eases quickly. And, if not forgetting, you would all go on living, even enjoying. Only I would really lose the most precious thing there is, my life and all that it might hold in the future. I have no wish to die, Arnie. It's that simple. But I tell you this. If I were to go back to Rita, if I were to stay with her, she would destroy me. Goddamit, I know this all sounds melodramatic, but hear me out. Then you'll know." He moved away from the window and came back to his chair. Facing me directly, he went on.

"It's a question of personality, Arnie. In that particular context, she is strong and I am weak. Or let us say, she is too strong for me. At one and the same time she is fire and brimstone or icily contemptuous and derisive. I'm inclined to be quiet-spoken, as you know, even reverent. She is outgoing, I tend to be withdrawn. She is practical, I am not. She is tough-minded and I am not. I could go on and on. But let me say simply that I cannot cope with her. She is too much for me. And she will surely destroy me in the end. Why she married me, I'll never know.

"As for me, I suppose, subconsciously, I must have wanted to lean on her. But it was all wrong from the beginning. Opposites are supposed to attract. But with us it's a clash of personality that can only end in disaster. When the battle is finally over, there must be the victor and the vanquished. And I know which of us will be which. Only the vanquished will be dead. I have faced the truth, Arnie, at last. I married the wrong woman, she the wrong man. For all our sakes, I have to escape now, before it's too late, before the field is strewn with all our bodies, hers and mine and Petey's and Blaze's. For the love of God, Arnie, I'm fighting to survive."

"And will she let you, escape I mean?" was the first question that came to my mind.

"I don't know, Arnie, I really don't know," was his reply.

I didn't know what to say to Jonny. He had the right to expect me to say something. And the pause was getting uncomfortable. Better to say something than nothing at all. I had to try. "You know, Jonny, ever since we were small kids, going back to our chippy-hunting days, you always placed women on a pedestal. You've never been able to bring yourself to insult them, hurt them or even argue with them. So I can guess how helpless you must be with your wife, the mother of your son. And I wouldn't even want to begin to guess why Rita was so crazy to marry you. The psychiatrists might have something to say about that. Also about your own role in all this, for that matter."

"But now that we're talking, I've watched you allow Rita to dominate you, to make too many important decisions, particularly where Petey is concerned. I've seen her assume the role of the boss in your home life, almost to the point of figurative emasculation. You're right about one thing though — she's one hell of a strong woman. What I can't understand, what seems to me truly ironical, is your brilliance in a court of law. There you can plead a case, argue powerfully, fight like a tiger to win. But then again, you're not fighting women, are you? At least not in the way we're talking. It beats me Jonny. Anyway, I guess we could talk all night and still not be enlightened. Tell me what you want me to do, how I can help."

Jonny was staring at me moodily. "I don't know yet," he said. "We'll have to play it by ear and see what happens."

I shuddered inwardly. All hell was about to break loose. And I was scared to death.

A thought flashed through my mind, one that was far too premature to bring up for discussion at this time. It only added to my concern. Jonny had been talking about a divorce, from Rita. If it worked, would it not also mean a divorce from me? Wouldn't it mean the final, irrevocable end of Temple and Berman, Attorneys At Law? Unquestionably Jonny would go back to California, to Blaze. One more of the little ironies of life. For no matter what, I knew that I would do everything in my power to help him.

Jonny called Rita the next morning. I was still in the apartment when he told her that he was back in Montreal and wanted to talk to her. I was watching his face for reactions but, except for a tightening of the jaw at one point in the conversation, he seemed calm and unperturbed. When he hung up he turned to me, smiling grimly. "She was rather cordial, as a matter of fact," he said, "invited me to come over as soon as convenient. But she did call me Jonathon."

I should explain something to you at this point. I don't think I've mentioned before the cute little trick Rita pulled when she was annoyed or angry with Jonny. At these times he suddenly became Jonathon. I used to cringe whenever I heard that strident voice of hers grate, "Jonathon," making the name sound like a blasphemy. Apart from the name, her tone was always deceptively sweet and soft. It was like the one-two of a boxer. First the feint, then the uppercut. The sweetness was the feint, the name-curse was the uppercut. And often as not, that mother-in-law of his was the referee in chief. Well, from the moment of that phone conversation on, he ceased to exist as Jonny and became Jonathon forevermore in that house.

I dropped him at his front door and then headed downtown to the office. I tried not to think of the allegory of the lamb being led to the slaughter as I drove. But the picture persisted in my mind. I've never been able to stand the sight of blood. By the time I reached the office, I was getting pretty damn sick to my stomach.

Petey was in school when Jonny walked into his house. And Marion, as usual, was in her bedroom. She seldom made an appearance before noon. So there was only Rita to greet the husband, father, son-in-law on his return home. The reunion started off casually enough, Jonny deciding immediately to ignore the frigid atmosphere. He would wait patiently for a thaw in the block of ice that was his wife. If there was to be no thaw, well he'd find that out soon enough.

"You're looking well, Jonathon," was Rita's opening."Obviously you and California got along well together."

Jonny searched her face but could read nothing there. "You look fine, Rita," he said. "How are Petey and Marion?"

"Oh, they're well enough," was the reply. "Petey missed you."

Jonny swallowed hard. Only Petey? He would not ask the question. "Yes, I missed him too," he said.

"Coffee? The perc's still warm."

"Yes, coffee would be fine."

They moved into the kitchen and Rita poured two cups. Still deceptively casual, she asked, "Are you planning to stay long?" Without waiting for an answer she went on. "I assume you came in last night and stayed with Arnie?"

Jonny was grateful for the lapse in the questions. He answered the second. "Yes, I got in about five. Arnie met me. We went to his place."

When Rita said nothing, Jonny felt it necessary to add, "I had to talk to Arnie. But I felt it would be better if I came here this morning."

"Of course," Rita said.

There was a long pause. The fighters were moving about the ring, each checking the other's style, gauging stamina, looking for an opening, praying for the opportunity to throw the punch that would give them the round.

"Are you going back to work?" Rita asked. "Is that what you had to talk to Arnie about?"

In court, Jonny would have been more alert. But with Rita, he fell into the trap, like an innocent. "No," he admitted, "we didn't discuss the firm at all."

"Well, what did you discuss then?" Rita asked ever so softly. "Was it me? Was I the subject of this important priority conversation?"

"Partly," Jonny mumbled. "Mostly it was about me, about the future, about everything."

Rita sniffed as only she could. "And naturally, you would choose to discuss all these things with your friend and business partner rather than your wife."

Jonny gagged. He was losing the round. Maybe he could still rally. But then came the first knockdown punch.

"You didn't answer my earlier question. Are you planning to stay long?"

Jonny went down. Desperately, he remembered to stay down for the nine-count. He didn't answer. And he couldn't have gotten up anyway. One look at Rita's eyes and he was ready to have the towel thrown into the ring. He had never been able to cope with her tongue; his youth with his mother had forecast that. And, as always, she was able to anticipate his thoughts and arguments. Now she was ready to pounce. She was ready with the uppercut.

"Look here, Jonathon," she ground out, "you'd better start talking. If you think you can just walk out of here and go to that tramp in Hollywood, and then come back when you're tired of her, you've got another think coming. I want explanations and I want commitments. And I want them now." The fight was almost over. Jonny knew it. He was hanging on the ropes, completely on the defensive.

"Rita," he choked, "Rita, for the love of God don't start jumping to conclusions. I didn't just take off for an extended roll in the hay. I had to get away. The whole damn world seemed about to come down on me. If I hadn't left when I did, I don't know what might have happened. I went away to get my thinking back in perspective. I had to think about what was best for all of us. And please, please don't call Blaze a tramp. She's anything but that. And Rita, you're wrong about one thing. I didn't come back to ask your forgiveness, I . . . I . . . Rita I came to ask you to divorce me. It's impossible to go on and we both know it. Why torture each other? It's best this way. We know that too. Rita?"

But Rita's reaction robbed Jonny of any hope of victory. Had she screamed and raved, he might have achieved the comeback. He might have pulled it off before the final bell. But he was facing a pro at the art of infighting. Her last flurry demolished him.

Cold as ice, she faced him. Her eyes flashed but her voice was low, foreboding. Grindingly she started to speak.

"You bastard. You have the nerve to come to me with a story like that. And you think for one minute I'll just smile politely and tell you how easy I'm going to make it for you? You honestly believe I'll just step aside and send you back to that whore of an actress? Oh no, you didn't get your thinking back in perspective in California. You went completely screwy to have thought up a plan like that.

"I'll tell you something, you miserable bastard. I'll never give you a divorce, never. You can run to that whore in Hollywood. You can sleep with every female from one coast to the other. You can wallow in filth for all I care. But one thing's for certain — you'll never give your name to another woman as long as I'm alive. You can have all the harlots and call girls you want. But I remain Mrs. Jonathon Temple. I keep my self respect and your name. No divorcee me.

"One more thing. By the time I get through taking you for every dime you've got, I doubt the whores will have anything to do with you. You're not that great a lover you know, that they should want to support you. How do you like that?"

A strangled sob escaped from Jonny's throat. His eyes bulged, the veins in his temples throbbed. "Rita, Rita," he gasped, "you can't be that inhuman. No one can. You don't want me, not really as a husband. Why should you want to destroy my life and Blaze's? You can't be so vindictive as to make life a hell on earth for me, for yourself, for Petey. The name can't be more important than a chance for happiness for you and Petey in the future. You can't hate me so much that in destroying me, you would destroy yourself and our son. You can't be that cruel."

Rita smiled enigmatically. "Can't I? You haven't seen anything yet. I'll destroy you, completely and finally so that nobody will want you ever again. But I won't destroy myself. My reward will come with your destruction. And you know what, Jonathon, my dear? I'll dance on your grave before I'm through. Contemplate that for a while."

Jonny staggered. He would have fallen had he not clutched the kitchen table for support. His stare was fixed on Rita, unbelievingly, while his head shook from side to side. He tried several times to speak but the words ended in a constricted croak. He tried again and this time a whisper was audible. "I'll leave," he managed, "I'll leave, I'll leave."

Rita smiled with pure pleasure. "Sure," she said, "you leave and I'll be here to explain things to my mother and Petey. The big hero, the virile lover will slink off to the arms of some slut and leave his forsaken wife to make all the explanations. It's a lot easier that way, isn't it? But, forgetting me, don't you think you owe it to your son to have some words with him? Couldn't you at least try for his understanding at this time? Or did you leave your guts in California along with your manhood?"

Jonny was on his knees by now. He held up a hand beseechingly toward his wife. "What do you want of me?" he cried.

Rita continued to smile. "Only to crush you," she said, "to grind you to a pulp, to stomp you under my feet until you're no more than a smear on the ground. That's all I want. But nothing less will do." She walked out of the kitchen.

Jonny sank slowly, slowly to the floor. He lay there inert, for a very long time.

How long Jonny lay like that can never be reckoned in minutes or even in hours. When, finally, he struggled to his feet, his mind was somewhat clearer, although filled with despair. Realization came to him slowly, and with the awareness, insight. His flesh crawled as he understood how wrong he had been. There was neither real hate nor vindictiveness in Rita's attitude. Far worse was her burning desire to dominate and to control. She was bent upon robbing Jonny of the initiative. Decisions, destiny, these were hers to command. He groaned aloud as the full impact of his thoughts crystallized. How do you combat a monumental ego? How do you convince, cajole, argue with someone who has the fixed idea that she is never wrong? How can you win against a closed mind? He looked up to find Rita in the doorway, watching him curiously.

Their eyes met, and Rita's attitude changed instantly from curiosity to malevolent scorn. Smiling contemptuously, she said, "Well Jonathon, I see you've recovered from your little tantrum. I'm beginning to understand what that actress sees in you. It must be the mother complex that draws her to you. She nurses and you suckle. Quite an arrangement, I would say."

Jonny remained silent. He had no words to rebut the bloodless woman facing him. And he was ashamed of his inability to refute her hideous implication.

Taking his silence for weakness, as always, she pressed on. "What I will never forgive you for, what I can never condone is your running from my bed to hers. It's not pride — it's anger, anger because you are a husband and a father, because you're thoughtless and have no guts. And yes, anger because I didn't deserve it. I made a good home for you and your son. I washed and cleaned and I tended this house. I took care of my appearance and I did all the wifely things. I commanded respect from those around us and made a place for us in the community. I did all that was required of me. Damn you, I didn't have this coming."

Jonny made one final convulsive effort to fight back. "Yes," he shouted, "you did all that was required but nothing more. And you left out the most important things like understanding and affection. No, I didn't leave my manhood in California. You took that away from me a long time ago. You ruined my relationship with Petey. You made me nothing in his eyes."

"That's ridiculous," Rita snapped. "You never had any manhood to begin with. You were a mama's boy. You still are."

Again Jonny was silent. He saw the uselessness of further argument. A refrain pounded in his head and would not stop. Goddamit, he thought, why can't I answer her, why am I dumb? Why do words fail me when I need them most? He started for the door. Pale as ashes, he foresaw the futility of his future. He closed the front door behind him, softly, sadly.

He wanted to see Petey very badly. But not at home. Not with Rita and certainly not with Marion. He invited his son to have dinner with him in a small French restaurant in downtown Montreal. Petey was glad to see him. Of this Jonny was sure. That night, their first together, alone, he was quite certain that a rapport with Petey was something to cling to, something desirable, worth fighting for. He studied the boy over his dinner plate. He had changed, was more grown up, confident, had the look of a man, a few straggling whiskers on his chin, the outline of a moustache on his upper lip, piercing eyes and . . . sullen.

Could he have been mistaken about Petey being glad to see him? No, he convinced himself, he had seen something in the boy's eyes as they met and shook hands. A flicker of joy at the reunion? A gladness to have him back? But why the sullenness? And, of course, he knew why. Two reasons. One was Rita's doing. She must have done her work well. There would have been any number of discussions concerning Jonny after he left. And he had no illusions as to how he had fared in those discussions. Glad to have his father home or not, some of the mother's contempt for her husband had rubbed off on the son.

The second reason, and perhaps the more normal one, was simply the age gap between the boy and the man. Petey was grown up now and Jonny was growing old. The boy was feeling his wings. He wanted to be rid of old influences, aged disciplines. He wanted to fly, to seek, to explore. Life was challenging and he wished to make his own life in his own way. He would do things better, he would improve matters, he would fan into life a vital flame and not allow it to be extinguished as the older folks seemed willing to accept. Part of his sullenness was due to his intense desires and his frustrating struggle to achieve them.

Then, too, the boy was aware of the failure of the man's life. His father had not met the challenge well. He was good at his work. So what? He had fouled up his personal life. He had failed as a husband and father, perhaps as a lover too. And in the eyes of youth, there are no acceptable excuses for failure, only scorn and disdain. There is nothing on earth so regrettable as the disillusionment of the young with the old. A rapport with Petey would not be easy.

Just how difficult it was to be, Jonny found out as the meal progressed. Petey had become increasingly silent, reckoning all the things Jonny had done wrong, had failed in, weighing them against the desirability of having his father back. And Jonny lost again. The hell with it, Petey decided, so he came back. Big deal. How long's he going to stay this time? Just long enough to try to talk Mom into the divorce? She'll never give it to him. So where does that leave me? With a bitter mother and no father again. Sooner or later, he'll run back to that broad in California. So what's with this big reunion? Screw it, there's nothing in it for me. He was getting angrier by the minute.

Slouching in the leather banquette, Petey eyed his father warily. He was determined not to make the opening. If his father was bent on having one of those nauseating, father-to-son, heart-to-heart chats, let him find the opening. It was stupid anyway. He and Jonny really had nothing to say to each other. Fact is, he didn't care a damn what Jonny did or said from now on. It was nothing to him anymore. He had his own problems. If the old man wanted to shoot his mouth off, fine. He had to listen, but he, sure as hell, didn't have to enter into conversation enthusiastically. Let the old bugger sweat. It was all the same to him.

"How's school, Petey?"

"It's okay, I guess."

"Been getting good marks?"

"Good enough."

"What else?"

"What do you mean, what else?"

"Well, I mean have you decided what you want to do after school, what you want to be?"

"No, I haven't decided. Look, Dad, if you have something important to say, say it."

"It's been a long time, Petey. I thought maybe we'd talk, man to man. I hoped I'd be able to make you understand. And I do care about you, you know."

"I'll bet."

"Why do you say that?"

"You're the one buggered off, not me. Do you really care? Do you Dad? Did you care about what was happening here while you were screwing around in California? You even made the movie magazines."

"Hold it, Petey. There's no need to talk like that. You're young, a schoolboy. You can't understand how circumstances sometimes make a man act the way I did. You don't know the reasons. You're young, you've a lot of living to do. And a lot of learning about life and how to try to cope with it. If I could, I'd like to help you avoid making the same mistakes I did."

"I know a lot more than you think I do, Dad. And I have no interest in knowing about your mistakes. They're nothing to me. And I don't want you to preach to me. You adults give me a pain. You foul things up, you make a lousy mess of your lives, you've made the world a rotten, stinking place to live. Your politics stink and your wars stink. And when you don't know what else to do you preach clichés. Oh, we've made mistakes, young people. But we're trying. The thing is not to rock the boat, don't fight the establishment. Because someday we're going to find the answers. Then there won't be wars any more, there won't be poverty, there won't be racism. Everything will be beautiful and the world will be a wonderful place to live.

"Only you know what, Dad? You won't find the answers. Because you don't want to. Because you don't know how even if you did. And there will be wars. And poverty. And racism. And lousy politics. Only maybe there's still a chance. Maybe we'll change things. We can't do any worse. It might take a youth revolution to tear down all the old, antiquated, outmoded ways of life. But we've got to try. We've got to make the world better. Or there may not be a world one of these days. One more thing, please stop calling me Petey. I'm not a kid any more. And my name is Peter."

Jonny stared at his son in shocked bewilderment. This was the most Petey had ever said at one time. And, my God, how he had lost touch with him. Or was it the whole younger generation's attitude that had changed? Had he been so wrapped up with his own problems that he had failed to realize that the so-called generation gap had caught up with him, had completely alienated his son from him? He would still try to reach his son. He had to.

Jonny got himself well under control and smiled. "You do a pretty good job of preaching yourself. . . Peter. And yes, things have changed. You young people are better educated, for the most part, more aware, less ready to accept status quo, anxious for change, more passionate than we were at your age. But one thing I won't buy. You don't really feel all that differently than we did, not basically, not way down deep where it counts most. Your desires, your hopes, your pleasures and your pain, your loves and your dreams are not so very different from ours. I wasn't much older than you when I tried marijuana, for kicks. I didn't stay with it, is all. I had the same dreams you have of changing the world and improving on it. And I certainly wouldn't have quarrelled with the slogan, 'make love, not war.'

"No, dammit, there isn't all that much difference. Except maybe that young people have no desire to communicate with their elders. You want to write us off, you want revolution for the sake of revolution, forgetting that you don't have all the answers and forgetting, too, that revolutions breed new evils which might turn out worse than before.

"And I want to tell you something. Parents never stop loving their children, even if that love is not reciprocated. They don't stop wanting to be good parents, wanting desperately to give their sons and daughters the benefit of their experiences with life, hoping to guide them and to help them prepare for their own futures. I tell you the love of a parent for a child is one of the great truisms, and nothing can change that.

"And I tell you that there is no such thing as a thirty-five-year-old 'hippie,' if that's the correct word, or is it 'militant?' Sooner or later you have to come to grips with yourself. You'll have to earn a living, maybe for a family. Then the decision as to whether or not to conform takes on a different light. You have the right to think the way you do now, nobody can take it away from you. But I promise you that you'll get older. And your thinking will change. And, believe it or not, my son, you are the establishment of tomorrow. The pendulum may have swung away from the past, but like all pendulums it will swing back again. And try to stop a swinging pendulum. It's pretty tough to do."

Jonny stopped talking and looked hard at his son. Petey looked bored, the lines of communication were still closed. There was no point in bringing up his personal problems, or trying to justify himself to his son. Petey had neither the capacity nor the will to care. They were lost to each other, the outside influences had won. Jonny took a long, deep breath that was almost a sob. He had lost again. Rita, Petey, Blaze. Jonny wondered dully where it was all going to end. How long a road did he still have to travel? As Petey looked at him contemptuously, Jonny buried his face in his hands. The old world, the new world, certainly his world was collapsing. He was marching down a cul-de-sac. When he came to the end, what then?

He closed his eyes. His whole being cried out for Blaze and

her image danced through his mind. But even as he reached out to her, the image faded. He called out to her. He exhorted her back. But she smiled and blew him a kiss. The image faded completely and only the remembrance of her scent lingered in the air. The scent grew stronger and he was choking, choking.

Jonny came down to the office the next day. He looked terrible. Reluctantly, and at my insistence, he filled me in on all the details of his conversations with Rita and Petey. As he talked, I grew more and more alarmed. His voice was dead and his eyes even more so. By the time he finished, I was in a sweating panic. Rita was one thing, but the loss of his son was killing him. Well, Petey would have to wait. First things first. Something had to be done about Rita. I had thought up a plan but I didn't know how Jonny was going to take it. It was obvious to me that Jonny was in no condition to get to work. In his state, his mind couldn't possibly function. He wouldn't be able to concentrate on law work for two minutes. If my plan worked, everything might turn out alright. It might be the saving of Jonny. So why was I so bloody nervous?

"Jonny, Rita refuses flatly to give you a divorce. It leaves only one alternative. Let me put Sidney Korvin to work on it. We need a case of adultery. Sidney can set it up. There's no other way, Jonny. It's your only chance."

"No." That one word tore itself from Jonny's throat and reverberated through the room.

"Jonny, I know it's pretty rough. And we'll have to scheme like hell to get Rita into a situation where we can trump up the photographs. It's not pleasant, but we've got a doozy on our hands. Jonny, you've got to let me try it. I have to help you and I don't know any other way. You must get free. That's all that matters now. You must get free."

"No," Jonny shouted, "no, Arnie. I can't do it. Not to Rita. Not to any woman. I just can't bring myself to do it, no matter what."

"Fine, Jonny, fine. We don't do it. But what the hell do we do? Something must be done. What?"

Jonny looked at me, strangely, for a long minute. He was smiling as he said, "Something will be done, Arnie. I promise you I'll think of something. Everything's going to be alright." He left my office and headed for his own. I remained where I was. It was warm in that office. But I was shivering.

Montreal, September 16th.

My dearest darling;

    I have waited to write to you because I've been hoping I'd have good news to tell you. I wanted so much to be able to write that everything is working out well here and that I would soon be holding you in my arms again. But I'm afraid it's not so. Rita is adamant. She will not consider giving me a divorce under any circumstances. I must stay here for now and try everything in my power to get her to change her mind.

I had thought to simply leave and fly to you as quickly as possible. But we both know why I returned and why a divorce still remains the only answer for us, for our future. Arnie tries to convince me to let him stage an adultery situation. But I know you, of all people, will understand why it is not in me to let him do that.

Don't despair my darling. Be patient. And keep on loving me as,

I love you,

Jonny.

    I look back on the events of that time, and I often wonder. There are so many ands, ifs and buts. I'm sure everyone does that sometimes — wonders about what might have been. . . if only. For instance, in spite of absolutely everything, I still believe that things might have worked out, might have turned out a hell of a lot better for Jonny if only he had left his home for good. There are many things I will never understand, but the most curious of all is the way he was drawn back to that house, as if by a magnet or a loadstone. Had he left and never returned, I can't help but feel that he would be living in California today, married to Blaze, and happy. What drew him, why did he go back? For what reason did he stay? The questions still haunt me to this day. And the answers continue to elude me.

    I wasn't there to see the kind of life Jonny now lived. But I could imagine. And by putting bits and pieces together, the picture became as clear to me as though I were actually living in the house, God forbid. You can dismiss Marion. She had ceased to bother her son-in-law. The fact is, Jonny didn't really care a

damn about her. He was more concerned about his own problems than hers. Even her nagging and holier-than-thou attitude
left him quite unmoved. He was no longer impatient with her,
her sloppiness didn't bother him. She lived there but, to him,
she had ceased to exist.

Rita stalked about the house, frigid and unbending. She
made her decisions, she issued her edicts in no uncertain terms.
Jonny could take it or leave it. She refused to discuss or to
argue. He was there but he wasn't there. Tight-lipped, eyes
unblinking, she looked right through him, and talked about him
as though he were dead. He was refused entry to the master
bedroom, and the tiny den-study at the rear of the house
became his vale of tears.

Only the mention of Blaze or the subject of divorce ignited
the slow-burning fuse always present, ever smouldering, just out
of sight. Then Rita became animated, raised her vitality level
and turned her withering scorn on the one who uttered the
forbidden words until he turned to the consistency of jelly. Like
a beaten dog, tail between his legs, Jonny would escape to the
den-study, to stay for hours, brooding and licking his wounds.
After a time, the uselessness of broaching the subjects began to
sink in. Wishing to avoid the inevitable eruptions, Jonny kept
quiet. It became a house of oppressive silence.

Only with his son did Jonny attempt to keep up the
struggle. It became fixed in his mind that he must re-establish a
rapport with Petey. He summoned all the last reserves of his
strength, he scratched and clawed and fought for a toehold in
the boy's affections. But the point of no return had been long
passed. Petey was casual, lethargic, indifferent. He could find no
pity in his heart for the man who was his father. Love and
devotion had very little to do with it. The old man had screwed
things up, had made a goddam mess of his life, had made things
bloody difficult for all of them. There was nothing he could do
about it. Let him stew in his own juice.

Well, what can I say? My own heart was broken. I loved this
man as though we had sprung from the same womb. His hurts
became my hurts, his pain mine. My desperate want to help him
became a living, pulsing force in me. I cried bitter tears that I
knew not what to do. I raved and I cursed the fates that had
brought him to this. I wept and I prayed for his deliverance.
And I watched him. Watched him even as he was inexorably
sinking, drowning.

I'm not sure of the exact moment when I realized I had a sick man on my hands. I had often wondered, almost casually, just how much a man was supposed to take. I suspected that Jonny could not go on like this indefinitely. I think the realization struck me one day when I came into the office and found Jonny sitting at his desk writing a letter. Had I not noticed before? Had I failed to see what was happening before my eyes?

Jonny looked dull and, for the first time in his life, unkempt. Looking at him critically, I was shocked to discern how much weight he had lost. He looked gray and old. And he looked sad, so very sad and miserable. He hadn't heard me come in. Nor did he notice me watching him as he made a visible effort to concentrate on the paper in front of him. Then he closed his eyes as if to rest for a moment. With his eyes closed, he fished in his pocket for cigarettes. Locating them, he brought them out and placed them on the desk. He opened his eyes and looked at them. Then he slowly pushed them aside, unwilling to exert the effort to light one. His eyes closed again.

I couldn't stand it a minute longer. I called to him softly. He looked up at me with a trace of the old Jonny smile. I moved over to him and put my hand on his shoulder. He nodded and his hand came up and covered mine. We remained like that for a long while. Then, very gently, I asked him what was doing.

He didn't answer immediately, but looked around the office. Then his gaze fell on the letter. He brightened perceptibly and nodded toward it. "Writing a letter to Blaze," he murmured.

Some God-given impulse made me do something I had never done in my life before. I said, "Could I read it?"

Jonny frowned. And then he reached over and pushed it nearer to me. I picked it up and began to read. And as I read, my whole life changed. When I finished it, I knew what I had to do.

My darling, my life;

You have been so very patient. You have waited so long. You have hoped, day by day, for good news. You have wanted this bad time to end and the good times to begin again. You are still waiting. And I am powerless to give you what you want. At least not yet. Why are you still waiting? Is it really worth that much? I wonder, truly I do. I would give my life to be able to write what you want so much to hear. And my life is such a small thing, compared to what you so willingly gave to me. It seems that I am always thanking you. And I do thank you, and God knows that is little enough to offer you.

I remember, Father Molino said, 'I will always remember that once Blaze Scotland kissed me.' I was luckier than he. Blaze Scotland loved me.

For all the tears I've caused you, forgive me. For all the heartbreak and the broken dreams, forgive me. For my shortcomings and my weaknesses, forgive me. Forgive me, if you can. And know, that in all my life, I've loved no one but you. I've loved you as no man has ever loved a woman. You were, and are, all of life to me.

And I'll love you all my life,
Jonny.

I felt torn apart as I put the letter down on the desk. But I looked at Jonny anxiously. I was stunned to see him extravagantly watchful and alert. He was looking off into space, listening with intense concentration. Even to my untrained mind, he was obviously having hallucinations. He was listening to someone.

"Who is it?" I whispered.

"Blaze," he whispered back.

I tiptoed out of the room and went to my own office, where. . . I reached for the phone.

CHAPTER 9

THE CHRYSALIS

Touch wood, I've been pretty healthy all my life. I've never been hospitalized for anything serious and I've never undergone an operation of any kind. As a matter of fact, I despise the sights and smells of hospitals. It's always been a big effort for me to even visit someone there. I feel uncomfortable and apprehensive and I can't wait to get the hell out. On occasion, for some small complaint, I've had to visit a doctor or have one visit me. Those occasions I could live without too. You see, I equate doctors with hospitals. One has an antiseptic atmosphere, the other an antiseptic personality. With both, I am out of my element.

Other professionals notwithstanding, doctors feel themselves a breed apart. They know something we don't know. And that makes them something special. Ever try to question a doctor? If they do deign to answer, it's often with a superior condescension that makes me feel like a goddam fool. It may be an age of specialists. We are, most of us, specialists in our own way. But why do they have to be so bloody patronizing? I've often wondered if doctors feel the way I do when they come up against a lawyer, an accountant, a rabbi or a priest? There are exceptions of course. Father Molino obviously was one. The other was old Doc Geller.

"Old" Doc Geller was Jonny's age and mine. We had known him in school as Carl Geller, a boy who had never wanted to be anything else but a doctor. Even as a boy, he had been destined to be one of those selfless, single-purpose, dedicated individuals who spend their lives in service to others, seeking truths, living only to do good. A modest, independent income made it unnecessary for him to make money a god. So he was able to devote himself wholly, unrestrictedly to his commitment, immune from common pressures.

As a young doctor, he had a standard fee for office visits — one dollar. Though times had changed, he was known forevermore as "One Buck Geller," to his hundreds of adoring patients. And because of prematurely grey hair, his friends, those of us who knew him well, referred to him as "Old Doc Geller." Carl was a big man, florid of complexion, with an equally big, gruff voice. And gentle as a lamb. And human. He was the only doctor I could ever stomach. One more thing about him, he was a G.P.

I dialed his number feverishly, hoping to God he would answer himself, pushing out of my mind the thought of Jonny sitting in his office, listening to the voice of Blaze. My prayer was answered. Carl picked up the phone himself.

"Doctor Geller," he said.

"Carl, this is Arnie, Arnie Berman. I've got a man-sized problem on my hands and I need your help."

"Sure, Arnie, sure. What's bothering you?"

"It's not me, Carl, it's Jonny Temple. You've got to see him as soon as possible. He needs your help, I'm sure. He's not sick physically, but he's under a terrific strain. I think he's cracking up, Carl."

"Why do you think that, Arnie? Tell me what you mean."

As quickly as possible, I sketched the last few years of Jonny's life for him and brought him up to date by describing the scene in the office a few minutes ago. "He's listening to Blaze, Carl, he really hears her. What do you think?"

"I can't make a diagnosis on the phone, Arnie, you know that, But I think I should see him immediately. The symptoms you describe may or may not be significant. Knowing Jonny, I'm inclined to think they are. There's an inter-relationship between grief and depression. It's the depression I'm concerned about. Grief, in itself, no matter how intense, is the healthy working out of a real loss, the loss of Blaze for example. Depression is an emotional illness, triggered most often by a loss, but out of control, a sickness that feeds on itself and that can warp a personality, disrupt a family, and at its worst, end in self-destruction. I'd say, get him over here tonight."

"I will, Carl, I will if I have to carry him. See you later." I hung up in fear. I knew that a reign of terror had begun. I knew, too, that I would live with it for a long time to come. Jonny, Jonny, friend of my youth, partner of my man's estate, beloved brother. Why? Why? Why?

I spent the rest of the day trying to figure out a way to get Jonny over to the doctor's office that evening without triggering unwanted suspicions. I had looked in on him several times during the afternoon and found him sleeping in his chair. I didn't know, at the time, if it was a good sign or a bad one. But I was glad of the time it gave me to think. At one point I thought of calling Rita and advising her of my concern for Jonny. Also of Carl's insistence on seeing him immediately. But I couldn't bring myself to do it. She was the last person in the world I wanted to talk to right then. And I wasn't sure I could control myself. Hating Rita, yelling at her, cursing her wouldn't help Jonny.

I didn't give a damn about Rita, I had only to think of Jonny. So the hell with her. She'd find out soon enough. What's more, she had created the problem, and I, who loved him, would have to try to solve it. I finally came up with the banal idea of telling Jonny that I was feeling sick and asking him to accompany me to Carl's office. His touching concern for me affected me deeply. I fought the good fight in holding back the tears. Jonny worried about me. A macabre joke. But I didn't feel like laughing. At that precise moment, I doubted I'd ever laugh again.

Jonny sat in the waiting room while I went into Carl's office. He had begun to doze almost as soon as he sat down. Carl and I used the time of my supposed examination to talk about Jonny and decide on a course of action. After an appropriate length of time, Carl came out to the waiting room with me and greeted Jonny. "Well, you old ambulance chaser, how the devil are you?" he grinned

Jonny stood up and shook hands. He grinned too. "Fine Carl, it's been a long time."

"Sure has," Carl agreed, "and it's probably been a long time since you had a physical checkup. Might as well kill two birds with one stone. While you're here, come on in and let me give you a one-two-three."

Jonny looked dubious but he followed Carl into the examination room. I blew out a long breath of thankfulness and relief. I guess I was looking for a miracle.

Late that night, after I had dropped Jonny off at home, Carl reached me at my apartment. I knew it was he before I answered. My hand hesitated on the receiver. What he would say to me was crucial. Miracle or despair? I hesitated because, frankly, I wasn't too hopeful. "Hello?"

Carl wasted no time on preliminaries. "Not good I'm afraid, Arnie. The symptoms you mentioned and my own observations leave no doubt in my mind that Jonny is in a depressive state, a defeated state of mind if you will. It's a damn shame it couldn't have been caught earlier. I'd say Jonny has been settling gradually into the condition over a period of time."

"But he seemed so good when he met you, Carl, so glad to see you. Can you be sure?"

"I wasn't at first, but I am now. The diagnosis of depression is rather subtle. And Jonny did his level best to conceal his misery, which is a symptom in itself. But considering various factors — fatigue, difficulty in concentration, his appearance, lassitude, the smiling face he wore in spite of what I know — I'm certain of my diagnosis. What I'm not sure of is whether the condition is mild, moderate or severe. But Arnie, he's going to have to be watched in case he should develop suicidal tendencies."

"Oh my God, Carl. What are you going to do for him? What do you suggest?"

"I suggest first of all that you get him out of his house. Take him in with you because he needs constant watching, day and night. I'm going to try supportive therapy and antidepressant drugs and see what happens. We'll watch him carefully, Arnie. If other measures need to be taken, we'll take them. But one step at a time. I'll treat him at my office for now. The main thing is to get him in with you. And bring him to me tomorrow. Got it?"

"I've got it, Carl. Be in touch with you in the morning. And Carl, I hope it's not too late. Please make Jonny well again."

"You know Arnie, it's never too late while there's life. We'll give it the old college try."

Getting Jonny out of his house and away from Rita was easy. I really laid it on thick. For a clincher, I warned her that Jonny might become violent, although I didn't believe that for one minute. But the thought that he might do harm to her, or Petey or Marion terrified her. Her relief, when Jonny was leaving with me, was so obvious that morning, I became enraged. Settling him in my car, I walked back to her.

Speaking quietly, so he wouldn't hear me, and pretty near choking, I ground out, "Well, you bitch, you've had your day. You took a fine man and ruined him. You took a sweet, gentle soul and crushed it. You've all but destroyed a beautiful, sensitive human being. May you rot in hell for it. And may God forgive me for allowing it to happen, for not killing you before your wedding day. If there is such a thing as retribution, I pray that you know only pain and suffering for the rest of your days. And know this. If anything more happens to Jonny, I may get to kill you yet. Contemplate that for the next while."

I couldn't go on, the bitterness in my mouth was overwhelming. As I turned toward the car, Rita was standing tall and proud, a cold enigmatic smile on her lips, icy, victorious. That was the last time I saw her. And that picture of her is stamped indelibly on my brain from that day until the end of time. Is there retribution in this world? I wonder. Oh God, I hope so.

During the day, a small thought that had been gnawing at the back of my mind became an imperious command. I had to go to California, to Blaze. A letter or a phone call was unthinkable. Besides, I'd never forgotten that once, a long time ago, I had played God with her life. I had torn up a letter from her to Jonny, a letter that might have altered the course of both their lives. I carried my guilt with me, stronger than ever now in the light of all that had happened. I had to see her, to tell her about

Jonny face to face, to comfort her as best I could. I would not mention the letter, it would only add to her pain. But in the giving of something of myself to her, perhaps, just perhaps, I might be allowed some small expiation for what I had done. Blaze. Blaze. We both love him. We will mingle our tears and the salt from them will form a mighty bridge. And our love for him will enable him to span the abyss. And he will walk back across it, to us, strong and free, and whole again.

I arranged to have Sidney Korvin stay with Jonny until my return. He was instructed not to leave Jonny alone for a single second, day or night. And to co-operate fully with Carl Geller. I wired Blaze and arranged for a flight for that same day. A few hours later I was on my way to California, rehearsing en route what I would say to her, and how I would try to say it.

It was early evening when the plane touched down, and the flaming sun lit up the tropical skies over Los Angeles airport. But I was in no mood to admire the scenery. As the plane taxied to a stop and the door opened to the ramp, I pushed through it, seeking out Blaze in the waiting throng at the gate, knowing with certainty that she would be there. And she was there. I spotted the fiery red hair and the beautiful face immediately. I began to run towards her. And, breaking through the gate, she ran towards me until she fell into my arms. We didn't speak; we just clung to each other for a long time, drawing nourishment and strength, one from the other, dreading to mention the name of the man who had brought us together, on whose behalf we would try to build a causeway of love.

Finally I held her away from me and looked down into her face. She was even lovelier than I remembered. My throat constricted as she smiled at me, sadly, pathetically. "I knew you'd come," she said softly. "The moment I read Jonny's last letter I knew you'd come. Thank you."

"You mustn't thank me," I choked, "please don't thank me, Blaze. I wanted to come to you, there was no question in my mind. We have some talking to do about. . . Jonny. It had to be together like this. I love him almost as much as you do, honey."

"I know," she replied simply.

Something in her eyes forced me into a quick decision. "Before we go, let's step into a bar and have a drink together," I insisted, "that way we can talk right away." She smiled at me gratefully and led the way.

It was mercifully dim in the tiny bar as we sat at a corner table. I could just make out the profile of Blaze's face in the gloom, the famous profile that was so well known to millions of movie fans all over the world. But she wasn't acting now. It was dark and there was just the two of us, two frightened people bound together by fear of the unknown and a common love. She was nervous. I could tell by the rigidity of her head and by the constant clasping and unclasping of her hands. My heart went out to the sublime girl who was Jonny's love and I reached over to take her two hands in mine and hold them tightly.

Not a word was spoken for a long time. Blaze waited for me to begin. And I didn't know how. All that I had rehearsed on the plane, everything that I had planned to say to her seemed so inane now that I was sitting beside her, so close, holding her cold hands. For me it's always been easier to rehearse than to perform. We sat. And we waited, for the dam to burst.

"How is he, Arnie?"

The words, spoken softly, hesitatingly, hit me like a splash of cold water in the face. I shook my head angrily. What the hell was the matter with me? I had come all this way to comfort a grieving girl. And instead of speaking the right words, I was sitting, inarticulate, mute, useless. I fought to pull myself together. The words were in my heart. I wanted desperately to speak them. But I wanted them to come out right, to offer solace, to alleviate the pain. But the battle was lost before I had begun. Words are only words, shallow and dull. Only the truth could be spoken now. There was no way to spare her. Jonny belonged to her. At this time, in this place, she had to know all. She was entitled. I told her, everything.

"Is there any hope?" A plea, a cry from the wilderness.

"There's always hope, Blaze honey. The illness is treatable. And Geller is good. He won't leave a stone unturned. We mustn't develop false hopes, but we must believe that recovery is possible, even inevitable. And then, if the gods should be so kind to us, I will bring him back here to you. And you will do for him what no other power on earth can do. Your body will heal him, your love will restore him. And in the future of your years, this time will be forgotten."

"And you, Arnie, would you stay with us?"

I did not hesitate. "Yes, I will stay."

Driving into town to the hotel, I was greatly relieved to see Blaze in far better spirits than she had been. At the same time I felt a pang of conscience. Had I ended the conversation with too much promise? Were my last words allowing Blaze to build castles in the air? No, I decided, this was surely a time for faith. If Blaze was looking to the future optimistically, so be it. Better that than despair. Maybe the words had come out right after all. Mountains had been moved by faith. Surely a bridge could be built on it.

"Are you very tired, Arnie?" Blaze asked anxiously.

"No honey, not at all. Why do you ask?"

"Well, I may have done something silly. I asked Father Molino to meet us at the hotel. He's driving in from Santa Barbara. He'll be there by midnight. Was it stupid of me, Arnie?"

My first instinct was to blurt out, "But he's a Catholic priest, Blaze." Just in time I recalled all that Jonny had told me about him, all that he had meant to him and to Blaze. "No it wasn't stupid at all. Actually it's quite fitting that I should meet him. He thinks enough of Jonny to drive in. I should like to know him. And Blaze, he lives by faith. Maybe he'll teach us how to live by it too."

The Father was all that I expected. I've never met a kinder, more compassionate man in my life. Small wonder that Blaze and Jonny thought so very highly of him. His presence bespoke faith and peace and serenity. He listened intently while I recounted all that I had told Blaze. And as I ended on the note of encouragment, he was nodding his head.

"Yes," he agreed, "you are right to feel that way. I have seen many such cases in my time. And I know that the right combination of loving care and medicine and therapy produces results that may seem miraculous. But we must maintain our trust. Can you do that, my son?"

"Yes, Father."

"And you, Blaze, can you keep faith?"

"Yes, Father, and I will."

The old man's smile was unclouded. "That is good," he murmured, "and it will help. Believe me, it will help."

Through the hours of that night, three people who cared struggled to build the causeway that would bring Jonny home to us. Because of that wonderful old priest, Blaze and I felt our doubts melting away. He spoke and we listened, with gladness in our hearts. He talked of the power and the glory of belief in the human spirit, of the transcendent living force of love. He conjured up a merciful God, the miracles of science, the might of the will to live. He lightened our load, he gave us a creed by which we might live. He taught us the articles of faith and he gave us the tenets of life. He strengthened our judgement, he lifted our hearts. He gave meaning to our days. All that night, as he battled for the soul of one man, he transformed the life of another. In the morning, I would be changed. I could never be quite the same again.

Father Molino said goodbye to me at the hotel while Blaze prepared to drive me to the airport. Even his farewell was fully typical of the man. "Bring Jonny back to us, Arnold," he said. "He will be safe with us. We will be praying for him. And Arnold, tell him that we love him, will you?"

As we drove off, I looked back. The Father was standing with both arms raised, looking up into the sky. I don't know what he saw or thought. But I remember thinking what the world would be like peopled only by men such as he.

At the departure gate, I watched Blaze closely. But Father Molino had reached her, too. She was in full control of herself and composed. Only the coldness of her hand in mine gave her away. I smiled down into her eyes. "Remember what he said to us last night, Blaze honey. And like he said, it will help. . . all of us."

"Yes, I'll remember, Arnie. And don't worry about me. I'll be fine. Only, Arnie, promise me. . . ."

I put my finger on her lips to quiet her. Then I kissed her. "I know honey," I said, "I promise. I promise."

The next weeks were a series of ups and downs, as far as Jonny was concerned. I made certain that either Sidney Korvin or I was with him every minute of every day. And the treatment that Carl Geller had decided on seemed to be having a good effect, although he warned me not to get prematurely enthusiastic. As he put it, there could be no guarantee that the treatment would be permanently beneficial or that an apparent cure would not end in a relapse. But, for the moment, suicidal tendencies could be ruled out. And for that we were most grateful.

If I live to be a hundred and twenty, there is one thing I will never understand, that is totally beyond my comprehension. Day after day passed and never a phone call from Jonny's home. Marion, forget about. And as for Rita, well what can I say that I haven't already said? But Petey. My God, he was

Jonny's son. It was inhuman that he should make no effort to inquire about his father. Rita must have done her work damn well. Jonny had been completely written off. It was as though he had ceased to exist. His family had put him entirely out of their minds. Rita was one thing. But that Petey.

Carl's words came back to haunt us. As he had feared, Jonny's condition deteriorated dramatically. One day he was coming along fine, the next a variety of symptoms manifested themselves. I first noticed the change when Jonny came in to breakfast one morning. He hadn't shaved and his clothes were dirty. This I was used to by now. But I was thoroughly alarmed when I couldn't understand what he was saying. What was it that Carl had warned me about? "Verbal retardation" was the expression he had used. He explained that Jonny might want to confide in me but that he might find it impossible to communicate. He might want to explain himself to me but be unable to do so. I phoned Carl to tell him that we were on our way to his office.

Later that day, Sidney Korvin was keeping Johnny company when Carl reached me at my office. "Problems, Arnie, problems," he reported. "I couldn't very well talk to you at my place. But there are a few things you should know. I've been a little confused because of the hallucinations you mentioned in the beginning. They're usually associated with severe depression. But they weren't repeated and no other severe symptoms developed. I've been watching for them, but so far so good. Because of the symptoms obvious to us, I've been treating Jonny as a case of moderate severity. I've been watching for signs of a suicidal urge but I have every reason to believe it's not present at this time.

"Why moderate severity? Well, I've become an authority figure with a capital A. Jonny puts on a display of bowing and scraping before me like you wouldn't believe. This leads to another problem. It could be the beginning of a hostility complex. Another thing. I found myself being very sorry that Jonny had come to such a state. And that in itself is significant. Empathy is part and parcel of this whole thing. Are you still with me, Arnie?"

"I'm still with you, Carl."

"Good. Now I'll tell you how you come into the act."

I was sweating profusely by this time. But I held on to that phone receiver for dear life. "Shoot, Carl."

"Okay. Now listen carefully. You can expect a number of things to develop. Things like reduced sleep, a decrease in appetite, falling weight, constipation, and anergia, which is loss of strength or lack of energy. Any of those things. Maybe several at one time. And complaints of muscular aches and pains. I don't want to get technical with you, Arnie, but don't worry too much about pains. Localization of the pain may be only symbolically significant to Jonny. It may simply be a tombstone of his lost love, an emotional fringe benefit, so to speak. You're likely to have a hypochondriac on your hands, Arnie. It's going to be rough. Can you handle it?"

"I don't know, Carl. I'm going to try like hell. I'll let you know."

Most of the work at the office was handled by the juniors now that I had to give so much attention to Jonny. It turned out as rough as Carl had said it would. I no longer attempted to take Jonny to the office, it was just too much for both of us. And caring for him at home was like caring for a small baby. Two things sustained me. My hatred for Rita, and my love for Jonny. I don't know how long I could have kept it up. I was also aware of Carl's increasing concern and vigilance.

I knew we were in trouble the day Carl phoned me and advised that he had called in a psychiatrist for consultation.

"That bad, eh Carl?"

"Afraid so, Arnie."

"What do you think?"

"Well, I want to go over the whole case with Doctor Torre. But I believe that Jonny has transgressed to an acute psychotic depression with attendant increased suicidal or homicidal risk. I'll get back to you as soon as possible. In the meantime, don't let Jonny out of your sight. Watch out for him. And Arnie, watch out for yourself."

The phone rang. I knew it was Carl. I also knew what he was going to tell me.

"Arnie, Doctor Torre has just left here. He concurs. We don't have any choice. It's hospitalization immediately, I'm afraid."

"When Carl?"

"Tonight."

"Which one?"

"Doctor Torre works out of the Douglas."

"Oh my God."

"Don't be stupid, Arnie. It's a good hospital. They do excellent work there. And Jonny will get the best of care. There's no reason to believe they won't be able to effect a cure."

"When I was a kid we called that place the insane asylum. Oh God."

"Well goddammit, Arnie, you're not a kid any more. So up. And get a grip on yourself. It's Jonny we're thinking about. Remember?"

"Okay, Carl. Sorry. You're right, of course. We'll be ready when you get here." I hung up. Then I picked up the receiver again. I dialed direct to California. I had promised Blaze. I was keeping my promise.

By the time Carl arrived at my apartment, Jonny was in an extremely agitated state. It was as though he sensed something and was employing delaying tactics. Carl immediately decided to delay the departure until the next day. We looked on helplessly as Jonny paced the room, wringing his hands, weeping, begging for help and understanding but in a way which permitted no full grasp to be taken of what he meant.

"Severe depression," Carl growled as he reached in his bag for his drug case. "We'll let him sleep tonight. He should be better in the morning. Let me know if you need me. Otherwise I'll meet you at the hospital around ten."

The drug had taken effect and Jonny was sleeping peacefully. I finally went to bed myself. That night Jonny and I were as one. Only for those few hours, my nightmares exceeded his.

In my whole life no other single day remains so firmly etched on my mind as the day I drove Jonny to the Douglas Hospital. It's as though it were yesterday. It was a drizzly, dark-grey, oppressive day in mid-November. I woke up and it was still dark in my bedroom. I fought the awakening because I knew, dejectedly, what the day would bring. Looking over to the twin bed, I sensed that Jonny was still asleep. Carl must have administered one blockbuster of a drug.

Moving quietly, so as not to wake him, I went into the living room and looked out at the street below. It was a foreboding sight. The maple trees were bare, stripped of the bright foliage of a few weeks ago. The driveways and the gutters were clogged with the dirty, fallen leaves. And the hedges around the lawns had been cut down or tied up for protection against the winter snows. I stood there for a long time, my thoughts as ugly as the bleakness of the day. With a long-drawn sigh, I turned away and went into the kitchen to make coffee.

Jonny got up with little hint of the agitation of the night before. When I explained to him that I was taking him to a hospital for a few days of rest and treatment that would do him good, he was almost eager. I couldn't even drink my coffee.

We walked out into a gusting, chilling wind that cut through us to the marrow. There was more than a hint of snow in the wet air. As we drove, in silence, I listened to the hum of my snow tires on the bare pavement. And the windshield wipers clicked like a metronome keeping time to the beating of my heart.

As I drove down the Decarie Expressway to the Bonaventure, I glanced over at Jonny. But he was hunched in his overcoat, oblivious, listening to his own secret thoughts. Partway down the Bonaventure Expressway, I turned at the Avenue de L'église—Boulevard de la Verendrye exit and entered the Montreal suburb of Verdun. Ironically, the stores were brightly lit with Christmas decorations and the coloured lights were already strung across the main street, Wellington. I say ironically because the gaiety of the scene was in bitter contrast to my own low spirits. Like a death's head at a feast.

Along the St. Lawrence River waterfront; past the children's swimming pool, Wellington Street becomes Lasalle Boulevard. And then we were at the gates of the hospital. Through them, the long driveway passed rolling green lawns, the staff houses and then the red brick and grey stone buildings of the hospital itself. As we entered the admissions pavilion, I was fighting a blank despondency myself.

Carl was waiting for us, talking to a hospital attendant. The attendant unlocked the elevator doors and we rode up to the second floor. The doors opened on the nurses' station; we turned right down the corridor to the admitting psychiatrist's office. Doctor Torre, a tall, handsome man, motioned us to chairs and took the file Carl was carrying. He glanced over it and pulled two printed forms from his desk drawer. There was complete silence in the room except for the scratching of pen on paper. Jonny sat like stone. His writing finished, Doctor Torre handed a form, the Medical Certificate, to Carl who signed it and handed it back. Then, while I stared in astonishment, the second form was handed to me.

Half strangling, I managed to blurt out, "You want me to sign? Is it the commitment papers?"

Doctor Torre looked at me briefly then down at the paper I held. "You are his partner and friend," he stated rather than asked. "That form is both administrative and a consent. It is preferable that a relative or close friend sign it. But I will sign it if you object. It's entirely up to you."

I stared at the form in my hand. Neatly printed. Neatly filled in. Sterile, hospital procedure, businesslike. A patient being committted to a ward for the mentally disturbed. Another case to be considered, therapeutic procedures to be decided upon. Hopefully a cure might be effected in this case.

I wanted to scream and beat my chest. This is not just another case. This is Jonny, Jonathon Temple. Blaze's Jonny, my Jonny. In the name of God, what am I doing signing him in here?

Carl must have seen some of the horror I was feeling. He got up and came over to me, and spoke very softly. "Arnie, would you like me to sign the paper? I know how you feel. But try to understand. This is a hospital, nothing more. Jonny will get the best of care here. This is not the end. It is only the beginning, perhaps the beginning of the cure. Isn't that what we want? But I'll sign the paper if you wish."

I shook my head savagely. I didn't recognize my own voice when I said, "No, I'll do it."

I looked at Jonny and he was staring at me curiously. I scribbled my signature and handed the form to Doctor Torre. Then I went next door to the bathroom and threw up.

When I came back to the office, Doctor Torre was setting up his own file. He looked up at me, I imagined apologetically. "The decision to hospitalize is a wise one," he said. "I am quite sure that it could be classed as an emergency. We will do our very best for him here. As a start, we will assign him to a room just off the nurses' station where he can be observed around the clock. As an added precaution, I will assign a nurse to remain with him for a day or two to avoid the risk of a suicide attempt. Please wait here while we take him to his room."

As he left with Jonny, I lit a cigarette. My hands were shaking violently.

In retrospect, I must admit that the thought and sight of the Douglas Hospital is far worse for relatives and friends than it is for the patients themselves. It's true that patients don't notice the atmosphere, they're unaware of the surroundings. They're sick, and so wrapped up in their sickness to be oblivious to everything else. But my hour was not over yet.

Doctor Torre returned to his office to advise Carl and me that Jonny was settled in his room. He told us that he had given Jonny a combined antidepressant and sedative and warned me that I would find him somnolent. Then he invited us to follow him.

I guess you could call it a room. In reality, it was more like a cell-cubicle in size. There was linoleum on the floor, a dullish brown. The walls were pale green. There were four articles of furniture — a white wood chair, a white wood night table, a small mirror over it. And in the centre of the room, a single white iron bed. On it, Jonny lay in a hospital nightshirt, drowsy, slack. Even to me, he was almost unrecognizable from the man-brother I knew.

I went over to the bed and touched his shoulder. His eyes wavered about the room and finally focused on me. "I'll be back later, Jonny," I said, "rest for now."

In spite of myself, my voice sank to a whisper as I continued, "Get well, Jonny. For you, for Blaze, for all of us, get well."

Carl took my arm and guided me out of the room. Jonny was grinning emptily. The drug was at work.

Doctor Torre conducted us to the recreation room down the hall. It was a large room and contained a television set, a radio, record player and card tables. Several patients were sitting at the tables, playing gin rummy. The record player was going full blast and a young girl was dancing a modern ballet in the centre of the room. The jarring note was supplied by three attendants in white who kept a constant eye on the patients.

"I brought you in here," Doctor Torre said to me, "to show you these patients. They are remarkably improved from what they were like a few days ago. A few days from now you may be playing gin with your friend. So be cheerful, you have nothing to reproach yourself for."

Be cheerful. That was a laugh. As we left the building and Carl walked me over to the parking lot, there was only one thing I wanted to be. And that was drunk as a skunk.

"Operator, I want a person to person call to Miss Blaze Scotland in Beverly Hills, California. I'll hold on."

"Blaze honey, this is Arnie. Carl and I took Jonny in to the hospital this morning. And things are looking up. Doctor Torre there thinks there's every hope for successful treatment. I think he may be right. So there's no need for you to be worrying yourself to pieces out there."

"Oh thank you for calling, Arnie. I have been worrying myself sick, ever since your call last night. Is it a good hospital? Does he have a nice room?"

"Yes to both questions. It's one of the best hospitals and his room is very nice. No problems."

"I've been thinking, Arnie, since I spoke to you. I want to come to Montreal. I want to be near Jonny, to see him as often as I'm allowed. I could leave tomorrow morning and be there by lunchtime. Would you reserve rooms for me?"

"No. I mean, it's too early for you to come, Blaze. Look honey, he just went in this morning. It would be better to wait a few days and see how the treatment works out. I promise I'll call you every night and let you know what's doing. Your coming here tomorrow won't solve anything, and it'll be awfully rough on you. What do you say, honey, will you listen to me?"

"I thought you'd say that, Arnie. Maybe you're right. But I can't stay here. I'll go to Santa Barbara. Call me tomorrow night at the Hermitage. I'll be waiting there. And Father Molino will look out for me. Arnie, you're sure everything's alright?"

"I'm sure honey, I'm sure. Speak to you tomorrow night."

I stared at the phone for a long time after I hung up. Blaze couldn't know it. But I was thinking I was a pretty damn good actor myself.

For the next few days, things seemed to be going well. The reports from Doctor Torre were encouraging. Jonny seemed to be responding to the new medication. All this was borne out by my own daily visits. Certainly Jonny looked a whole lot better. He was brighter, more alert than he had been. He complained less and begged for help infrequently. His interest appeared awakened. He even asked me for details concerning our office activities and law practice. As a consequence, my phone calls to the Hermitage each night became cheerier and more hopeful. Once Father Molino answered my call and his relief must have rubbed off on Blaze. She sounded positively joyous as I repeated the conversation to her. If I seemed surprised that Jonny remained in the close-observation room near the nurses' station and that he never mentioned Blaze, Doctor Torre placed no great significance on either. He remained confident. It turned out to be the lull before the storm, the calm before the hurricane.

Carl Geller phoned me at the office. He caught me just as I

was reaching for my overshoes and winter coat and heading out
to lunch. My therapy, the thing that kept me going in between
bouts of heavy-heartedness, was total immersion in the daily
routine of the office. Concentrating on law problems kept my
thinking straight and gave me strength for my visits to the
Douglas.

"Arnie, this is Carl. As a matter of courtesy, Doctor Torre
has kept me informed of all aspects of the treatment he's been
prescribing for Jonny. But something's come up I think you
should be in on. Could you skip lunch and pick me up right
away? I think we should get out there right now. Can you make
it?"

"Be at your place in fifteen minutes," I answered. The
questions could come later.

Carl filled me in on the latest developments as we drove out
to Verdun. He concluded by saying, "As you know, Torre has
been watching Jonny very carefully. Several new symptoms
have manifested themselves, or rather I should say several
changes in symptoms have taken place. Not the least of which is
that there have been no recurrences of agitation. On the
contrary, Jonny has become very self-contained. Supported by
various evidences and having tried numerous antidepressants as
well as psychotherapy, Torre has now reached the conclusion
that very energetic treatment is required. He recommends
ECT."

My withering hopes and nervousness made me bark at Carl.
"What the hell is ECT?"

"Sorry, Arnie," Carl replied gently, "I should have said
electroconvulsive therapy."

I ran through a stoplight while Carl's words sank in. "You
mean, shock treatment?"

"That's right," Carl agreed, "and don't get into a panic. It's
a perfectly safe, effective form of treatment. There's absolutely
nothing to be concerned about or Torre wouldn't be suggesting
it. But talk to him. He'll go into a more detailed explanation for
you."

I said nothing. But I thought, how much more? Hell's sweet
angels, how much more?

"Six to eight treatments ought to do it," Doctor Torre was
saying. "I am convinced ECT is necessary both from the point
of view of physical condition and the risk of suicide. I assure
you it is not a hazardous procedure. What's more, you, the

patient, and I will all feel that something big is being done about the case and this is much more satisfying and reassuring than nursing this longstanding depression on medication. It's likely to make the difference to Jonny; it certainly should hasten his recovery. I plan to start the treatments tomorrow morning."

While Doctor Torre was talking, some small memory nagged at the back of my mind. What was it I had heard about shock treatments? Who had told me, what? Suddenly a pounding dread seized me, and I turned to Carl.

"But isn't it true that this ECT may leave Jonny amnesic?"

Torre answered the question. "To varying degrees, it is possible. I cannot guarantee it won't happen, but I don't think so. In any case, the probable benefits outweigh the possible evils. Any other question?"

I felt like yelling, "A million of them doctor, a million." But I said nothing. My insides had turned to stone and they were weighing me down. I sat for a long time. I couldn't even try to get up.

I could have won the Academy Award that night, as I talked to Blaze over the miles that separated us. It was a good thing we were on the phone. Face to face, I could never have made it. Looking into the beautiful eyes, seeing the questioning hope in them, I'd have broken down for sure. As it was, I held on to the receiver for dear life, keeping my voice light, my conversation hopeful. I didn't mention the ECT. It was impossible for me to explain it to her sensibly, charitably. Especially since I didn't quite understand what had made it necessary myself. One minute, Jonny seemed to be coming on fine, the next shock treatments were deemed necessary. Obviously I couldn't see what Doctor Torre had seen. But surely he knew what had to be done. And was there any choice? He was the doctor, he had made the decision. And I could only stand by and wait, and trust. As I put the phone down finally, I was wishing mightily that Father Molino was with me, here in Montreal, now, to-night. I could have used some of his strength and wisdom. I needed it desperately.

I lay awake the whole long night. There was no sleep in my tortured mind. So long ago, we had been kids in school, with our dreams and our hopes ahead of us. So much water under the bridge in the years between then and now. Such terrible suffering had come to Jonny. Strong, handsome, brilliant Jonny. Why? Why did some people live out their years in comparative contentment, with peace of mind their reward? Reward for what? Were they better than those who walked with sorrow, whose final bed was made of nails? Conversely, why were some of us born for pain and anguish and knew nothing but all our lives. Good questions. I doubted if even Father Molino had the answers. It was morning when I fell asleep. And I had the answer. It was that there is no answer. Some are born for this, some for that. And the One who decides has not told us why.

CHAPTER 10

VALLEY OF THE SHADOW

In the final analysis, it was the words and the beliefs and the teachings of Father Molino that sustained me. The ECT treatments were never completed. One night, Jonny just . . . died.

I had visited him in the afternoon and he slept most of the time I was there. Certainly there was no cause for alarm that afternoon. On the contrary, if anything there was reason for hope in Doctor Torre's report. I decided to drive back to town for dinner, promising that I would drop in during the evening. I returned to the hospital around eight o'clock. No sooner did I reach the second floor when I saw a flurry of activity in the vicinity of Jonny's room. Nurses and attendants scurried in and out, equipment was being wheeled in. At one point, as the door was opened wide, I saw Carl Geller and Doctor Torre on either side of Jonny's bed. I knew something was wrong, very wrong.

A nurse told the doctors that I was outside the door and Torre came out to me a few minutes later. Shaking his head, he looked at me miserably. "He's very ill," he said. "We are not certain yet, but we suspect a coronary. Why, we don't know either. But it happened very suddenly. We're doing everything possible for him, Mr. Berman. Please make yourself as comfortable as possible in my office. We'll keep you informed."

I dreaded asking the question, but I had to. "Does it look bad, doctor?"

"I must say his condition is critical," was the reply.

Sitting in Torre's office, chainsmoking, I kept thinking back to that night in California, so long ago it seemed, that Father Molino had talked the night through. I had to try to remember what he had said, what he had wanted me to live with. Otherwise I might have become Doctor Torre's next patient.

Hours later, or maybe it just seemed like hours, Carl Geller came into the office. I looked up at his face and I didn't need words to tell me that it was all over.

"He's gone, isn't he?" I whispered. Carl nodded and his expression turned to anger.

"And I'll be a sonofabitch if I know why," he growled. "I'm still not fully convinced it was a coronary, even though there are a number of indications that point to it. Now I have a request to make of you, Arnie. It's going to be a bastard, but Doctor Torre and I want you to get permission from Rita for a post mortem. I know, I know, but you've got to try to convince her. It's important, Arnie. Will you try?"

"I'll try, Carl," I answered, "but give me a few minutes alone. And Carl. Don't hold your breath."

Random thoughts crowded my brain as I sat there in Doctor Torre's office. It was incredible. The mind refused to wholly accept it. Jonny gone. The labours of so many down the drain. What price the words of Father Molino now? But perhaps his words did have the deeper meaning. We are not to question why. Nature and destiny. Destiny and nature had, finally, won out over medical science. We are mortal. And in our mortality, the whys and wherefores, the questions and answers, the known and the unknown elude us. What would I say to Blaze? What would Father Molino have to say to me? A man who didn't want to die had died. Why? I pondered over this for some time. Maddeningly, though I sensed I knew the answer, it continued to evade me. But I also knew that when it came to me, I would be able to live with it. In the meantime, rest Jonny, rest in peace my brother. Go now to your heavenly Hermitage and wait. Wait for us.

The time was past to curse Rita, to hate Petey. That couldn't help Jonny who needed no help from anyone any more. Keeping it to the simplest common denominator, Jonny Temple had married the wrong woman. I call heaven to witness that it was she who destroyed him. Once I had called her a vampire. I didn't know then how close to the truth I was. It was Jonny's blood that she needed to sustain her. Well, she had won, the victory was entirely hers. If she could live with herself, so be it. I was beyond caring about her any more. But one last thing had to be done. The post mortem. Even she wouldn't refuse that. I breathed deeply, and dialed her number.

Well, of course, Rita refused her permission. She took the news of Jonny's death calmly, inhumanly so. She flatly rejected my suggestion that I pick her up and bring her to the hospital to sign an agreement for a post mortem. I figured her refusal might be based on fear or shame, or guilt. Maybe she just couldn't face us. Would she be willing to telegraph permission? No, she wouldn't do that either. There was no use coaxing that non-feeling vixen. I said nothing more. I just hung up on her.

"It's a damn shame," Carl Geller said when I reported my conversation. "As doctors, we feel an obligation to society to know exactly why he died. And it helps us with others. Well, we can't force her. So that's that."

Doctor Torre was nodding agreement. "From a medical standpoint I would have liked a post mortem," he sighed, "but there is another point of view. Perhaps his wife is trying to expiate her own guilt by telling herself that 'they' have done enough to him already. Or perhaps she really believes that Jonny had to be sacrificed instead of her. Whatever she thinks, we are rather helpless now. There are so many things we don't know. That's why it's a shame."

As the two doctors were talking, a stunning realization came upon me. The evasive answer was clear. "But I know," I said. As the doctors stared at me, the words spilled from my mouth. And I knew they were the right words, that I had somehow found the truth.

"The simple fact of the matter is that Jonny Temple no longer had anything to live for. His case became, not medical but philosophical. Don't you see? He had sustained a terrible loss. He had been the recipient of grievous bad news. Disappointed beyond belief, having been torn, literally, in two, he turned his face to the wall and proceeded over a period of time to die . . . of loneliness and misery." The doctors were nodding agreement as I walked out of the room.

EPILOGUE

I left the hospital and started back to Montreal. As I drove, I thought of all the people who had played their parts in the brief, tormented life of my friend. But most of all I thought about Blaze and Jonny. I was remembering the time Jonny had first told me about the Hermitage and Santa Barbara. I had felt so lousy then. There had been a wistfulness in his eyes and a yearning in his voice that was heartbreaking.

All of God's children should have their Hermitage and their Santa Barbara, at least once in their lifetime. I know this, I believe it even though it may never happen for me. But what bothers me, and concerns me deeply, is why does it have to end? Why is it always so short-lived? Why is the time of joyful happiness and tranquil contentment so short and the time of ugly reality so long? Why must all good things come to an end? Why? Why? Why? I guess if I had the answers I, Arnold Berman, would be the most sought-after man in the whole world.

There is one question that cries for an answer. Is there no place in this big, wide world for the dreamers and the humble hearted? Must it be given over to the practical and the strong? I say yes to the first part and no to the second, a thousand times. Some time and in some place the day will come when men may possess their own souls, when the dreams and yearnings of all will be fulfilled. And I say this. If ever the meek are to inherit the earth, it better be soon. Or there will be no earth to inherit.

But isn't that part of the dream? That those who care, those with the generous hearts and compassion will find the way to lead us to our Hermitage? It may come too late for most of us, for you and me. It's too late for Jonny. But we had better believe it will come. Else we're in deep trouble. And when that Hermitage is found, will it not be permanent and for all time? And will it not be far, far better that what we have now?

Well, Jonny and Blaze had their Hermitage, briefly. The Spanish house on the shores of Santa Barbara, overlooking the Pacific, stands today silent and locked. It is still a place of solitude. And only the flowers and the sea keep it company. It was the only promise to Blaze that Jonny ever broke. They never returned to the Hermitage.

Some day it will crumble and the sea will claim it. And the dreams that it nurtured, for just a little while, will long have been forgotten. They will have been buried too. And except for the endless sound of the waves, all will be silence.

These words, all of this, and all that I have told you, I call heaven to witness.